THE
DETECTIVE
& THE
PIPE GIRL

ALSO BY MICHAEL CRAVEN

Body Copy

THE
DETECTIVE
& THE
PIPE GIRL

A MYSTERY

MICHAEL CRAVEN

BOURBON STREET BOOKS

An Imprint of HarperCollinsPublishers
www.harpercollins.com

HarperCollins books may be purchased for educational, business, or sales promotional use. For information please e-mail the Special Markets Department at SPsales@harpercollins.com.

FIRST EDITION

Designed by Michael Correy

Photograph on pp. ii–iii © by Trevor Smith

Library of Congress Cataloging-in-Publication Data is available upon request.

ISBN 978-0-06-230559-6

14 15 16 17 18   OV/RRD   10 9 8 7 6 5 4 3 2 1

THE
DETECTIVE
& THE
PIPE GIRL

1

I was in my office in Culver City, sitting at my desk admiring my new Ping-Pong table, when a man appeared in my doorway. I work out of a warehouse that used to house three Porsches owned by a movie producer. So the entrance to my space is a big, metal sliding door that a car, or even a pretty big truck, can fit through. I do have a couple windows on one side of the building, and a proper door, but I keep the big slider open almost any time I'm in my office. It really opens up the space, lets in the breeze and the sun, and gives me a wide, clear view all the way across the parking lot to a couple other warehouses.

The man standing there was backlit so I couldn't see him fully. I could tell, however, that he wasn't in the greatest shape. He made for a big, pearlike silhouette.

"Come in," I said. "Walk all the way in."

He walked deeper into my office, moving swiftly and delicately. He barely made a noise as he danced across the slick concrete toward my desk. A quick and agile big man. Light on his feet. A quality I admire, by the way. As he got closer, this shadowy figure began to transform into an actual person. Now that I could see him, I noticed he was odd-looking in ways other than his shape. He was probably six-three, pale and double-chinned, with a baby face and eyebrows that were too arched and lips that were too red. Up top, he had a mop of curly black hair—his hair popping against his clammy white skin. He wore schoolboy khakis and a pressed blue oxford.

I almost told him to go back and stand where he was before so I couldn't see him as well. I think I liked that better. This guy—he was a big white blob all ready for Sunday school.

I pictured him wearing a diaper, shaking a rattle, rolling around in an enormous vat of baby powder, giggling maniacally.

I have no idea why.

"What can I do for you?" I said.

"You are Mr. John Darvelle, I presume?"

I thought: I presume?

So this was a pear-shaped, nimble, *pretentious* manchild.

I sighed. "Yes. I am."

The man went on, "My name is Mountcastle. Paul Mountcastle."

He stuck out his hand. As my face stretched into a

skeptical frown, I shook it. I let go as quickly as possible. I thought, okay, introductions done, now I'll hear what my misshapen visitor wants. But I didn't. Not right away. Instead, he just stood there.

Awkwardly, I might add.

I looked at him. His face had an expectant quality to it. You know those people who, mid-conversation, just kind of smile and stare at you? Who don't give you any indication that they are *hearing* what you are saying? That they are *processing* what you are trying to communicate? But rather seem to have some pedestrian observation about something *else* lingering behind their shifting eyes and creepy smiles? You know those *annoying* people?

You know those annoying people.

Mountcastle was one of them.

Finally, finally, he said, "Are you familiar with the name Arthur Vonz?"

This wasn't like asking me if I'd ever heard of Pablo Picasso. Or the pope. But Arthur Vonz was pretty damn famous. Especially in this town.

I said, eyes half lidded, "Yes, Mountcastle, I am."

With the same expectant smile, and now with a touch of surprise, and more than a touch of condescension, he said, "You know his work?"

"Yes. I've seen a lot of his movies. Who hasn't?"

I thought to myself: I might punch this guy.

Mountcastle then lightly inched closer to my desk, put his hand on the back of one of the chairs that sits in front of it, and said, "Mr. Darvelle, may I sit down?"

From under my desk I pushed out one of the chairs with

my foot. Mountcastle eyed it, sat. He then somewhat dramatically looked around my space. "So," he said. "Is it just you? Do you have others who help you?"

"Mountcastle. What do you want? Does Vonz want to talk to me?"

He smiled at me again and raised his eyebrows, like I'd just made a brilliant observation. Like I'd just exhibited amazing intellectual dexterity.

"Yes, he does."

"When?"

"Tomorrow morning, ten o'clock. At the house in Beverly Hills."

The house. Not *his* house. *The* house. That's what you say when you've got more than one house. Not a problem Vonz and I share.

He continued. "Does this time suit you? Well, before you answer that. Are you interested in speaking with Mr. Vonz?"

"Give me the address. And I'll be there."

Out of his shirt pocket he produced an index card. He handed it to me. I took a quick look. There was an address typed neatly on it. I put it on my desk.

I tested him. "So, he wants to hire me. Do you know what it's about?"

He put an index finger up in the air. "I didn't say he wanted to hire you. I just said he wants to *meet* with you. And I don't know what it's about."

Normally putting an index finger up in the air and pointing something out to me would have irritated me. But he was doing right by his boss in *this* situation. He was still a supremely annoying guy, don't get me wrong. But he was protecting his boss right then so I was okay with it. As for whether or not he knew the nature of the meeting? Not sure. Most assistants, helpers, man-child baby-faced house-boys, have an idea of what the boss man is up to.

I thought he was lying.

He continued, "So. You will be there in the morning? At ten?"

I nodded.

"Do you have any more questions?"

"Just one."

Mountcastle looked excited.

I said, "Do you by any chance own an enormous baby rattle?"

Mountcastle frowned, "I'm afraid I don't understand."

"Never mind. I'll see you tomorrow."

Mountcastle got up, turned, and began to slide lightly out of my office. He was now right next to my new, bright blue Stiga indoor-only Ping-Pong table, which was between my desk and the sliding door, but off to the side. He looked at the table, then looked back over his shoulder at me.

He said, "Do you play, or is this an ironic homage or something?"

"I have no idea what that sentence means."

He tried again. "Do you play Ping-Pong?"

"Yes. As much as possible."

He gave me the smile again. "I used to play. In my basement as a kid. Nifty game."

I would have bet my life right then and there that he was terrible.

"I'm pretty good," he said.

Now, normally I would have blown this off, but Mount-castle just bothered me. So I got out a couple of paddles, nothing serious, just middle-of-the road Killerspin bats. Some decent rubber on them, but nothing too advanced. Just for casual play. Then I grabbed a couple Halex three-star balls. You don't want to use one- or two-star balls. They're cheaper, and have a thinner shell so when you hit them it doesn't give you that solid crack that you're look-ing for. That satisfying pop. That perfect thwok. One- and two-star balls have a floaty, weak, unsatisfying feeling. Not good, friend. Not good.

After seeing Mountcastle hit one ball, one ball, I knew that my detective's intuition had been correct. He blew. Just terrible. Watching him take a swing made me want to throw up. We started and, despite focusing mostly on what Arthur Vonz might want, I beat him 21–4. I know, I know, official soft paddle games are to 11 these days. But 21's the way to go for casual play. For any kind of play. You just can't get into a rhythm when you play to 11. Nobody can.

After the thumping, Mountcastle proceeded to tell me he "didn't play with paddles like this," he "couldn't see because of the sun," he "wasn't warmed up." Standard excuses. So, I let him select a paddle out of my quiver, I lowered the metal slider so there was less glare, I rallied with him until his pale, white face was covered in sweat.

Then I focused, I focused hard, and beat him 21–0. I know, I know. Skunks at 7–0 and 11–1. But I've been down on skunks lately. They're not really fair. Anyone, even really, really good players, can lose a lot of points in a row and later come back to win.

That's not an opinion.

But back to my 21–0 trouncing of Mountcastle. See, people always think they're better at Ping-Pong than they actually are. And these same people always insist on telling you this. And then, when they lose, they always hit you with a ton of excuses—even if you beat them badly. And the worst part is, if *you* don't play your A-game, and you allow these people to hang in there just for fun, they never, ever realize you are going easy on them. They just say, after a not-so-horrible loss, "See? And I haven't even played in a while." So every now and then, when I see a cocky, misguided glimmer in someone's eye, I make it sting. That's why, on the last point, I leaned into my forehand so the ball went off the table and hit Mountcastle in his flabby white neck. A little red circle was forming as he looked at me, his eyes holding a shocked and betrayed expression.

He then gathered himself, nodded, and without a word scooted under the lowered slider, somehow got in his little Honda Civic, and drove off.

2

Arthur Vonz was one of the top film directors in the world. Like Spielberg or Scorsese, if he wanted to make a movie, he pretty much got to make it. And if he was involved in any way in any entertainment project, as a producer, consultant, whatever, the project instantly had more credibility. Vonz was a full-on member of the Hollywood community too. You'd see pictures of him, or TV footage of him, at Hollywood parties and industry events hobnobbing with other big shots, working the town, relishing in, and using, his clout. You'd see him at non-Hollywood events too. Art openings, dinners for causes, gatherings where he could socialize with other people who worked in different fields but were esteemed in their own right. The guy was *involved*, present, a man about town out there mixing it up.

Thing is, contrary to what often makes you a big deal in the Hollywood culture, he wasn't known for massive box-office smashes. He wasn't known for working inside the studio system to create hits, to create franchises that could produce six movies and billions of dollars. Or to be at the helm of an idea the studio offered him because they owned the property and needed a good director. This guy wasn't toiling away on the big-screen remake of *The Facts of Life*, or racking his brain somewhere to reimagine *Cagney and Lacey* for the movies. Arthur Vonz was one of those rare birds who could do basically whatever he wanted. And the studios would give him the money, the time, the freedom. And the big stars would line up to cut their fees, and work on *his* terms. When *he* was ready.

Sometimes his movies hit big, made money. But that was never the intent. Because all of them, even the ones that had some obvious commercial potential, had weird edges. Had artistic ambition. If you went to a Vonz movie, you could expect a bold, intense, challenging, even strange experience. Music that made you a little uncomfortable. Notions that you hadn't ever contemplated. Or better yet, notions you had contemplated but had never told anyone.

Bergmanian. Kubrickian. Vonzian.

Vonz once followed a massive World War II epic with a subtitled film about a suicidal tribe in the Amazon. His World War II film made a bunch of money and won a slew of Academy Awards. His Amazon film bombed spectacularly. But I remember very specifically seeing an interview with him where he said something like, "You know, I think both of the films turned out pretty good. Not sure if I'd say great, but pretty good. But if I *had* to say, I'd say

I like the Amazon picture a little better." And you didn't feel like he was being pretentious or trying to cover up a failure. You believed him.

As you might have guessed, I'm a fan. I respect his work. Some of his movies are among my favorites. All-time favorites. *Starlight*. It's in my top ten. About a guy who decides to turn his whole life upside down by sleeping all day and living his life all night. Not some vampire bullshit either. Just a story about changing your perspective literally—with the hopes that it will change your perspective philosophically. Really interesting. Really weird. Really good.

Vonz, appearance-wise, had sort of an absurd vibe. He had a big shock of white hair and he wore massive, old-school seventies Robert Evans glasses. He wore ascots with no irony. Velvet blazers. I'd seen pictures through the years of the man showing up at industry events sporting a cane.

And not because he was injured.

The man absolutely did not have a tweaked ankle. He was feeling fine. He was simply the auteur dandy. But he didn't seem like a fool. That's the thing. You know why? You know why? Because when you saw one of his movies you left the theater impressed. Moved. And sometimes a different person from the person who walked in. So sport the cane, Doc, I could give two shits. Just keep doing what you're doing.

At nine-thirty the next morning, I left my office. Gave myself thirty minutes to get from Culver City to Beverly Hills. People say everything in L.A. is twenty minutes away. That's total bullshit. Everything's at least thirty minutes away and most things are forty-five minutes away.

This misperception is one of the reasons people in L.A. are always late. Drives me fucking crazy.

I am never late. And I do not respect people who are. Actually, you know what? I don't stop at disrespect. I full-on dislike people who are late.

I got in my car. 2010 Chevy Cobalt. Epically generic. Gray. That's the official name of the color. Gray.

I said to the guy when I was leasing it, "Gray? That's it? Not Cloud Gray or Deep Gray or something?"

The guy looked at me for a long time. For a second it got very quiet on the lot. The only sound came from the distant cars driving by on the road that ran next to the dealership. And then the guy said, "I think of it as Mountain Gray."

I looked at him. His face held a combination of false confidence and total doubt. I said, after another long pause, "Yeah, let's go with that."

I lease a new American sedan every three years or so. Almost time for a new one. No one, no one, can ever remember what I drive. My rides have names like Cobalt. Lumina. Azure. Azbalt. I made up the last one. But sometimes I tell people that's what I drive and they don't question it. Ever.

They say, "Hmm. An Azbalt. Sounds nice."

And I say, "Oh, it is. It's real nice."

I always find it odd that private detectives drive cars that really stand out. It doesn't make a whole lot of sense. Scratch that, it makes absolutely no sense. Let me tell you, as a P.I., you spend a lot of time following people around, and sitting outside their houses or offices, or bars or hotels they've wandered into. You're going to do that in a yellow

Ferrari? In a red and white muscle car with part of the engine sticking up out of the hood? I don't think so.

I drove toward Beverly Hills, toward the address Mountcastle had given me on that neat little index card. Headed north up La Cienega, swung a left on Sunset, then right on Benedict right next to the Beverly Hills Hotel. I was headed up now into *the* Beverly Hills. The fanciest section of one of the fanciest neighborhoods in the world. The grass in this part of town seemed greener than the grass in other sections of town. That's not a metaphorical way of saying I was in the up-market part of the city. The grass actually looked greener. The lawns were a bright, vivid almost lime green. Go check it out for yourself.

How did they do that, I wondered. How did they make the grass *glow*?

I headed up Benedict, up the little mountain toward Mulholland. The houses that lined the streets were big, old-school Beverly Hills with columns and bright flowers and cantaloupe-colored doors. About halfway to Mulholland, I swung a right on Portola Drive. Almost there.

And now, there. A big white wall and a gate covered in ivy. I pulled the Cobalt right up to the entrance and the gate magically opened. I guessed Mountcastle was probably spying on me using one of the house cameras. Or maybe he was peering at me from a lone window upstairs. Standing there giggling, binoculars in one hand, his enormous baby rattle in the other.

I drove on in and was presented with a wide, beautifully manicured lawn that a driveway twisted through. I went back and to the left, a fortress revealing itself. Gray-shingled house, two stories, Cape Cod vibe, with white shutters and trim. But this was Cape Cod with an asterisk. Because the house had offshoots and extensions and wings that turned it into a compound. You just sensed a pool back there somewhere, and a tennis court. The big front door was bright red. I parked, got out, looked back toward the main gate, my eyes focusing on a steel sculpture sitting in the yard. It was a massive half sphere standing randomly in the middle of a section of the lawn. It was like a giant smooth silver coin cut in half sitting upright.

"I like that," I said aloud.

I walked over to the door and was about to ring the bell or knock with the massive knocker, when the door swung open. Mountcastle, again, at the ready.

I sighed.

"Right on time," he said.

I didn't respond.

"Please come in."

He scooted back and away and I entered. I stood in the foyer, looking around. In terms of design, floor plan, it was similar to some other nice houses I'd been in. But the way it was decorated, put together, was unlike any house I'd ever seen. I looked to the left, the living room I thought, or *one* of the living rooms. My eyes found the couch. It was immense. Eight or ten people could sit on it side by side. It was bright blue. The floor it sat on was wood, but painted shiny black. A bright white rug covered most of the floor. Other pieces of furniture sat around randomly almost. I was taking it all in quickly, scanning the room. A hammock, an actual hammock, some big colorful pillows on the floor, a painting that I think was a Manet.

And no, not a Monet, a Manet. Strange and seductive.

Mountcastle said, "Mr. Vonz is in his writing studio. This way please."

I followed Mountcastle through the house. Various rooms that most houses have, but all made explosive by the Vonz touch. Rooms with beauty and tension. A dining room. A sitting room. A library. The library had dark walls, leather couches, surprisingly things you'd expect. But right in the center of the big wall across from the books was a very large painting of an aristocrat on a horse. It seemed too normal for the Vonz estate. But after a few seconds of looking at the picture, I noticed that the horse had a very human face and the man had a very horselike face. The painting came alive suddenly, it almost seemed to move and breathe.

"Jesus," I said.

We then went through a section of the kitchen and out a back door. And then, through a beautiful back courtyard full of foliage and flowers, a pool and a tennis court sitting in a chunk of the estate off to the left. See? There they were. A perfectly groomed California hardcourt, and a shimmering, inviting pool. Big, but still elegant.

We arrived at a relatively modest back house. Mountcastle stopped, gave me that baby-faced expectant smile, and motioned for me to head in.

"Walk right in, John. No need to knock. He knows you're here."

I looked at Mountcastle. The man-child. Who was this guy? How old was he? What kind of twisted shit was he into? Did he have a little room upstairs where he skipped around giggling and playing and prancing and throwing

15

things in the air? Was he truly twisted, like actual mental issues that could lead to violence? Who knows, man? Who knows? I turned and knocked on the door.

"No need to knock. Just go in," Mountcastle said, smiling, eyebrows arched up.

So I did.

3

There he was. Arthur Vonz. The great Arthur Vonz. The artist. The auteur. Winner of a zillion Academy Awards. He looked, believe it or not, younger in person. He was sitting behind his desk, holding a pencil. He was a longhand guy. Old school. Pencil, paper, and his ideas. His office, his little back house, was quite small. Desk, two chairs in front of it, big comfortable chair over in one corner. But it was still handled in the same way as the rest of his house. Wild color combinations. Unusual choices. One wall was a painting. It didn't have a painting on it, it *was* a painting. A massive Galapagos turtle looking right at you and sort of smiling.

Shit, I'll take it over that man-horse thing any day.

Vonz stood up. About six-one. Like me. He stuck out his hand.

He said, "John Darvelle. Nice to meet you."

"You too."

We shook.

"Have a seat."

I did.

"Thanks for coming to me. I mean driving over. Do most people come to your office when they hire you?"

"It depends."

"On what?"

"I really don't know."

He thought for a long second.

"So," he said. "My story."

I nodded, and unlike a lot of times, I was actually interested. Thing is, I can usually guess the general idea of what someone wants from me. I have a knack for it. Some guy walks in, I think: Wants to know if his wife is cheating. Some other guy walks in, I think: Corporate problem. Wants the competition looked into in one way or another. You get the idea. I know: Exciting cases. But, whatever, my point is, I'm usually in the ballpark, oftentimes right on the money. But right now? No idea. Could be anything. Stalker. Woman on the side. Rival. I didn't have an innate sense.

Vonz said, "Two years ago, I had an affair."

I looked at him. No acknowledgment, no judgment, I just looked at him.

"It was brief. And, I'm going to tell you this because it's relevant . . ."

He took a deep breath, looked away to the left, then looked back at me. "It was electric."

This guy was sucking me into his story.

He continued. "Most people think everyone in Hollywood has lots of affairs. Why? Because lots of people, like me, have plenty of opportunities. What is it that Chris Rock says?"

"You're only as faithful as your options."

He laughed. "It's a good line."

"It is," I said.

"And me? Well, I'm a director. So it's a bit of a double whammy. There is a tangible connection, a tangible reality, to what a tryst with me might get someone."

I nodded. Not because he was saying anything particularly insightful. More to let him know I was listening. Following along. But I *was* thinking: I'm glad he didn't patronize me by asking me, or confirming, that I knew what he did or who he was. He was respecting his audience's intelligence. That appeared to be his way.

"But until the affair I just mentioned, I was never unfaithful. I never took any of the opportunities I was given. In fact, I began to relish almost in *not* taking them. It gave me a certain pride, but more so, a certain *energy*, to not do what I knew I could do. And to not do what . . ."

"Everyone in the world expected you to do."

He looked dead at me. "Exactly." And then, "Are you married, John?"

"No."

He left it at that. I had been married. Once, for six months. But he didn't need to know that. My guess is he wanted to have a quick bonding session of the marriage-is-hard-no-matter-what-it's-easy-to-get-tempted variety.

"Well," he said. "Back to the story. One day, about two years ago, my ability to resist the temptation changed—in an instant. When I met Suzanne."

He paused. Then continued, "Suzanne Neal."

I said, "Suzanne Neal."

He looked at me, puzzled, but with a wry, maybe even hopeful, expression. "Do you know her?"

"No. But I like her name. Suzanne Neal. I like the way it sounds."

"I do too."

"Both the way it sounds when you say it, and the image it creates. She sounds attractive."

Vonz, very matter-of-fact, said, "She is."

And then he sat there. Still. Staring into some kind of void. Like he was on pause.

I said, "So, you broke your streak, and had an affair with her."

It was a statement, not a question.

"Yes," he said, back on play. "I met her on one of my sets. She was an extra on a movie I did called *Undertow*."

"I liked it a lot."

"Really? That one some people got and some people didn't."

"I got it. It was a typical adventure movie, B-movie type plot, B-movie archetypal characters. Only the movie was made really, really well. With all these sophisticated touches. With all these things that you typically don't see in a B-movie. That was the idea, I'd bet. That was the concept. To take a genre-type story and infuse it with really artistic direction."

"That's right. That was the idea. That's exactly right."

"But *Starlight*. That to me is your best movie."

"Thank you. That's one of my favorites too. It's one of the only movies I've made, maybe *the* only movie I've made, where I made exactly what I set out to make. It's not to say that I don't like, or even love, some of my other films. It's just that they didn't turn out quite how I envisioned they would. Except for *Starlight*. That one did."

Vonz looked out the window, again to his left, for a second. Thinking. Maybe contemplating that notion. Or maybe thinking about what he was going to have for lunch. I really didn't know.

He looked back at me.

I said, "Suzanne Neal."

"Yeah. It happened out of nowhere. Toward the end of the filming of *Undertow* I spotted her, we chatted, she charmed me, I took her to the Bahamas."

I thought: Replace the Bahamas with a Motel 6 next to the freeway and it's just like any other affair.

Vonz continued. "Like I said, it was electric. Primal, even. It was like the manifestation of all the affairs I had never had wrapped up into one. It was an exorcism to a certain extent. Subconsciously, I was mad at myself for getting myself into a position where women came with the snap of a finger—and then never doing anything about it. Inside my body, my biology, quite frankly, was pissed off at me. I had turned down all these opportunities and, as I said, part of me, my conscious mind, was energized by that. But another part of me, my id, was depressed and angry about it. I had rejected and suppressed millions of years of evolution. But then . . . Suzanne. I couldn't resist. The dam broke. I let it all out."

Okay, I thought. He's intellectualizing his decision, his cheating. A redneck, barefoot in front of a 7–Eleven, would have just said, "I was horny, bro." But Vonz was indeed in a unique situation. The wandering-eye scenario *was* a bit different for him. It's not everyone who has the most beautiful women in Hollywood proposition him.

"So," I said. "It ended?"

"Yes. My wife caught me. Gina. That's her name. Gina caught me."

He shot a look out the window, this time the window behind him, behind his desk. "My wife who isn't here, by the way." He looked back to me. "So, she caught me. I was willing to deal with the consequences. Because I didn't regret my decision. I believed I had to see what it would be like to follow my primal urges rather than suppress them. And it was great—as I said. It really was. But the truth is, the electricity of the sex abated. As it always does. And feeling that, knowing it for sure, comforted me. Made me happy that I had a wife I loved. A wife I wanted to stay with. And, as it turned out, a wife who was willing to forgive me. She never threatened to leave. She just wanted me to end it. So I did. But here's the thing. Suzanne and I kept in touch. I cared about her. I had connected with her, and I cared about her. Gina, of course, didn't know about this. But . . . I liked Suzanne. And I liked knowing what she was up to, giving her advice, helping her if I could. After all, she had helped me. So over the course of the last year or so, I introduced Suzanne to some industry people, helped her get a new agent, chatted with her from time to time. Just loosely kept an eye on her. Stayed in touch."

"And now you haven't heard from her in a while?"

Vonz didn't exactly answer. He kept talking, but he didn't exactly answer. "John. Do you believe in karma, signs, signals from the universe?"

"Yes," I said.

"Me too. And . . . I don't know, something *feels* off to me. Suzanne and I have had periods where we didn't talk much. And, yes, right now is one of them. I haven't heard from her in a while. And the number I had for her stopped working recently. But for some reason I feel like something's up. I don't know. I'm worried. I want to know that she's okay."

Or maybe, I thought, who she's dating.

"And you don't want anyone to know you're looking," I said.

"That's right. I don't want my wife to know. I don't want my assistant Paul to know. They think you are here to look into a little problem I'm having at my production company."

"Paul told me he didn't know why I was here."

"He lied."

I thought: Or you did. One of the two.

I said, "Paul. Interesting dude."

Vonz chuckled. "Yes. Well, Paul's been with us a long time. Gina didn't think it would be wise for me to have a beautiful young *female* assistant. This was before I ever strayed from my marriage—before she even had an inkling of suspicion. Just a smart wife being a smart wife. Paul's the son of an old friend of Gina's. He needed a job. Let's face it, he's not the type of guy who's going to be running a boardroom in New York. He's more the type who still reads comic books and lives at home with his parents. So I hired him, at first as a favor. But turns out he's a great assistant. Best I've ever had."

I nodded and moved on. "I charge seventy-five an hour,

plus expenses, which I document. An example of an expense would be: Say I'm following someone and he or she goes to a Dodgers game. I would expense my ticket. Some examples of things that aren't expenses: the gas in my car, the food I eat while on the case, my cell phone bill. It's very rare that clients dispute my expenses. Almost never. I invoice you when I'm finished with the job. On the invoice, as far as pertinent information goes, it will say your name, a number I assign to the case, and the amount you owe. No case details on the invoice itself. You can terminate the relationship any time you want. And so can I."

He nodded. "Great. Thank you for being clear. Let's do it."

"All right," I said. "What can you tell me about Suzanne? You have a number, an address, any family friends I can talk to? Anywhere she hangs out? A picture?"

He turned to his side, opened a drawer, and carefully pulled out a picture. He handed it to me and I looked at it.

Yes, a beautiful girl. Long blond hair, bluish-green eyes, bright red lipstick. She was on a balcony, high up, the sky behind her, the ground below her. She was looking right at the camera, smiling. She didn't appear to be posing. She didn't appear to have a pose that she had perfected. She looked natural. Now, I'm not being judgmental here. I'm being objective. She *was* a beautiful woman. But I didn't get a visceral reaction from the photo. I didn't think: Oh yes, I see why you risked your entire marriage on this one. She looked, in this picture anyway, like a pretty California blonde. Sort of typical. Like you see, oh, twenty to thirty times a day in L.A.

"You take this?"

"Yeah," Vonz said. "Keep it. And I've got the old phone number, if that helps. I've also got the name of a bar where she took me a couple times. The Prince. In Koreatown. And let me give you my number too, my cell."

I pulled out a pad, old-school, small, reporter-style spiral. And a pen. Bic, felt tip. I wrote it all down.

As a detective you need to write things down. That's pretty obvious. But I write things down, thoughts that occur to me, ideas that pop into my head, that have nothing to do with cases. I didn't always do this. But now that I do, I could never go back. Because oftentimes a thought comes to you out of nowhere. Sometimes it's useful to your life, sometimes it's a moment of clarity about something you've been mulling over, sometimes it's just a notion that you don't want to let go of. And if you don't write it down, something incredible can happen. It can disappear. Not for a moment, but forever. Like it was never there in the first place. These thoughts appear to you without warning, and if you don't zero in on them, in fact make them physically real by writing them down, they can vanish like a punishment. And it's a painful punishment because these thoughts, sometimes your most original and insightful, seem like they are retrievable. Like they will reappear if you think hard enough. But they won't. They're gone. And they're the worst kind of gone. Because they are *just* out of reach.

"What about an address?" I said. "Where does she live?"

Vonz laughed. "I don't know. She always just said Santa Monica. When we began our affair, I got a suite at the Four Seasons."

I held up the picture.

"Right," he said. "I took it on the balcony. We'd meet there. Or she'd already be there. I'd come home at night, of course. Sometimes she'd stay, sometimes she'd leave. It was our secret little place."

I looked at the picture again. Yeah, the earth behind and below Suzanne looked to be the area just west of Doheny, just west of the Beverly Hills Four Seasons.

Vonz said, "So, how long have you been a detective?"

"Eleven years."

"How do you become a detective?"

"You know, I think there are lots of ways. There are companies out there that employ sometimes hundreds of detectives, and they get people all sorts of ways. Ex-cops, ex-military, people who think they have an innate sense for it. And then, they just train them. Or sometimes people just hang a shingle, put an ad in the paper, and give it a shot. Me? I did a little of both. Went and worked at a big agency here in L.A. Six months later, I resigned and started my own agency. It took a long, long time before I really got it going. But if you stick with something, if you commit to actually doing the thing you say you want to do, it eventually starts to flow."

"Yeah. That's how I became a filmmaker. By just diving in. I didn't work in the studio system. I didn't work as a TV director. I just made indie films. It took a lot of work. But more so, time. Things go much slower at first. It could take years just to get barely enough money to start. But eventually, things started to flow."

I nodded. "I'm going to go look for Suzanne Neal."

4

All right, maybe he was telling me the truth, or some of the truth. And maybe not. I wasn't really sure. Maybe he's still involved with her, and she's avoiding him. That was my first thought. Or maybe she simply got a new phone and now her old one doesn't work and it's got his mind racing. You know? Is she sick of me? Is she seeing someone else? Am *I* not good enough?

Believe it or not, people who are in their sixties and have won Oscars and have given speeches to a billion people still have the same little fears and vulnerabilities we all had on the goddamn playground. It's amazing. Helps me in my business quite a bit. Not just in getting cases—paranoid cat walks in my office and pays me to follow his girlfriend. But in trying to figure out why somebody might have done something. Go back to the playground, John. That's what I tell myself sometimes. Go back to the simple, pure emotions we felt as children. That's where a lot of motives live.

Of course the possibility existed that he had indeed felt something and she was really in trouble. We'll just have to see. Yes, that's what we'll do. But no matter what, I'll tell you this, it didn't seem like it was going to be that hard to find her.

Back in the Cobalt now. Oh yes, look at that beautiful Sahara Beige interior. The *official* color of the interior was cleverly named "beige." I named it Sahara Beige. Better, right? So now I was sitting in a Mountain Gray car with Sahara Beige interior. You'd think that would be an unharmonious contrast. The mountains and the desert. Yet it was a perfect blend of visual comfort.

I called a friend of mine named Ken Booth. He's a Hollywood agent who represents TV actors. I've never had any small talk with him. None. Ken is all business, always. It's kind of nice. I call him when I want something, he calls me when he wants something, and we either help each other or we don't help each other, and that's it. I literally know nothing about him. Kids, wife, gay, straight, likes to put sexual conquests on a spinning knife board and throw things at them. I have no idea. I've only *seen* him once—the first time he hired me. Simple case. Find his ex–business partner so the cops could arrest him for trying to extort Ken. I found him pretty quickly and used a trick on him that I use on a lot of people I suspect have no real street experience. Within five seconds of meeting him, I pulled my gun on him and said, "Get on the ground with your hands behind your back or I'm going to shoot you." He was terrified, did what he was told, and I took him to the cops.

Ken appreciated it: I had my check within twenty-four hours. Not to mention more business from him over the years on behalf of his clients. The most valuable payment I got out of that first case, however, is that Ken uses his Hollywood connections to help me from time to time—on the house. But let's get back to the beginning of this little story within the story, to the fact that I don't have any personal relationship with Ken at all. That never once have we so much as engaged in ten to twenty seconds of pre-actual-conversation chitchat. Never once.

And yet, I like him a lot. I feel like he's a friend. I feel like if I called him with a serious problem he'd drop everything and help me. Weird how that works. It's just a feeling. It's something that isn't there, but is there. I thought about Vonz, who had said he *felt* something was wrong. Whether or not that was true in Vonz's case isn't the point. The point is, those invisible sensations are often real.

"Ken. John Darvelle."

"Yeah, my assistant told me. What's up?"

"I'm looking for an actress named Suzanne Neal."

"Is she commercial, TV, film, what?"

"Suzanne Neal. She just sounds hot, doesn't she?"

I can't describe to you the level of silence on the other line. Like outer space in a soundproof capsule. Ken would absolutely not get off track. He was just *not* going to say, "Yeah, she does sound hot."

I moved on, basically glad that Ken didn't break character. If he had agreed with me, or started to tell me some story about a girl with a great name, it might have freaked me out.

I heard some typing, and then: "She hasn't done much. A few commercials, a couple, looks like, indie films. Yeah, indie, never heard of them. Probably didn't get released. Her agent is Karen Alves at TT Talent. Hmm. Pretty big agent. Here's Karen's number."

He gave it me and I said, "Thanks, Ken."

"Yep," he said, and clicked off.

Hung up on me.

I switched my phone over so it would read "private" and called TT Talent—Karen Alves's direct line. Today so far I had met with a huge director and now I was on my second call to a Hollywood agent. Jesus, I was a player all of a sudden, I was a guy in a terry-cloth robe making a poolside call, I was Lew Fucking Wasserman.

Karen's assistant answered. A guy. Eager-sounding. "Karen Alves's office."

"Yeah, I'm calling from Dowd Casting. Actually, let me back up. You represent Suzanne Neal, right?

"When she feels like working we do." He laughed. I had no idea why.

"I have her down to be at an audition here at Dowd and she's not showing up."

"Hmm," he said. "She has an audition today. But not at Dowd. The only reason I know that offhand is she hasn't been going out much lately, and she is today. I guess it's possible she double-booked. Hmm. When it rains it pours. With most of Karen's clients, I'd know what's up, but with

Suzanne you never know. She meets people, gets called in, and doesn't tell us. Let me look here . . ."

Typing. Shuffling. Hmm-ing. "I don't see anything. What's it for?"

I said, "Film. Indie. It's called . . . *Cobalt.*"

Cobalt? Nice bullshitting, Darvelle. What are you going to tell him next? There's this hot new movie coming up called *LeSabre*? A terrific new film with the intoxicating title of *Oldsmobile Cutlass Cierra*? Dammit.

The assistant didn't see a problem with the title. He said, "Hmm. Well, she's supposed to be at Raleigh in Hollywood right about now. Or a little while ago. She may have left already. I just don't see anything about an audition at Dowd."

"Okay. Well, maybe her audition today is for a national commercial or something. Those can happen out of nowhere. And I guess make you forget about your indie audition."

"No, it's for a studio movie called *Friendship.*"

He paused again. Then: "Let's see. I can't give you her number. I *can* call her, but . . ." He laughed again. "That doesn't always do much good with Suzanne. What is your name, by the way?"

I had what I needed. Time to get off the call.

"Hello," I said. "Did I lose you?"

I know. Not that original. But it works.

"No, I'm right here," I heard the assistant say clearly.

"Shit," I said.

Now to an imaginary person in the room: "Think I lost the agent's assistant. She's over at Raleigh. Going to give them a call and see if she can come over after her audition . . ."

Click.

Raleigh Studios in Hollywood. A bunch of soundstages and casting rooms. You had TV shows and movies being filmed on part of the lot. You had TV shows and movies being cast on other parts of the lot. And you had commercials happening too. There were plenty of people kicking around hoping and praying and sometimes begging for their first break—getting the lead in a diaper commercial.

Like all studios these days, there was a security gate and a puffed-up security guard monitoring it. I couldn't think of anything to say to the guy, so I didn't turn in, I just drove right past. I think I might have even been whistling as I drove by to appear casual and not at all interested in entering the studio's lot. I took a right at the first block past the lot and parked in a little residential area that bordered the studio. I walked over to the back wall of the studio, perpendicular to the security gate, and climbed up a jacaranda tree that hugged the wall.

Side note: Jacaranda trees. Cool.

I exited the jacaranda and hopped onto the top of the wall. Then: Down on to the ground on the other side. I was in. Amazing security. Jeez. I hope someone doesn't want to show up on the set of some random sitcom one day and spray gunfire. It would be too easy.

I was in the parking lot now, the security entrance that I had bypassed over to the right. Big warehouse-y stages to the left, production bungalows and casting offices up ahead. I walked up to one of the little gray bungalows, opened the door, and walked in. There was a receptionist there. Fifty maybe. Attractive, but a little rough. Look in her eye that said: I've seen it all, babe. Hollywood glamour. Broken promises. Heartbreak. With a dash of: And by the way, don't fuck with me.

I said, "I'm here for the *Friendship* audition."

And then I thought: What if today's auditions are only for women? Shit, Darvelle, this isn't your best day.

She said, "Your point?"

Total smart-ass. I respected it.

"Sorry. Do you know where it is?"

"Didn't security tell you? When you enter through security, they tell you where to go."

Man. Another snafu. Yeah, that's right, I used the word "snafu." I said, "I'm an actor. I don't listen to others. Like the security guy. Didn't hear a word he said. When people talk to me I smile and nod, but I'm really just thinking about myself."

"Well, you kind of look like an actor, but you're not an actor, because actors don't talk like that. Actors actually *do* that, but they don't *say* they do that. And by the way, if what you just said is true, how are you going to hear what I'm telling you?"

"What?" I said. "I drifted off."

She gave me a sly look, called security, and asked where the *Friendship* audition was. Then she told me. "Walk across the lot to stage seven, then go through a door marked A."

"I think I can follow that."

"Like I said. You're not an actor."

I smiled. "Thank you. I appreciate it."

And I did. And I thought that, despite her remarks, she bought my story. I walked out the door.

Across the lot, I walked through the door marked A—I'd found the audition. Flanking one of the big stages, the waiting area was a stark, bleak, gray-walled room. Actresses and actors sat, some reading their scripts, some just blankly staring into the stark bleakness. Suzanne was not one of them.

The room housed a door that opened periodically to reveal the actual audition room. I'd catch intermittent glimpses of smug-looking black-turtlencck types determining the careers of people. But no Suzanne in there either. Must have missed her. I sat down in the waiting area; no one seemed to mind.

A weary, bearded casting director wandered in and out of the two rooms. Calling people in, sending people out. Man, this was depressing. No wonder actors and actresses were such freaks.

The thing is, though, this was a pretty big audition. For a real movie. That's the reality. Even some of the biggest Hollywood pictures were cast in environments like this. For starring roles. Hard to believe if you've never seen it. If you took a tourist here and said: Do they cast big movies here or torture people? You'd get a 70–30 split—in favor of the torture.

I caught the bearded casting director's eye. He looked at me. He seemed to know I didn't belong there. "Can I help you?"

"Wait. This is the audition for *Friendship*?"

He nodded. He looked exhausted.

"Sorry, wrong room. This place is confusing."

I walked back out to the lot and hung around. I stood between a Toyota Prius and a pickup. I felt obvious, but the reality is no one even gave me a second look. I watched people mill about the lot, casting people, Hollywood types, actors, actresses, randoms. Nobody walked by in costume like you see when people are on Hollywood lots in the movies. No aliens. No Roman gladiators. No bald strong man sporting a curly mustache and a wrestling singlet. I leaned on the pickup, watched the door to the *Friendship* audition. A young actor who I'd seen in the waiting room emerged. He would be filed under the "quirky" type. The pudgy-white-guy-with-a-charmingly-unkempt-Afro-friend who says outrageous yet somehow honest and real things. I watched him get in his car, an old red Jeep Wrangler. He cranked it up and headed toward the entrance I had bypassed. I took off. Ran back over to the back wall, climbed it, jumped over to the jacaranda, then dropped to earth on the other side. I got in the Cobalt, fired her up, took off, and yanked her around to the street where the gated entrance was.

The Jeep had already exited the lot and I just caught it going left at Sunset, two blocks up from where I was. I stomped on it, got up to the Sunset intersection fast, then ripped it left, in front of, way too close to, some oncoming cars. Had to, otherwise I would have been waiting forever. The guy's red Jeep was at a light one block down Sunset. I put the Cobalt right behind him. I followed him for a bit, left on La Brea, right on Beverly. A couple miles later he parked. I copied him—parked ten spaces up on the same side of the street. Then through the glass of the Cobalt watched him head into the King's Road Café. Coffee shop slash lunch spot. Hipster Heaven. Don't even fucking walk in without the proper amount of irony. They should sell pencil-thin mustaches and pencil-thin cardigan sweaters at the door.

I got out, got my slim jim out of the trunk, walked down to his Jeep, and broke into it.

It took less than ten seconds. I looked inside for some headshots, figured he brought some to the audition. Found them. Right next to, you guessed it, some other headshots. A stack of black and white shots, no smile, his serious look, and a stack of colored shots where he sported a big smile that said: Hey, I'm a loose, fun, funny cat. I went color, looked at the picture, looked at the name on the bottom. Clay Blevins. Friendly-looking. Like I said—shaggy, curly hair. And, yeah, overweight. Charmingly overweight. The slacker friend. Perfect for the scene where the character is sitting on a couch, the remote control to the tube out of reach. And instead of getting off the couch and walking over to grab it, he grabs something within arm's length, a nearby broom or rolled-up newspaper, to try and hook the remote and drag it over to himself, so he didn't have to actually move.

Not a judgment. Look, I've pulled that move. More than once.

I looked on the back of the headshot, where Clay's résumé was stapled. He'd done a few things. Couple sitcoms, some commercials, an indie flick or two.

All right, Clay, time to introduce myself.

I walked in King's Road Café, pretending not to see him, but getting a look at him. Already seated, and now noticing up-close his wardrobe. Big old cargo shorts and a massive T-shirt. He was kind of gazing off into space. Contemplating his audition. Or maybe thinking about what porn site he was going to go to later. Or maybe picturing himself in a perfectly fitted tuxedo, with a sharp part in his curly hair, entering and then winning a tap-dancing contest. I really didn't know.

I grabbed a cup of coffee and walked over to his table. "Clay?"

He looked up at me, smiled, sort of eager.

"Yeah."

"Hey, man. I'm Tim."

He smiled. He was polite. Nice. He really, really didn't want me to know that he had no clue who I was.

I continued, "I work at Raleigh. I'm one of the casting directors. Came in at the end of the *Friendship* call."

He stood up and said, "Tim! Nice to see you, man."

"Yeah, you too. Nice going in that Bud Light spot."

"Dude, that dog could actually ride that bike. There was no CG."

"Ha!" I screamed. "So how's things? What else is going on?"

He started to give me the life-as-an-actor-in-Hollywood spiel. How you never know. How you just keep going day to day. How Johnny Depp was living in a tiny apartment one day and driving a Porsche the next. My eyes began to glaze over. Actually, that's not true. It was much worse than that. I almost killed myself. I swear I did. I almost just ran out onto Beverly and threw myself in front of a bus. And let it rumble over me and tear me to shreds.

I said, "Well, I hope you get the *Friendship* gig. Good to see you, man."

I started to bolt and then, casually: "Say, do you know Suzanne Neal?"

"Yeah. God. She's . . . Man, she's just so hot."

I laughed. It was so honest. It's like he couldn't *not* say it.

"I mean it's just not fair," he continued. "It hurts me. It hurts me to think about her."

Probably true, but moving into routine-ville now.

"Yeah," I agreed. "No doubt. I needed to talk to her after her audition today, but missed her."

"I didn't see her today. I heard she was in though."

"What's she up to these days? She working?"

"You'd know more than me probly."

That's how he said it. "Probly."

And I didn't say anything. Sometimes that's the best way to get someone to keep talking.

It worked. He went on, "But I really don't know. A bunch of us used to all be in the same acting class. Suzanne would show up every now and then. Man, she skipped a lot of classes. But we'd all hang out with her some. You know, go have beers after class or whatever."

"Where, the Prince?"

"Ha. Yeah, once actually. She likes that place."

See, Clay, see, I really *do* know her.

"But we'd all see each other at auditions too. People from that class. But that was a while ago, man."

And then, like he was having a fond memory, "*Suzanne* . . . She was always cool. Nice, I mean. Even though she was, you know, so totally hot. We'd be at a bar and like ten guys would ask her out. Celebs and stuff too. So who knows what she's doing. I did hear she bought some sweet condo in Santa Monica like right on the ocean."

"Good for her," I said. "Maybe she got a big part or something."

"Yeah, maybe. I don't really hear from her much. I wish I did, but I don't."

"Well, I need to talk to her. Possible print shoot for her. You don't have her number, do you? I've got one but it doesn't seem to work."

"I don't have her number, man. And she never got into Facebook. I've checked. She doesn't need it, you know what I'm saying?"

I nodded.

And then he said, "Sorry, dude, I definitely recognize you, but what did you say your name was again?"

I had no clue. I stood there looking at him. A long time seemed to go by. I was looking right at him and he was looking right at me. It was a universe of time, and it was the universe that did me a favor by dropping my fake name back into my memory bank.

"Tim," I said.

"Right. Cool."

We shook hands.

And I split.

And I knew what I had to do.

And it scared me.

5

What scared me? I had to call my real estate connection Linda Robbie. Linda Robbie is a fifty-one-year-old master of Westside real estate. She's buxom, brunette, and sports a perma California tan. She's definitely not afraid of a lift, a tuck, or a pull. And that's just her sexual exploits. Sorry. Sorry about that. But it's true. In that she's known for some bedroom acrobatics. She's also very open about her self-improvement, which, of course, disarms the situation completely and makes her beautifying downright charming. And let me say this: She gets it done right. She doesn't look like some freakish Frankenstein-ian creation. She looks pretty damn good. But, if I'm being honest, and I am, she looks a little *unreal*.

She's also not afraid to get married. Four husbands in

her past. But currently single. I've helped her out quite a few times over the years. And she's helped me out quite a few times over the years too. You'd be surprised how often she and I need each other's services. I think it's fair to say we use each other. It's a full-on you-scratch-my-back-I'll-scratch-yours deal. Although, unlike Ken Booth, Linda seems highly interested in a more personal relationship.

"Linda, it's John Darvelle."

"Please tell me this isn't a business call and you want to take me to a fancy hotel in Palm Springs and have your way with me."

Linda is direct.

"Where's the subtlety, Linda? Where's the innuendo, the coyness, the old-fashioned suggestion?"

"Oh shut up, John."

"Hey, I'm just asking a question."

With some sexual topspin she said, "I'll give you something to question."

Sometimes Linda tries to find double entendres in regular sentences. Actually, she does that pretty much all the time. Sometimes she hits: rarely. Sometimes she misses: often. I think that was a miss. In that I had no idea what she meant.

I said, "Babe, I got a real question."

"All right, hurry. I'm about to sew up a deal on a three-point-fiver in the Canyon."

Three-point-five-million-dollar house. Santa Monica Canyon. That's what she meant.

"You are good at your job, Linda."

"I know. So are you."

"Listen. Have any condos been sold to a Suzanne Neal

in the last three months? In Santa Monica. I'm thinking Ocean Avenue, but I guess check the PCH too."

"There aren't many condos on the PCH, John. Not that are technically Santa Monica anyway."

"Okay, let's go Ocean Avenue."

"I need twenty minutes."

"All right. Please also check for Arthur Vonz. If Arthur Vonz bought anything."

Linda's voice changed. It got serious, intense, you could hear the focus. "Is Arthur Vonz in the market? Was he looking recently? I didn't hear that."

Linda, irritated that she hadn't gotten the listing—if there had indeed been one. I mean, look, she's good at her job. She's a millionaire many times over, by the way. A real estate machine.

"I don't know if he was in the market. This is something I'm looking into. But please also check if he's bought a condo. Same location."

Again with a sexual twist: "What do I get in return?"

She always says this. Even though that's not how we operate. We just do whatever the other person needs. Within reason.

I moved on. "Call me when you get something."

"I'll give you something to call."

Having absolutely no idea what she meant, I hung up.

She called me back twenty minutes later. She had said twenty minutes. She called, I think, exactly twenty minutes later. Love that. I didn't love her news though. No one by the name of Suzanne Neal had bought anything in Santa Monica in the last year. And then:

"Nothing by Arthur Vonz either, doll."

"Do you know if he—"

"Already owns one? He does not. I checked."

"How many condo sales on Ocean Avenue have there been in the last six months?"

"Somewhere between twenty and thirty, I'd say," she said without missing a beat.

A lot. And very hard to tell, even with the names attached to the sale, who exactly they were for. Especially if it was a purchase that the person doing the purchasing didn't want others to know about.

Hmm, I thought. What to do? Linda answered that for me.

"Look," she said. "There's a relatively new building on Ocean. They just sold it out this past month. A few of the recent purchases were there. Four or five. 78630 Ocean. Maybe that's not a bad place to start."

"Yeah. You're right. That's not a bad place to start."

6

I drove over to the condo. Nice. White. Tall. New. Not really my style. It was fancy and probably had some Lakers living in it or something. But for some reason I pictured a really rich old lady with a face-lift sitting high up in one of the condos, looking out at the sea, sad-eyed, by herself, and then saying out loud, "Yeah, yeah, I remember . . ." to no one in particular and then walking back into her bedroom and going to sleep.

I have no idea why.

I parked at a metered spot across the street from the tall, bright white condo. It was right on Ocean Avenue, thus the address. But Ocean Avenue isn't quite accurate. Ocean Avenue is actually a road that runs parallel to the Pacific Coast Highway, but up a big cliff. And then, on "Ocean

Avenue," up the big cliff, all the condos and buildings are on the east side of street. On the west side of the street is a long park that runs essentially the whole of Ocean Avenue.

I thought, you know, even though these condos are really expensive and desired, you're not *really* on the beach. The beach was across the street, down the freaking cliff, *and* across the Pacific Coast Highway. So, yes, on most floors you had the view, and you had the nice park right across the street where you could watch lovely ladies jogging and stretching and stretching, but you didn't really live *on* the beach. You lived up a cliff and across a street from the beach, with a *view* of the beach. I mean it's okay if you're a "view person," which I'm definitely not, but it's almost a tease. You know what I'm saying? To get to the actual beach, you're going to have to walk basically just as far as someone who lived two, three blocks inland on a regular old street with a regular old name like Second Street. Or Third Street. Or the appropriately named Fourth Street.

Jesus, man, why do I give a shit where someone else lives? Why am I wasting mental energy on this?

Let me just say one more thing before I move off this point. People who are obsessed with "views" or "the view" from a particular place are just generally irritating. You ever have someone show you their pictures from a trip and there are a bunch of shots of "the view" from their deck or whatever? You know what I say, eyes half lidded, after the third shot of the lake? I say: Listen, dude. Or lady. Please go grab a shovel, come back, and hit me in the face with it as hard as you can. Please. Please do this.

Let's get back to the story.

I exited the Cobalt and walked across Ocean Avenue

and went in the main door of the new building. There was a security guard sitting there, reading a paperback novel. He had a glazed look on his face and his mouth hung slightly open.

I thought: I want this guy's job.

He lowered the book and offered me a slightly awake expression.

"Can I help you?"

"Hey, has Suzanne come back?"

"Suzanne who?

"You know who I'm talking about. She's like a ten. *Suzanne.*"

He gave me a flat look.

"Suzanne Neal. That's her name."

"I don't know who that is."

And now he gave me a long, glazed-over, mouth-breather stare. Sometimes dumb people can almost throw you off your game. They can betray a certain calm, or behave sort of unnaturally, or just stare at you blankly and interminably. You can mistake it for wile and gamesmanship. I had a feeling, though, this guy just simply didn't have much going on upstairs.

He said, "Let me look her up."

"Cool," I said. "Thanks."

He started to look her up on the building's computer directory. "Suzanne who again?"

"Neal."

"Don't see her," he breathed.

"Maybe it's under S. Neal."

I thought to myself: Sneal. That would be a hip last name.

"Yeah, good idea, I'll check that."

I thought, yes, it was a brilliant idea.

"Don't see that either, guy."

He shot me a bizarre, crooked smile. "You sure she lives here?"

I looked right at him. "Positive."

"Well, I don't see her."

"Maybe it's under someone else's name. I think her parents helped her with the down payment."

"Wouldn't that be the same name, though?"

Chalk one up for the mouth breather.

"Stepdad," I shot back, now in a completely unnecessary mini-war. Time to let this one go. "I've got to run. I'll just call her."

"You want me to leave a message for her in case I figure out she lives here?"

I thought: Does what he just said even make sense? Actually, I think it does . . .

He continued, "What's your name?"

I repeated, "I'll just call her."

I left, went outside, crossed Ocean, and stood next to my car. Now, right next to my car, in the park, a yoga class had started. It was a tan, attractive woman teaching a group of mostly tan, attractive women to twist into lots of lovely shapes. I watched for a moment. My bottom lip curled involuntarily and I stared with what I knew instinctively was a transfixed, trancelike expression.

You ever sneak a little steak to a dog under the table at a dinner party? And then, hours later, I mean *hours* later, the dog catches your eye from across the room and he gives you that look of hope, desperation, and longing all rolled into one? That look that says: Whatever you need me to do, my man, I'll do it.

That's how I looked right then.

I got in the Cobalt. I drove a little ways south on Ocean toward Venice, flipped a U-ey, and parked. I had a clear view of the building I'd just exited ahead of me. I had a second Ocean Avenue condo right next to me. And a third right behind me, across a little side street, visible in the rearview. Maybe, I thought, she lives in one of the three. It's all I had for now. And, yes, if you must know, I could also see right across Ocean to my left, the yoga class, the ladies bending this way and that.

So that was nice.

Looking at the building I'd been in and sort of the yoga class, I called my friend Gary Delmore. Gary's a TV director who's been out here a long time. Wanted to be, basically, Arthur Vonz when he first arrived. And he got off to a great start. Directed a small indie movie that got a lot of attention. The lead actress got nominated for an Academy Award. Gary was hot. He quickly signed on to a big, big movie to direct and almost just as quickly it failed spectacularly. Not entirely his fault. It happens. But he never really got another chance for big-screen success. He had the failure connected to him like an appendage. But Hollywood let him into the TV world—Hollywood will do this—and he did well. Worked well with the studios. Made some friends. Directed some episodes of big shows that won some Emmys. Now, years later, he works in TV all the time. Directing sitcoms, dramas, dramedies, comedramas, sci-fi, sci-com, sci-dram, everything. If it's got a freaking script, Gary gets a call. He makes a shitload of money, lives in a big house, has dyed white teeth, a perma tan, and big eighties hair. He dates a different actress each week. And, of course, drives a mid-life crisis–style sports car.

But he knows who he is. Embraces his cheese. Hugs his shallowness. Makes out with his vapidity. And that's why he's great. Gary's one of my connections. But he's also become a friend. He loves Ping-Pong. He comes over to my office from time to time and we drink a few beers and hit around. And, yes, he sets me up with an actress or two occasionally. Guilty. Guilty as charged.

"Gary, John."

"The Darv. How's life in the exciting world of P.I.-dom?"

"Not too bad. Have a quick question for you."

"Yeah."

"You ever come across—sorry, bad choice of words for you—you ever *meet* a beautiful actress named Suzanne Neal in your many experiences as a director or as a dater of young-will-do-anything-to-make-it actresses?"

"It's hard to remember all their names," he said in a faraway tone. He wasn't kidding. He really meant that. "Hmm. I really don't think so. Suzanne Neal . . . Hey, but let me tell you this story. So this past Saturday I'm at a party in Marina del Rey . . ."

"I gotta go," I said, and hung up.

Something unusual, interesting, something, something caught my eye. And that's what we do in the P.I. biz. We look for stuff that catches our eye. Our private eye. A guy in a brand-new Maserati pulled into a spot five spots ahead of me, same side of the street. He got out of the car and walked over to the parking meter. Fumbling around. He looked like he didn't know what he was doing. He looked like he'd never paid a parking meter before. Staring oddly at the meter, looking at his change like it was currency from another planet. But that's not really what caught my eye. This guy, this rich guy, was trying really hard *not* to be seen. Trucker hat pulled low, glasses, head pointed down, moving around quickly and frantically.

And nervously.

Why did this interest me? Well, it was either be interested or sit and stake out three buildings at once that Suzanne may or may not live in. See what I'm saying?

I got out of my car and walked toward the guy. His glasses were just huge. Not Vonz-style, not old-school movie producer, more modern, more ironic. Big ski glasses. Hiding a face that was handsome. I could tell. I got nearer, then right next to him. I walked straight on by. Not whistling this time. I stopped, casually looked back. He figured out the parking meter, paid it, then turned and walked toward the middle condo. Not the one I'd been in, the one next to it, the one right next to my car. Also nice, pretty new. Also quite a snazzy address if you didn't have the problems I did.

Walking down the hill, across the PCH, all that bullshit.

He went in the building. I followed, ten, maybe twelve seconds behind him. I walked up to the entrance, opened the door, went in, caught him getting in an elevator. He hadn't stopped at the doorman character—this one an old man, maybe sixty. No way. He wouldn't be at the elevator if he had. Been here before, I thought. I turned around and walked back outside.

An hour and a half later the guy walked out. I was now

on a bench in the park across the street. The yoga class had ended about a half hour ago. It had made the waiting time fly.

The guy walked over to his car. Not as nervous, as fidgety, more of a glide to his step. He'd gotten a parking ticket, I'd seen it go down, hadn't put enough dough in the meter. The guy didn't react, didn't seem to give a shit. Grinning, he snatched the ticket off his car, got in, buckled up. In a moment of recklessness, and vanity, he removed his shades and his hat and looked at himself in the rearview. And then he turned quickly toward me, not looking for me, but looking to see if anyone was watching him. I was. I looked right at him.

And I made him.

Jimmy Yates, one of the biggest movie stars in the world. I smiled and waved at him. He covered himself up, quickly all hat and shades again. He cranked up the Maserati and roared out of there.

All right, folks, let's look at some possibilities. One, Jimmy Yates has nothing to do with my story. Very possible. He's just a famous guy sneaking into a building incognito. Maybe for some extramarital activity. Jimmy's married. To a famous actress. He's one of those guys. He's famous and so is his wife and they're just *so* happy. And you can tell they're *so* happy by the numerous pictures snapped by gossip photographers which capture them walking through airports with their children who are wearing classic rock T-shirts and mini Chuck Taylors.

I can be cynical.

Or maybe it's not about having a girlfriend on the side. Maybe he's got a meeting he doesn't want anyone to know about. Could be—happens all the time. He's sneaking in to read a script. Meet with a director. Set up a project. Why would he sneak around to do that? Because these guys take themselves really fucking seriously. That's why.

But that glide to his step. That no-longer-nervous thing. That I-just-got-laid vibe. Looked to me like, with these two aforementioned options, possibility A was more likely.

Or.

Or maybe it *is* about getting a little something on the side in a way that *does* fit into my story. Let's get crazy here and connect some dots. Arthur Vonz is an A-lister. Jimmy Yates is an A-lister. These guys know the same people. And the big shots have a tendency to fall in love with the same women. What's that girl's name, Pattie Boyd? Who dated, like, every rock star in the seventies? Broke up a couple marriages and, let's not kid ourselves, inspired some good shit while doing it. All right, getting off track. But maybe Vonz bullshitted me and the truth is he's just suspicious that Suzanne's hanging out with somebody else? Somebody who's also a player with a ton of influence *and* who's handsome and not pushing seventy.

This is what you do in the P.I. business. You guess. You guess a lot.

I looked at my picture of Suzanne. This girl might possibly have two Huge Shots tied in knots over her. I don't know, man. Like I said. Attractive, sure. But I wasn't seeing anything I hadn't seen in a thousand headshots, in a thousand faces wandering the Grove. You know, the hottest babe in high school who came to L.A. to get famous. That's what Suzanne looked like.

So what.

I walked across the street, put some more change in the meter, and stood next to the Cobalt. Now what? This is another thing you do a lot as an investigator. You say: Now what?

I didn't want to walk into building two, the Jimmy Yates building, and pull my bullshit-the-doorman routine. But I wanted to see if Suzanne lived there. I thought, maybe I'll pull the info out of a neighbor, switch it up a bit. I got in the Cobalt and sat there.

Even though I'd just put more money in the meter, I moved the car again. Restless. Parked again. Still had a line on all three buildings. But now there was no yoga class and no movie stars awkwardly parking and giving me hope. There was a dead, empty feeling in the air. Like maybe I had made literally zero progress.

I thought: Let's let this empty feeling grow. I put on a playlist I'd made of some of my favorite Lou Reed songs. I found "Lisa Says," the Lou Reed solo version, not the Velvet Underground version. I listened to it four times in a row, then let the playlist ride. Lou's strange, interesting phrasing, his unusual, exotic melodies took me away from the case. The music took me on an hour-long emotional journey. I thought about my life, some epic college moments, one of the actresses Gary Delmore had introduced me to, my six-month marriage. It felt good. Introspective. A little melancholic. But good.

And then I saw a beautiful blond woman walk out the front door of, you guessed it, Ocean Avenue condo two. She leisurely walked right out the same door Jimmy Yates had come skipping out of.

7

She walked right in front of the car parked two cars up from me. I watched her. She crossed the street and headed into the park. She went to the edge of the park, where a low-slung wooden fence provided a little support to lean on—and prevented you from walking straight off the cliff and tumbling down to your death. It was a small fence, decoration, a reminder really. You could climb it easily, step over it or through it, and throw yourself off if you really wanted to. People had. One guy drove his car right through it and headed off the edge into gravity and, of course, pavement. That's what I heard anyway.

The blonde leaned lightly against the fence and looked out at the ocean.

I grabbed my digital camera, nothing serious, tourist-style, got out of my car, crossed the street, hid behind a tree, and snapped a couple photos of her. Mostly from behind, and a few of the back quarter of her profile. Then I walked over to her.

"Excuse me," I said.

She turned to me. Suzanne Neal. For sure. And no fear or suspicion in her eyes at the hello of a stranger. Just a smile and some lifted eyebrows to suggest: How can I help?

I said, "Would you mind taking my picture? Want to get a shot with the ocean in the background. I'm visiting."

"Sure," she said.

I handed her the camera, then leaned against the fence, getting ready for my close-up.

"Where are you visiting from?" she asked.

"Jacksonville, Florida."

Pretty good choice, right? A big city, but kind of unexpected. Like there's no way that's bullshit. Truth is, my aunt lives there. And I've been. My aunt found some trouble once. I'll tell you about it sometime. But it's a good, just-off-the-radar, totally believable fake hometown—and I can answer the follow-up questions about it if necessary because I've been, I've experienced it.

And sometimes there are follow-ups.

Suzanne Neal didn't have any.

I did the standard forced smile and she snapped the photo. She looked at the camera, at her own work. "Pretty good shot if I do say so myself."

She smiled at me. And in an instant I knew what Vonz, and maybe Jimmy Yates, were all crazy about. She was beautiful. And sexier than her picture let on. But also real and special and in no way typical. She had a magic in her eyes, and a mischief. But the thing that exploded out of her was the ability to make *you* feel special. Like she really liked you. Like you were the only person who mattered.

Like you were the only person in the world.

You know people like that? You know people like that.

I said, "I'll be the judge. Let me see."

I looked at the shot. "Not bad. Take one with me."

I scooted over next to her and held the camera out pointed back at the two of us. She was game, didn't mind. I popped off a shot. I looked at the picture. Me with the over-the-top smile, her with the over-the-top, lips-ready-to-kiss, playful sexy look. My eyes stayed on Suzanne.

Her image was heartbreaking.

"Thanks," I said. "I'll cherish it forever. The one of just me, I mean."

She smiled. I nodded and respectfully headed off. Even though I wanted to ask her to move to Mexico with me and start a family.

"What's Jacksonville, Florida like?"

Well, well. There *was* a follow-up.

And was this Arthur Vonz affair-having gorgeous young woman engaging me? Me? John Darvelle, P.I.? Yes, friends. Yes, she was.

I turned around. "It's great. Great town. Sort of has a hidden gem, undiscovered quality."

"What do you mean?"

Damn. She actually cared. She wasn't just making conversation.

"Well, it's in North Florida, so it doesn't look like what you expect Florida to look like. It has big oak trees and sort of a beautiful Southern look. But at the same time, it's on the Atlantic. So it does have the Florida sunny beach thing. But it's a different kind of beach from the rest of Florida. It's big and wide and pretty great."

I was overdoing it. Because I wanted to keep talking to her.

"What, are you a travel agent?"

I laughed. "Do those still exist?"

"I grew up in Charlotte. I know exactly what you mean about the Southern beaches and everything. I miss it. I love L.A. I do. But L.A. is . . . complicated. And for some reason it makes you feel lonely sometimes."

She was right.

I said, "I've had a nice visit. Checked out Hollywood yesterday. Had to go to Mann's Chinese. Santa Monica today. Got a picture with you. Had some good celeb sightings too. Actually . . . you know who I just saw?"

No reaction from her. She just smiled and said, "Who?"

"Jimmy Yates."

Her smile didn't leave her face. Her face didn't stretch into any new configuration. But there was a shift in her eyes. And therefore a shift in her expression. It just happens, you can't help it. You cannot help it. It's so subtle, but so obvious. Kind of incredible—human emotion is hard to tamp down.

"Wow," she said in a very genuine way. "That's a big one."

"Now if I can just figure out a way to see Scott Bakula I can go home totally satisfied."

"Ha. Right," she said.

I held up the camera. "Thanks again."

Back in the Cobalt. Found her. Got a picture of her. Got a picture *with* her. Mr. Big Shot Arthur Vonz would be impressed. Or not. Maybe he knew it wouldn't be that hard to find her.

I drove back to my office. Opened the big slider, sat behind my desk, let the afternoon sun stream in. Had a quick memory of demolishing Mountcastle in Pong. I had made it hurt and had zero regret. That's a good feeling. Zero regret. I dialed up Vonz. To my surprise, he answered. I don't know why that surprised me. Maybe I suspected Mountcastle would intercept the call. Devious fucker.

"Mr. Darvelle," Vonz said.

"Mr. Vonz," I said in a way that showed I didn't like him playing around with my name like we're old friends.

"What can I do for you?"

"I found Suzanne."

"That didn't take long."

"Often if doesn't. If the person isn't hiding."

"Well, tell me about it."

I started to, and then he interrupted me. "You're in Culver City, yes?"

"Yes."

"I'm leaving on a flight tomorrow evening from the Santa Monica airport. Not too far from your office. Maybe you could meet me there and we could talk? I'd like to talk to you about something. I'd . . . I'd like to give you something."

The Santa Monica airport was not LAX. This was a

small airport for private planes. Props and jets. For aviators and rich people. On the property, there was one pretty big building, the terminal, I guess you'd call it, and a few smaller surrounding structures. The big one housed some offices and a nice, sparse waiting area where you could hang out while your eighty-five-million-dollar jet got all fueled up. The building also housed a popular restaurant, a groovy but upscale California Thai place, Typhoon, with big widows out to the runways so you can watch the planes land and take off. Watching planes land and take off—it's actually more enjoyable than you'd think. There used to be a sushi joint called Hump that sat high up on the third floor of the building, the top floor, with a little outside patio for, yes, plane viewing. Hump shut down, though—something about selling whale meat illegally. By the way, it wasn't called "The Hump." It was just called Hump. I used to say to dates, "I'll pick you up, we'll go to hump, and then maybe after we'll grab some sushi."

Yeah, I know, it's not that great. Whatever.

I said to Vonz, "Sure, what time?"

"Let's meet at Typhoon at five. We'll have a drink, watch the planes come in."

See? Even this guy enjoyed it.

"Until then," I said.

8

I walked into Typhoon at 4:59. Running a little late, quite frankly. It was on the second floor. Hadn't been here in a while. Great vibe. Great design. Dark wood everywhere, good lighting, and the whole back wall essentially one big window looking out onto the runway. It was beautiful—planes coming and going up through and down through an orange and purple sky just beginning to darken over Santa Monica.

Vonz was on time, earlier than I even, sitting in a booth at the right side of the big window. The best seat in the house. He looked over at me, grinned, and raised an eyebrow—glad to see me, it seemed. Maybe he was impressed that I took care of his assignment so quickly. Or maybe he was just a charming bastard and that's how he got you to do what he wanted. The latter almost certainly.

I sat down. Before I said a word he flagged over a waitress. Not tough when the staff is basically staring at you.

A pretty girl said, "Can I get you a drink, sir?"

"I'm having a scotch and soda," Vonz said.

I said, "I'll have a Bud Light."

"We don't have that here."

"Do you have any domestic beer? Bud, Bud Light, Coors, Coors Light?"

"I'm afraid not. We have an assortment of Thai beers and just one domestic, from a microbrewery in Northern California."

I almost got up and left.

Here's the thing. A classy restaurant, a truly sophisticated establishment, has cheap American beer as well as that other bullshit. Almost nothing pisses me off more than when a restaurant tries to raise its sophistication level by only serving Japanese beer or some fucked-up micro brew or, this is the worst, just Amstel Light and Heineken. It's such an uninspired, middle-class, ersatz mentality to think that sophisticated people wouldn't want a goddamn Budweiser just because they're at some restaurant. It's such a mistake. It betrays such a lack of knowledge about what's really happening in life. About what it really means to *get it*. About what it really means to be "classy." Go to Dan Tana's in Hollywood, go to The Polo Lounge in the Beverly Hills Hotel, go to an old-school New York–style restaurant that understands service and people. Sure, you can get a Heineken, you can get a Beck's or whatever, but you can also get a cold, crisp Miller Fucking Lite if that's what you want. Yes, rednecks in Florida drink Budweiser, barefoot in front of their trailers, listening to Edgar Winter and arguing with each other at high decibels before noon. But you know who else drinks Budweiser? Me. And I've read a book by Thomas Pynchon. I didn't understand it, but let's not split hairs. It makes me a whole lot more sophisticated than most of the assholes in most places.

Except for maybe Vonz. He's probably read a Pynchon book or two.

I took a breath, looked out the window. I pictured running as fast as I could, crashing through it, and landing on the tarmac two floors down. Then getting up, shaking off the glass, and just quietly, very quietly, walking off.

But I didn't do that. I took another breath, got my shit together, and looked back at the waitress politely. It wasn't her fault, after all.

"Gin and tonic then."

The waitress scurried off.

"You don't like the beer choices?" Vonz asked.

"I like beer that I can have a lot of. Light and crisp. I'm not interested in drinking a beer that makes me full after one. I'm not interested in drinking a glass of bread."

Vonz looked at me. He might have been slightly scared. He said, "I like that." Then: "So. You found Suzanne?"

"Yes." I told him essentially how I found her. And where she lived. I left out parts I didn't think he needed to know. Like the Jimmy Yates part. My assignment so far was to find her and that's what I had done.

"You sure it was her?"

I produced my camera and showed him the picture I had taken of her and the picture I had taken of me *and* her.

"Ha!" he said. "You're good. A picture of her to show me you found her. And a picture of the two of you to prove to me in an absolutely certain way that the first picture was current and not something you found somewhere."

"Bingo."

Our drinks came. I took an enormous sip, half the drink. I was still pissed off about the beer.

I said, "There's a couple more shots in there if you scroll back."

Vonz did, to the sort of profile shot that I'd taken before introducing myself, where Suzanne looked out over the cliff toward the ocean. In this voyeuristic, more straight-up P.I.-style shot, there was a pensiveness about her, even though you couldn't fully see her eyes. You could *feel* something kicking around in her psyche. And as he looked at it, you could see a pensiveness in Vonz's eyes too. For just a moment, as he took in the picture, this man who was very accustomed to examining images, this man who'd seen them all, was captivated. He was somewhere else—in the movie he'd made from his memories.

Then he looked at me with the sparkle back in his eyes, the Vonzian charm back in his smile. "Did you talk to her?"

"Not much."

"She's really special, I think. Beautiful, sure. More beautiful in person. I bet you realized that. But a rare and special energy about her."

I agreed. But I didn't say that. I just let him go.

"Well, I'm impressed you found her so quickly. I'd like you to do something else for me. I'll continue to pay you, of course. I'd just like you to do one more thing."

I wondered what the one thing was going to be. A message perhaps? I looked at Vonz, thinking, what does he have up his velvet-blazered sleeve? He looked at me, then up and to the right of me, and said, "Hello, lovely."

I turned to see a very stylish older woman now standing at the head of our table. Just to my left. Mrs. Vonz. For sure. Gina. Appearing out of nowhere like a vision. Looking sleek, sophisticated, hip. Downright decked out. White suit, white hair, tan skin, silver and turquoise necklace. Glamorous. And still foxy. A Helen Mirren quality.

To Vonz: "You and the detective. Meeting again."

Vonz laughed. "Yes, this is John Darvelle. John, my wife, Gina."

I stood up and extended a hand.

"Hello," she said, gripping my hand in a way I could only describe as sexy.

Her hand was cool. She held my grip and looked me over, observed me, with a charming smile.

"I like your look," she said. "I like your hair."

It was her way of saying that she liked my *lack* of hair, that she admired, I suppose, that I was losing it but didn't hide it with a comb-over, implants, a rug, or some other trick. I just kept it short. Zipped it down myself with the half-inch guard on my Oster head shaver every three days. My receding hairline left me with some power alleys up top, a veritable Hair Peninsula on my head. My friend Gary Delmore once used my Hair Peninsula as a facsimile for the state of Florida. He showed a girlfriend of his how to get from Tampa to Miami by tracing with his finger from the middle of my peninsula, Tampa, to the bottom of my peninsula, Miami. I think he even showed her where you would turn off of to visit the Everglades. I just stood there. It wasn't a great moment for me.

You're probably wondering, well, what are you going to do when you *totally lose* your hair up top? Are you going to be one of those guys with a moat of hair wrapping around the sides and back of the head? Like Terry Bradshaw, or Captain Stubing?

Here's my answer to that: YOU'RE GODDAMN RIGHT I AM.

But let's get back to the story.

Gina Vonz said, "Yeah, I like your look. Ever thought of going in front of the cameras? Most people who live in L.A. consider it at some point, even if they don't admit it."

"Really?" I said. "Have you?"

Vonz chimed in. "She's been in a couple of my movies, John. Surprised you don't recognize her."

Gina said, "Well, it was a while ago. His early stuff. And the parts were pretty small."

She gave Vonz an affectionate, flirty look to say: You could have given me slightly bigger parts.

"She could have done more, could have been a star, I think," Vonz said. "Even without my help."

She smiled at Vonz. They still had chemistry.

"So," she said to me. "Have you ever been bitten by the acting bug?"

"No," I said. "And I'll tell you why. When you're an actor, your whole life is waiting around for someone else to *allow* you to do the thing you want to do. I'd never do that. My drug isn't stardom. It's freedom."

Gina looked at me.

Then Vonz again said, "I like that." And then, "John, walk us out to the plane."

We both downed our drinks and got up. Vonz motioned

to one of the waitstaff, who nodded. Guess he didn't have to pay right then and there. Ah, the life of the elite. Maybe he didn't have to pay at all. That's what happens to a lot of these rich guys. They get rich and *then* everyone starts buying them stuff. You ever noticed that? The rich, famous guys getting the free drinks, free dinners, free this, free that? You've noticed that.

We left Typhoon, walked down the outside steps to the parking lot, then swung around through a ground-level door that Vonz used a magnetic key fob to get us through. We were now underneath the restaurant. We went through a clean, simple waiting area, then out the door on the other side, and ended up, essentially, right on the tarmac and runways.

Thirty yards away, a gleaming, crisp, white jet, engines humming, slid into our eye line. It stopped, the door opened, the stairs unfolded down, waiting for Vonz and Gina. The jet looked like it had just been just washed, pellets of water visible, which made it sort of glisten and shine. Almost like it had been sprayed down for aesthetic purposes.

Talk about freedom. It looked like a vessel to freedom.

We walked toward the jet.

"We're going to New York for a couple days," Vonz said.

"Okay."

"Some meetings, some restaurants, some real city life."

Vonz was bullshitting until Gina got on the plane. I just kept walking. We arrived at the jet, the stairs to freedom. Gina trotted on up.

"Be right there, G," he said.

At the top of the steps, she turned and smiled at him, and smiled and flickered her fingers at me. And then she disappeared.

Vonz, his back to the plane, to the windows, discreetly pulled an envelope out of his blazer.

"Please get this to Suzanne for me."

He was close to me. Having to raise his voice over the engines, but not much, surprisingly. The engines would prevent Gina from hearing him, but I could hear him fine. I guess that's what you get for sixty, seventy, eighty mil.

"What is it?" I said.

"Why do you ask?"

"I need to know if it's something illegal. Occasionally I will do something illegal. Okay, maybe more than occasionally. But when I do it's because I know what's happening, and I choose to do it. I don't know enough about this story yet."

I grabbed the envelope out of his hand.

"So if this is anything illegal, deliver it yourself."

He nodded and said, "It's just a letter that says I miss talking to her and, well . . . John, we had a connection, and, as I've told you, hell you know now, there's something about her. So if she's through talking to me, I want to tell her just one last time that she's . . . great. And that I'd like to talk to her from time to time. And that if she ever needs anything to call me. That's it. I don't want to send a letter she might not get, or that will come back to my house for my wife to open. And I don't want to deliver it myself because if she doesn't want to talk to me, if she feels she needs to end all communication with me, I doubt she wants me just showing up."

"Stalker."

"Right."

"Can I open it and read it? I'll put it in a fresh envelope to deliver it."

"Yes. If you need to do that, fine."

Gina Vonz reappeared at the top of the steps. Like: Let's go. I held the envelope openly. Always the best way to go. Nothing to hide. Maybe it was just a payment from Vonz.

Vonz turned around and headed up the steps. Halfway, he looked back at me. "Thanks, John."

I nodded. And Vonz and Gina went in.

Almost instantly, the stairs retracted, the door shut, and the plane began to head out to the runway. So fast. None of that bullshit you get on a regular old flight.

Then I noticed a profile in one of the back windows—Mountcastle. He was already on the plane. He'd boarded with the crew. He wasn't creepily looking out at me. He was just sitting there, like a good little schoolboy, all buckled up and ready to go. Man, these big shots take their assistants everywhere. So they never have to do *anything* the rest of us do.

Then, just moments after the stairs had been enveloped by the plane, Vonz, Mountcastle, and his wise, glamorous wife rocketed skyward in a zillion-dollar machine, parting the darkening orange and purple sky, the water on the jet of the plane catching sunlight and sparkling, the wings for quick moments looking like they were covered in fireflies.

I followed the plane for almost five minutes until it was a black dot in the distance.

And then I turned and walked back to the Cobalt.

9

Dusk as I drove back to Suzanne's Ocean Avenue condo. Thinking: Hmm, how do I get this letter to Suzanne without blowing my tourist cover that I used to get her picture? Or did it matter at this point? Don't know.

Why did I feel like I'd need the cover later? Don't know that either.

Some obvious information: Sometimes it's better to use a cover when you're trying to get information. Especially early in a case. Because you don't want people to clam up when you say: I'm a detective and I'm on your case. Which they do. And you often don't want people to know that you're looking into something at all. Because often that's when they tell you exactly what you need to know.

Some not-so-obvious information: Sometimes it's better

to tell people exactly who you are and what you want. Especially later in a case. This approach allows you to be yourself, to not have to keep up with your cover. And it allows, when the circumstances call for it, to instill some fear.

Back at Suzanne's. Back out front in a spot, same side of the street as her condo. Sitting. Waiting. Again. I put Pavement's *Brighten the Corners* on. That song that goes: "Sherri, you smell different . . ."

"Type Slowly"—that's what the song's called. Just love it. I listened to it six times in a row, then let the CD play.

I just sat there, thinking, listening to the music. The letter sitting on the Cobalt's passenger seat, unopened. "Suzanne" written on the front, in Vonz's hand. Hmm. What to do. How to do it. Dark now. Watching cars pull out from behind her building into the little side street next to it, one after the other. And then, in my rearview, a new, three-series BMW appeared. First on the side street, then behind me, right on Ocean Avenue. Light caught the driver's face and I could see it was Suzanne. Just a moment of her, but an unmistakable moment, the headlights from another car doing a pass across her face.

She headed north and I followed. She took a right on California, another right on Lincoln, then left onto the 10 Freeway. The 10 Freeway that went all the way from Los Angeles on one coast to Jacksonville, Florida, on the other coast.

Jacksonville, where my aunt lives.

But back to L.A. Back to me following Suzanne. It was about seven, and for L.A. not much traffic. She took the 10 to the 405 North, then got off on the Mulholland Drive exit. Mulholland—that famous snaking road that crested the Hills, giving you beautiful looks of L.A. to the west and to the east.

We took it east, winding atop the mountains, from Sherman Oaks to Bel Air to Beverly Hills and now into the Hollywood Hills. We were near Nicholson's house and Brando's old place and you could feel that special, magical, haunting L.A. vibe. This part of Los Angeles had a spooky, seductive mysticism to it—especially at night. And, even now in the present day, you just got the feeling that some combination of Fleetwood Mac was somewhere nearby having a small but lively orgy.

We crossed Laurel Canyon and about a half mile later she turned left into a driveway. A big metal gate opened and closed, taking in her BMW. Lots of gates in this world. Keeping people out. But keeping people in too. This particular gate protected what just *felt* like a compound. Some multimillion-dollar fortress tucked away in these glamorous Hollywood mountains.

I drove on past, swung a U-turn, parked on a shoulder, stayed focused on the driveway. I stared at the gate. Not just any old gate this one. A big ornate mess with crisscrossing lines of steel and copper and who knows what else. It was hideous. Forty minutes later it opened, allowing Suzanne to leave. I picked her up and followed her all the way home.

She pulled into the alley behind her condo, parked under the building. I pulled back around, this time across the street, on the side of the park, and looked once again at the front of her apartment building. Some moonlight, or was it a streetlight, shone into my car and put a spot right on the envelope still sitting on my front seat. I thought about reading the letter, but didn't. I wondered what kind of bewitching, artful love letter the maestro Arthur Vonz could write.

I thought: Should I just knock on her door and give her the letter? Blow my cover? Or maybe give it to the security guard, then hang around and make sure he gives it to her?

I grabbed the envelope and got out of the Cobalt. Going security guard route. Make *sure* he hands it to her. Yes. I knew she was home, and I was reasonably sure I could get a confirmation of delivery. I'd think of something to tell the guard so as to not reveal my identity. No problem.

Some cars were coming down Ocean Avenue so I stood in front of the Cobalt looking at her building still on the other side of the street. There was a soft breeze coming in from the ocean. It felt amazing. I looked up at the palm trees swaying in the wind, set against the sky and the lights of Santa Monica. The kind of night that makes people come to California—and stay. The California dream, in handy, beautiful nighttime form. And the moon was out. It had been moonlight on the letter, not streetlight.

I stood there for a moment looking up at the moon, just sitting there glowing, a yellowish orange. I imagined it briefly as a portal to somewhere else. As a hole in the sky that was a tunnel to another dimension. And then I moved my eye over to Suzanne's building. And there she was.

She was standing on her balcony. I did a quick count up, looked to me to be the twenty-first floor. The wind moving her hair. Up there, you could look out at the big green sea and hear it too probably. The palm trees below you, the cliffs of Malibu to the right outlined, accentuated, dotted by lights. California magic from hundreds of feet in the air. I guess that's why you buy these places. Forget what I was saying earlier. You know about having to walk down the cliff and cross the PCH just to get to the water. I bet it was great up there.

She was taking it all in, I could tell. Through the iron bars in her balcony I could see most of her body. I could see what she was wearing. White shorts and a light-colored T-shirt. The streetlights and the building's lights and the moonlight silhouetted her, so instead of really seeing her I was taking the image of her face that I remembered and putting it on her way up there in the sky.

And then a man appeared behind her. He too was in shadow, in silhouette, but I could see that he was pretty tall, and I could see the outline of a curl in his hair, and an intermittent flash of reflected light off his watch. I took my camera out and snapped a picture of both of them. I looked at the picture—you could make out Suzanne but the man behind her was nothing more than a shadowy outline. I looked back up at the balcony. Suzanne turned around to face the figure behind her. The man held out his arms, like he wanted to hug her. Or maybe he was gesticulating as he talked. Very hard to tell. And then, Suzanne walked back in the apartment. As she entered, the man put his hand gently on her back and guided her through the doorway.

Is that why I had been dicking around down here, not getting to giving her the letter? Had the cosmos told me that someone else was up there with her? Had it been a message that had come through that orange portal in the sky? Probably not. But *maybe*. I asked myself: Was that

Jimmy Yates Movie Star up there? Could be, again, *maybe*, but don't think so. Seemed like a different guy. Different hair. The curl. But could not be sure. Could definitely not be sure.

So, had another player entered my story? Just. Not. Sure. Was Suzanne some kind of kept woman up there in her Santa Monica pad? Or was she some kind of real professional? Man, if she was either one, Arthur Vonz definitely did not appear to know that. Then again, I didn't know that either.

And the other question was, the more pressing question was: Do I give her the letter anyway? Again, don't think so. Don't think Vonz would appreciate that. And that's who I was working for. Shit, given the circumstances, if it *was* Jimmy Yates up there, or maybe another suitor, or even a friend, Suzanne probably wouldn't appreciate it either. A letter handed to her unexpectedly from a private corner of her life, right in front of her guest. I decided to wait, and give her the letter the next day.

I drove home.

10

I live in Mar Vista. Just east of Venice, just inland a few miles, but still decidedly west of the 405. Decidedly Westside. It's the perfect place, location-wise, to live in Los Angeles. I've thought about this. I've thought about this a lot. You're almost to the beach. But on the south end of town. South of Santa Monica, Brentwood, the Palisades. All that nonsense. And, like I said, just inland from the funkiest place in the city, Venice. Just a quick drive or bike ride to Abbot Kinney, the canals, the Venice Pier. So you can easily enter that one-of-a-kind groovy scene. That scene that still has its roots in the culture of hippie, artsy seventies California. Yes, it has become trendy and full of hipsters and there's too much irony, for sure, but it's still good. Still has a great beach. Still has charm out the wazoo.

Still a great place to grab dinner. Drink a beer, do a shot, say hello to a lovely lady or two. But then, you can retreat. Away from the scene, the ironic mustaches, the noise, and, these days, the expense of Venice.

Mar Vista's still overpriced, but you get a real house, and a little land, some room to breathe.

And Mar Vista is near Venice Boulevard. So, sure, you can head west and be at the ocean in a couple miles, but you can take it the other way into Hollywood as well. And you can do it stealth-style. Much less traffic, much less hassle than taking more popular east-west roads like Pico, Olympic or the god-awful Wilshire. From Mar Vista, you pop onto Venice and slide into Hollywood. Slide, my friends. Slide. Unnoticed. Through funky hoods, by Cuban restaurants, around far less people.

From the great Mar Vista, you can also get right on the 405, and then the 10. To go anywhere in the city. You simply have lots of options to get places. Options that are much less traveled.

And, this might be the biggest thing. In Mar Vista, you aren't trapped in a section of the city. You are free to operate. People who live in other Westside neighborhoods, take Brentwood for example, always talk about how beautiful it is. Problem is, Brentwood is essentially inaccessible. You're always fighting poor urban design. Only a couple streets in and a couple streets out all surrounded by clogs of traffic. I need better access than that. It's just that simple.

That goes for the Palisades and Santa Monica too. Certainly beautiful. Uniquely Californian. Nice to visit. But knotted. Hard to get to. Inconvenient. Awkward. If you're there, and you want to go somewhere else in the city, it's a headache. You are at the mercy of the system. At the mercy of streets and designs that make no sense.

You will not find me living in one of those places.

Mar Vista is quiet, chill, a hidden sanctuary amid the insanity of L.A. Beautiful trees and streets and funky seventies ranch houses built on lots, as I mentioned, with a little size to them. And not oversized, just right. People always say to me: Mar Vista is boring. Mar Vista is old school and doesn't have the California flash of some of the other Westside neighborhoods.

And I always say: You just don't get it. You just truly don't get it.

And then I often say: Please get away from me—forever. No, really, please do not talk to me again.

My house is on the end of a cul-de-sac. It's a seventies California Craftsman, but remodeled by me. One story for most of the house, with vaulted ceilings throughout. On the bottom floor, I tore down all the walls except for the two bedrooms. So the den, living room, and kitchen are all one room. With big windows out the front and back. Dark hardwood floors with dark blue carpets. I don't have a lot of furniture. Just a few things. I have a nice, really nice, indoor-only Stiga Ping-Pong table in the center of the room.

A nice Ping-Pong table is like art.

Over the garage is my master. Good-sized room with some sliding doors to a balcony that overlooks my backyard. Pretty big backyard. Marked off by trees, yucca, palm, jacaranda. There's a big deck, surrounding a deep, rectangular pool with a black bottom. I swim in it mostly at night. In the summer, with a warm breeze coming in from the ocean, and the stars out even in L.A., it relaxes me, helps me think about my cases, and distances me from all the things that annoy the ever-living shit out of me.

I bought the house at auction. I fixed it up slowly. And now it is my kingdom of chilldom, my sanctuary of calm, my escape from the madness.

I walked inside, grabbed a Coors Light, sat down in my big main room. I drank the beer in four sips, grabbed another, sat back down. My cell rang. Vonz.

"Arthur," I said.

"You give her the note?" he said. I could hear that New York City sound behind him. The cabs, the traffic, the city. Unmistakable. It's alluring, that sound, and for a second I wanted to be there. Be in a dark bar in the East Village listening to some Clash. Listening to "Death or Glory." "Clampdown." "Washington Bullets."

"Not yet," I said. "Tomorrow."

He didn't ask why. I was impressed.

"Okay," he said. "Let me know when you give it to her. And . . ."

"And what?"

"Well, I just want her to read it. To know that she read it. And that she didn't just toss it. So if there's any way to know . . . to know that she read it . . ."

Man, for a guy who said he was thrilled that his wife took him back, he was acting like a little kid. I thought: I probably shouldn't tell him that there's at least one other guy in her life, and that guy is, for sure, over at her place right now.

"I'll try. Incidentally, that's why I didn't give her the

note tonight. I didn't want to just drop it off. I wanted to hand it to her personally. And I couldn't make that happen tonight."

Again, he didn't ask why.

"Good," he said. "If it's right in her hands, she'll read it."

I heard more of New York behind him. It had been a while since I'd been there.

"Where are you?" I asked.

Before he could remind me that he was in New York City I said, "I mean where in the city? It just sounds . . . good."

"Yeah, it's nice to be here. I'm at Pete's Tavern near . . ."

"Gramercy Park."

"Yeah."

"Great place."

"Yep. Dinner with some friends. It always amazes me . . . It's 1 a.m. here and every table's taken."

"Right. People still arriving for dinner."

And then he said something that surprised me—in a good way. He said something that a friend would say to another friend. He jumped topics and just kind of gave me an observation.

"John, I've been all over the world many, many times and I think the most beautiful women, if you had to pick one city, are in New York."

"Paris," I said. "Los Angeles? Buenos Aires?"

"All full of beautiful women, but they don't beat NYC for my money. Here in New York you have samplings from all over the world. You have the *best* from all over the world. Europe. Asia. America. Listen. I think L.A. is underrated. People always say that L.A. is just blond bimbos, and that, of course, is absurd. Look, there are beautiful women in big cities everywhere, but New York, I don't know . . . There's something about it. The fashion. The sophistication. The unspoken competition created by the crème de la crème from all over the world crammed onto a little island."

"It sounds like you've put some thought into this."

"I've made graphs! I've made charts!" he joked.

Arthur had a buzz on.

"Gotta go, John. Let me know when the eagle has landed."

Yeah, he had a buzz on. Speaking in P.I. terms now. A little cheesy.

And for the record, it always bothers me when people say "Gotta go" or "I'll let you go" when *they* called *you*.

I blew it off. "I'll call you when she has the note."

"Good night," he said, and I could hear the sounds of the city disappear as he hung up.

I had another beer, then took a long swim in my pool. It was quiet and still outside and I lay on my back in the water, floating, looking up at a black sky. I got out, dried off, went upstairs, and got in bed. I closed my eyes and began to think about how exactly I'd deliver the letter the next day. In minutes I was out.

The next day when I woke up Suzanne Neal was dead.

11

Here's how I found out. I got up early, went for a five-mile-run around lovely Mar Vista. Then: Showered, slid over to Starbucks for an enormous, nerve-wrenching coffee, and headed to Suzanne's condo, the letter from Vonz still riding shotgun.

When I arrived I could not immediately see that a crime had taken place. I parked, put a baseball hat on, and walked into the building. Immediately, trouble. Two police detectives talking to the condo security guard. I had to think fast. I didn't know what they were talking about, but you know that feeling when you just *know* the thing you're seeing is the thing that's a part of *your* story even though you don't actually know it yet? You know that feeling? You know that feeling.

I know a lot of cops. But I didn't recognize the two talking to the security guard. Head down, I walked straight by, toward the two condo elevators. The security guy didn't bother me. Instead, he just kept talking to the police, a stunned, almost contrite look on his face.

Another resident was getting on the elevator at the exact time I was. He pressed seventeen, then looked at me.

Head down, hat bill blocking me from elevator cameras, I said, "Twenty-one."

I had no confirmation that the two cops were part of my story. Yet. So I was proceeding as planned.

"You're on her floor," the guy with me in the elevator said.

Her floor? Was he talking about Suzanne? Of course he was. And I'd estimated her floor correctly. I went with it.

"Well, I don't live here in the building, but my friend does."

"Pretty crazy, huh?"

"I didn't hear the details, but yes, for sure."

"Shot."

"Yeah, I heard that."

"She fell all that way."

We got to the seventeenth floor, the doors opened, I wanted to confirm what I somehow already knew was true. So I said, awkwardly, "She was a beautiful girl."

He looked back at me on his way out. For a split second I thought I'd taken my swing and missed. But he nodded and turned out of view.

The doors shut and I stood still, thinking. The elevator headed toward twenty-one. There were probably some cops in her apartment, on her floor. I wasn't ready to see them. Especially if I knew them. Which I might. I hit twenty. Shit, I was too late. Shit. It got to twenty-one. The doors opened up. I moved over to the side wall of the elevator, still keeping my head down.

I heard, down the hall: "Someone's coming off."

The doors couldn't be closing any goddamn slower. I heard footsteps nearing. Nearing. Nearing. The doors shut. The elevator headed to twenty. The cops maybe thought there was no one on the elevator, but I doubt it. I pressed twenty-one again, then twenty-two, twenty-three, twenty-four, and twenty-five to send the elevator I was exiting first back to Suzanne's floor, then to a bunch of other floors above her. I got off on twenty and quickly hit the down button to get elevator two to take me the hell out of there. The other elevator came and I rode it down to the ground floor. I was hoping either the cops blew off elevator one when it came back to twenty-one, or got on it to take it to the ground floor to ask security who had gotten on— and now he, she, or they were stopping at a bunch of floors he, she, or they didn't want to go to.

Lobby. I walked back past the cops and security guard. I never saw elevator one reach the lobby floor again. If it had indeed come back down.

Outside. Unscathed. I got in the Cobalt and drove to my office.

Now, I wanted some answers but I had to be careful who I asked, how I got them, and how much I told them about what I knew. You give away too much now and it screws you later. Trust me. Related side note: Dispensing information properly and processing information properly are two of the most important things in life. And very few people do either one right.

I called the *L.A. Times*, a reporter I know named Larry Frenette.

"Larry, John Darvelle."

"Darvelle! What's up, buddy?"

"Have a question. Any murders reported last night? Actually, of course there were murders last night, we're in L.A. But supposedly an old friend . . . an old client of mine may have gotten it. Name was Christine Logan."

I heard typing. Checking the paper's news feed.

"Nope."

"Hmm. I wonder if someone is fucking with me."

"With you, John? No way."

Sarcasm was his native tongue.

"Was there a murder last night? A woman? Westside. Venice. Santa Monica maybe."

I heard slurping and eating. Newspaper guy. And then he said, "A woman named Suzanne Neal."

I already knew it, but for some reason it hit me in the chest.

"Hmm," I said. "Don't know her. Well, thanks, Lar."

"Anytime, slime."

I hung up and called Vonz. Got his cell's voice mail. Left a message, simply to call me when he could. I got out my MacBook Pro and typed out the whole story—so far. From the moment Vonz hired me to right now. I wrote it out exactly. Everywhere I went, every observation I had made, and everyone I had come in contact with. It took me eighty minutes. I pressed the command for print on my keyboard and my cell rang at the same time. Like my pressing the button made my phone ring. Vonz.

"Arthur," I said.

"So, you gave Suzanne the letter?"

"I did not." This time I didn't hear the sounds of New York in the background. It was quiet on his end. But I did feel something in the silence: Vonz just slightly losing his cool.

"Listen, John," he said. "I'm in my hotel now, Gina and Paul stepped out, but they'll be back shortly. So I do have a *quick* second, but when I'm traveling with Gina it's not that easy to talk to you."

"Arthur. I don't know how to say this other than to say it. Suzanne has been killed."

Now there was silence on the other line, but a different kind of silence. After an interminable ten seconds or so: "What are you talking about?"

"I don't know much about what happened. Her murder is not my case. I went to her apartment today to give her the letter and there was a crime scene. A neighbor of hers told me that a beautiful girl had been killed the previous night. Then I was able to find out it was Suzanne by calling a newspaper reporter who is a friend. I can tell you everything I saw, everything I know, but it'll take some time. Do you want to do that now?"

He said, calmly, with no irritation, "I'll be back in L.A. in two days. Paul will call you to arrange a meeting. Okay?"

I thought about saying, "I'm sorry for your loss" or some trite sentiment, but I really didn't know anything about this man, or Suzanne, or much about how the two of them related to each other. I just knew she was dead. That was the one thing I knew for sure.

I said: "Okay."

We hung up. I looked at the printout of my notes. I took another pass at them and condensed down what I had written to crisp bullet points. It took forty minutes. I printed two copies of my new, shorter version. I drove to a pay phone seventeen minutes away from my office. I called the LAPD. I told some cop who answered *some* of the things I knew. The information I thought the police needed to know to investigate her murder. I said I lived in the building, but didn't give my name. I told him Suzanne went to a house on Mulholland the night of the murder, and I gave him the address. How did I know that? Um, she had shown me the house at an earlier time, that's how. I told him there was a man in Suzanne's condo at approximately 8 p.m. How did I know that? I just did. I told him that, curiously, I had seen the actor Jimmy Yates in our building earlier in the day, don't know if that helps. The cop on the line started pressing me for who I was. I hung up on him and went back to my office.

12

Two days later I was back in the Cobalt heading to the Vonz estate. I went through mostly the same routine. Through the gate, then guided by Mountcastle through the house. But this time, Mountcastle didn't guide me into the Vonz study. Because after exiting the back of the house he didn't have to guide me anywhere—I spotted Vonz sitting outside, to the left of the study entrance, underneath a parasol by his pretty blue pool.

He gestured to me. I walked over and sat down across from him. Mountcastle disappeared back into the main house.

Vonz was reasonably decked out. Crisp dress shirt, blazer, handkerchief. And today, outside in the sun, blue-tinted shades. He seemed calm, or actually, deflated.

"Thanks for coming back," he said.

I nodded.

"And . . . I know you're still on the clock. I'm paying you for this time."

I nodded again.

He pulled out a pack of Parliament Lights. "I started smoking these before they somehow entered popular culture as a fashionable choice. Bizarre how that happens."

Yet again, I nodded.

He held out the pack for me. I wanted to take one. I used to smoke. But I had to quit. One, it kills you. Two, during my time as a smoker, all I wanted to do was smoke. Just sit somewhere and smoke. One after the other. I loved it that much. I remember I used to go to restaurants and mid-dinner, instead of enjoying the atmosphere, not to mention the food, I'd be standing out back by the Dumpster taking a big drag off a smoke, thinking: I've never been happier. I was a cigarette's bitch, plain and simple. So I had to quit. I wasn't free when I smoked. I was the slave of a little tube of tobacco. So I just stopped. Took it day by very difficult day. That was four years ago.

I declined his offer.

Vonz took a big drag and said, "So what happened?"

I told him my story. Didn't need my notes. First I told him that I'd seen Jimmy Yates leaving Suzanne's building when I initially got her picture. But that I wasn't certain then, or now, that he was a part of the story. Then, I took it from the moment I left him at the Santa Monica airport. That I had followed Suzanne to a house in the Hollywood Hills. That later that evening there was a man with her on her balcony. A man I believe was not Jimmy Yates, but that in reality could have been. And that I didn't give her the letter because of seeing the man.

I didn't give Vonz any theories, or any maybes, that had passed through my mind. I'd learned, the hard way, that possibilities only rarely turned into proof.

Finally I told him that I had gone back to give her the letter the next day and discovered, and confirmed, that Suzanne was dead.

DEAD.

It's a strange, fascinating concept when you allow yourself to think about it. When I was a child I used to think about what it meant to be dead all the time. I couldn't understand it. I couldn't fully grasp the notion of being dead. Gone. Zapped into the infinite. Forever. I used to say to my parents and my friends, "But what happens *after* you die? Because time is still happening, so where are you?"

No one ever gave me a proper answer and that always annoyed me. Truth is, they just didn't know.

I stopped thinking about it as I grew older. But now, now that I have a job that brings me close to death often, I think about it almost as much as I used to.

Vonz looked at me. Lit another cigarette. And then he took off his sunglasses and looked me dead in the eye. You could see fatigue surrounding his bright eyes. He didn't speak for what seemed like a long time. And then he said, "This hurts."

He was talking about her death, sure, but was he also talking about discovering the other man, or men, in her life? Didn't know. Probably. Yes.

After another long pause Vonz said, "I loved her."

I continued to simply listen. I looked at Vonz. He looked

much older. He looked exhausted. And that charm, that Cheshire pop in his face, had momentarily vanished. I instinctively looked over toward his house.

"She's not here, it's okay," he said. "But thank you for looking out for me."

"Maybe I was looking out for her, not you."

"Either way, it means you have a soul."

He took another long pull off the Parliament and then said, "You know, when you're really honest with yourself—about who you love—it's a very interesting conversation. How often—really—does it strike? You know?"

It was rhetorical, he wasn't looking for an answer.

"Suzanne and I had more than a casual affair. That was a lie. Probably an obvious one. I hope you aren't insulted."

"I'm a detective. People rarely tell me the truth."

He nodded. "The rest of it was true. How we met. Where we would meet up."

I didn't respond.

Vonz, after a moment, continued. "She was so *alive*. At least I felt that way. And consequently that's how I felt when I was around her. Alive. But she felt it too. You can't deny it, you can't lie, when it's real. It's just there. The feeling. After our first few encounters, I thought about her all the time, and I quickly realized I was in love with her. But I also thought about her because our relationship stirred me up in another way. It made me look at my wife, the mother of my children, in a new light. And sadly, I guess maybe tragically, it made me admit to myself that I wasn't in love with my wife. And that I never had been. As hard as I tried to be, as hard as I tried to be in love with her, as much as I really do care for her, I'm just not. And that made me think. Made me say to myself: How often are you really in love? How often in an entire lifetime does *it* happen? That energy. That lightning. That mystery. It's magic. And, I'm sure of this, it has absolutely nothing to do with anything other than that mysterious connection. It's not logical. It's not scientific. It's not about background, or intellectual connection, or age. We tell ourselves it is, but that's a lie. That's a way for the conscious mind to keep you safe. And put you in a situation that works. So you can create a life with a house and children and social options. Truth is, people fall in love in seconds. With people who don't speak the same language as they do. With people from wildly different backgrounds. It's amazing really. It's one of the truly amazing things about life. And like I said, you can't fake it. It's like a real laugh or a real feeling of surprise. It just *is*. And that's what makes it so special."

I knew what he was talking about. And like a lot of things I believed to be true, it hurt a little to admit it.

"It fucked with me, John. I thought about it a lot. I couldn't stop thinking about it. And I concluded the thing about love, the thing that makes it so special, is that it makes you feel like you're not alone. I don't mean in a simplistic way, a physical way. I mean it makes you feel like you're not alone in the universe. That's really what it is. The sex, the passion, all that stuff, is great. But it's the realization that you are not alone in the universe that makes it so powerful. When you fall in love, you have connected with another person in a higher way that is nothing short of life-affirming. It makes everything make sense. It makes you want to keep living."

Another drag. Another pause. And then, "The irony. The irony is, when you're in a relationship or a marriage where the love isn't truly there, take mine with Gina for example, yes, you are physically together, you are physically not alone. And that can help to keep you distracted enough to not be lonely on a surface level. But if you dare to dig a little deeper, you still feel alone. And if you really look at it, you realize you're more alone than ever. Because that real light isn't there. And in your heart, whether you like it or not, you're looking for it. It's why there have been a million stories, songs, poems, on and on, about it. And it's why there will be a million more."

Okay. He's dramatic. He's emotional. But in this moment I felt for him. Because it takes a lot, or a trauma, to admit you don't love your wife. I still didn't say anything.

Vonz continued. "It happens so fast. Like I said, sometimes in an instant. I felt it for Suzanne after one weekend. Our first weekend together. But, really, I think I felt it right away. John, our entire relationship was six months. Maybe. Yet it was bigger than anything else I ever had."

I pulled out the letter. Unopened. I held it out to Vonz.

"Do me a favor, John. Throw it out for me. When you leave, get rid of it. Gina'll be back soon and I'll have put it somewhere and forgotten it. Or I'll burn it and she'll catch me. Or I'll shred it and she'll find it and it'll be a conversation I don't want to have."

"Okay."

"It's just a quick note. On the surface, hey, I'm here for you. But really I hoped it would get her to call me again. Get her back in my arms again."

"Let me ask you this, Arthur. If you loved her so much, why didn't you stay with her? Why didn't you try to be with her permanently?"

He gave me an ashamed smile. "Another irony, John. I lied to myself. Told myself I was crazy. That I was overcome with passion or lust or whatever. Then I told Suzanne I could never leave my wife. And that we had to end it. It's a mistake that lots of people have made since the beginning of time. Denying your feelings. At the time I thought I had broken her heart. But it wasn't until later, right around the time I decided to hire you, that I realized I had broken my own."

Vonz grabbed his blue-colored shades but didn't put them back on. He sat there for a moment, still, quiet. And then he said, "Well, I've got to run, John. I'm headed to Paramount. Meeting with some money people about my next movie. Thank you for coming by. Thank you for your work. Talk to Paul on your way out. He'll get you your check."

We both stood up.

He stuck out his hand. I looked him in his tired eyes and shook it.

He said, "Do you think the cops will figure out what happened to Suzanne?"

"Depends on how hard they try. I've given them the information I have. Anonymously, pretended to be a friend, and without any mention of you."

He nodded. "Do they usually try hard?"

"Yeah, they usually do."

"Well, I hope this is one of those times."

He put his shades back on and his visage went back to the dashing auteur. The fatigue and anguish on his face hidden beneath blue glass.

13

An hour later, I was sitting at my desk, staring out the big slider. Pretty quiet on the property. I saw a few vans moving some stuff in and out of a warehouse across the lot. They were far enough away that I just heard the light drones of their engines. What was I thinking about? Well, I was trying not to think. To just let go for a moment. To enjoy the slight breeze coming in my office. To enjoy the sun slanting in and popping off my slick concrete floor.

I looked down at my desk, looked at the unopened letter that sat there. Vonz and Suzanne rattling around in my mind—whether I liked it or not.

I looked up and said aloud, "Oh shit."

My friend Gary Delmore, the large-haired, white-toothed TV director, had appeared in my office. He was holding his Ping-Pong paddle, striking an aggressive pose, his head tilted in a way that said he was ready to fight.

"That's right, Darvelle. You ready?"

I didn't want to play. I wasn't in the mood. I was thinking about something that I hadn't quite gotten my mind around. But I rarely turn down a Pong challenge and I never turn down one from Gary Delmore.

I shook my head, pulled out the bottom drawer of my desk, and grabbed my best bat. A two-hundred-twenty-five-dollar Killerspin with thick rubber, beautiful wood, and no fucking mercy. I then produced a couple orange Halex three-star balls, and took my position at the table. We started hitting, warming up, and the rhythm of it, as always, felt good, nice, downright therapeutic.

Gary wasn't that good. He had a decent serve, a solid backhand, but a weak forehand and—his biggest problem—an average understanding of the game at best. I could beat him giving it about forty percent.

"I don't know if this is fair," I said.

"Why?"

"Your teeth are blinding me. They're an unnatural, glowing, strange-looking white."

"I think it evens out."

"Yeah?"

"The power alleys on your balding head send an equal, actually an even more intense, glare at me."

Gary and I enjoyed insulting each other.

"I'm going to make this hurt, Delmore. I'm not really in the mood to play right now. And I was working, so I'm annoyed. You're going to experience a pain equal to watching one of your TV shows."

"Hey, serious question. Have you gotten married and divorced since the last time I saw you? I mean I saw you about a week ago, but your marriages are pretty quick."

"I'm going to punch you in the face."

"Just don't mess up my hair, pal."

"Three out of five?" I said as a formality.

"Yep. And remember, I've beaten you before. You're not that fucking good."

Gary had beaten me once. Once. I made the mistake of letting him hang in there for fun, assuming I could end the match as soon as it got too close for comfort. But Ping-Pong, like most things, can be unpredictable. Can take turns you simply cannot see coming. Gary hit a couple good shots, then hit a couple lucky shots, then hit a miraculous shot and won. I was stunned. Gary never stopped reminding me of it. And it never stopped bothering me. It's been a couple years now. It's sad, really, that it affected me like that.

We P-I-N-G-ed for serve and started up. Near the end of the first game I suddenly realized I was about to lose. For the second time. I was drifting off, distracted. It was 19–16, him.

Shit, my mind was elsewhere. I was thinking about what Vonz had said. About love. About how it really only happens, if you are honest with yourself, a couple times in a lifetime. In a *lifetime*. I know it had happened to me only a couple times. And, like Vonz, I'd been guilty of not respecting it too. Letting it go. Letting my mind trick me into thinking it wasn't that important, or that it wasn't even happening. Not with my marriage—that was a different story. But with a woman whom I met after my marriage. I told myself, and I told her, that I "wasn't ready." I know, such a lame, trite, unacceptable phrase. And an even lamer excuse. And so I lost her. Not like Vonz, she wasn't dead. But the magic was, so in a sense it was the same.

I forced myself to focus. Served the ball with spin I knew Gary couldn't handle. Took the first game 21–19. The next two weren't particularly close.

On his way out Gary said, "Well, I have to go to work. Point a camera at some people and make way, way more money than you will ever make. Then later, I'll probably take one of the actresses, beautiful, beautiful actresses, back to my very large house."

"You're compensating for the sting of defeat, friend."

"Maybe, but I'll be compensating in the arms of a ten whose only goal in life is to be on an after-hours Showtime movie."

I laughed. "See you, dude."

"Yeah."

He left.

I sat down at my desk, then, moments later, looked up to see I had yet another visitor.

It was a cat that belonged to one of the owners of a nearby warehouse. Not just any cat, though. This cat had been badly burned in a house fire. So random sections of his body had no fur, just skin. It was a strange patchwork of fur, then skin, then fur, then skin. He also had a twitchy left eye and a gimpy front right leg, both injuries caused by the mayhem of the fire. So when he walked he tilted way up, then way down, his left eye twitching all the way.

It was an amazing sight.

It was literally like nothing you've ever seen.

His name was Toast. And when his owner visited the warehouse and brought him, Toast usually weeble-wobbled down to see me—which I very much appreciated.

I went over and picked up the charred little creature. He looked at me, eye twitching, and did one of those bizarre cat hisses.

CAAAAAAAAAAA!

But I held him till he relented and just let me pet him and give him some affection.

"I love you, Toast. If you got killed I'd find out who did it."

I put him down on a shaded part of the concrete that was nice and cool to the touch. He lay down on his side and stretched out his arms and legs—even the gimpy one. And then his eyes fought sleep, the twitchy one bouncing up and down, struggling to stay open. But Toast let it happen and drifted away for a little snooze.

I went back to Vonz's question. Would they find out who killed Suzanne? She was a compelling woman. Vonz was right. So engaging. She affected you—in seconds. It was fascinating really. That charm, that energy.

But what was her story? What was she hiding? How did all that stuff I'd seen connect together to make sense, to give a reason for her death? Jimmy Yates. That trip to Mulholland. The man on her balcony.

Was I going to look into this myself? That was the question, wasn't it? I met her face-to-face right before she got killed. I saw with my own eyes the activity before the murder.

Even if we don't like to admit it sometimes, we want to know what happened to people we care about. Exactly what happened. And if it was something bad, we want the people who did it to pay. Vonz cared about Suzanne. And even I cared about Suzanne. I'd looked into her eyes and joked around with her on a beautiful Southern California day. I wanted whoever did it to pay. Turn the other cheek? No thanks. I wanted her killer to pay. I know Vonz wanted it too. He left that out of his discourse on love, but I know he wanted it too.

I thought, Darvelle, listen to yourself. Investigate the case. Go. Now. Do it.

So I did.

14

To work effectively as a private investigator you need connections. People who can give you information you otherwise couldn't get. Reporters, people in real estate, people who work at the courts, people who have access. Sometimes it's a cop, sometimes an ex-criminal, and, yes, sometimes it's a current criminal. You've seen me use a few of these already. It takes a long, long time to create, and then to nurture, these relationships. Because most of the people who work in and around my world are pretty jaded fucks. Not Linda Robbie. She's not jaded. She's horny, but she's not jaded. But most of my connections are. Even so, the truth is, if you give back, if you show you can keep a secret, if people know you're in it for the right reasons, and you're there to help them sometimes too, they *want* to help you out. Yep, another irony, folks. The jaded ones are the hardest to get through to, but once you do, once you prove yourself, they usually end up being the most helpful. Trust me, you still have to go through the dance. Even after they trust you. It's almost comical. You get reminded that you're being helped, told you're a pain in the ass, told over and over and over that passing along information, that bending a rule, is putting their job on the line.

But the truth is, when you, or your connections, help someone out in a not-necessarily-legal way, it's not a bad thing. It's a good thing. And everyone inside the circle believes that. Because you know and they know it has to happen sometimes to keep the fight alive.

And we are all in this to keep the fight alive.

One of my connections is a guy named Elliot Watt. You guessed it—he works at the morgue. He shows me pictures. He gives me the coroner's report. He tries to help me. And I pay him off in various ways. Cash, a front-row seat at a show Gary's directing, sometimes just the skinny on what I found out because of his help.

I drove to the morgue. A strange place most people never see. A building full of drawers with dead bodies in them. Next time you drive by the morgue in your town, think about that. A massive dresser full of dead, formaldehyde-injected bodies. With arms and legs and eyes and hearts. It's pretty damn creepy if you let yourself focus on it.

I walked in and Elliot got up from behind his desk. He looked like a morgue guy. A very thin man with deep-set blue bug eyes, black hair, pale pasty skin, a big mouth with too many big teeth. Maybe he looked like that and then just said to himself: You know what? I *look* like a morgue guy. I'm going to go get a job at the morgue.

"Yo, John. I can't let you look at the body. Cops are coming back down to look at it some more. Here's the report and the pics."

Not the original. A copy he'd made for me, of course. He handed it to me.

I said with a grin, "Not just a quick look at the body?"

"Not unless you want to get caught and never get access to here again."

See what I'm saying? He said it with real bite. He was tired, irritated. Like I said, you have connections, but it's still a challenge to use them.

"Anything you saw that was out of the ordinary?"

"Yeah, John. I mean, murder is out of the ordinary."

He gave me a blank, bug-eyed look, then calmed down a bit. "But not really. She was assassinated. Shot in the back of the head with a nine mill."

I thought: Jesus. Brutal.

He went on. "Broken femur, three broken ribs, cracked mandible, broken ankle. All from the fall. None of which affected her death. She was dead when she fell. Had she *not* been, the damage from the fall would have been worse. It's always worse when there is a conscious struggle."

I thought again: My god.

He continued, "No drugs in the system. Nothing really to see in the pics other than the wounds. She has a couple tats, they all do these days. Oh, and . . . she had sex the night of the murder."

"Was it . . ."

"Not rape. Sex. No sign of struggle on the body or anywhere else."

I looked at this strange, bug-eyed man. No expression as he told me the details of the autopsy for a beautiful young woman whose head had been blown off and whose body had been cracked into pieces.

I said, "Why are the cops coming back?"

"No reason. Happens all the time. You know that."

"Yeah, I know that. But sometimes there *is* a reason. You don't think there's a reason this time?"

"Oh. If I had to guess I'd say it's because they're not that thorough in the first place and they try to be all cool and cop-y and not ask too many questions like they know what they're talking about when it comes to corpses when they really don't. And then they get back to their desks and realize they haven't retained anything I said when they *did* decide to ask me questions, because they were too cool to write down my answers. So they tell me they want to come back for another look but usually they just want to come back and ask me the same questions again so they can get the same answers I already gave them. But that's just a guess, John."

I smiled. Elliot was wound pretty damn tight. I found his rants amusing, and often true. When they weren't directed at me, that is.

I held up the packet he had given me, nodded, and left. Back to my office to look at photos and an autopsy report of a dead Suzanne Neal.

Now at my desk, I opened up the folder. There she was, the beautiful girl I saw in a park overlooking the Pacific. But now pale, purple, and dead. And with an exploded head and face. I looked at the pictures. I read Elliot's report. Shot in the head, died, technically, for a couple reasons. Brain dead, loss of blood. But really, in layman's terms, because someone had put a gun in the back of her cranium and pulled the trigger.

Violent. Horrible. Sickening.

I looked at the pictures of her naked body. Not nearly as gruesome as the shots of her head. Just the lifeless flesh of a young girl, of a dead body. You couldn't really even notice the broken bones. They weren't compound fractures. I continued to scan her body. There were the tattoos. One small tat on each ankle. Left outside ankle, a rose, not terribly original. Right outside ankle, what looked to be a small rendering of a pyramid. I didn't want to be cynical in this moment, but I thought the pyramid was probably one of those attempts people make with their tattoos to be spiritual. Her version of Asian lettering. Hey, nobody's perfect. In fact, a slip like this, a bad decision, could even be endearing.

Because we all make them.

I looked over the report again, looked at every photo again. I didn't really know what I was looking for. But that was okay. That's what I do all the time. Look at stuff others deemed inconclusive and try to make something out of it. Sometimes I find something. Sometimes I don't.

I got out my case file where I'd put both the long and short versions of the events of the case that I had typed up. Looked at it. Found what I was looking for. Right, that was his name, Clay Blevins. And he had auditioned for the movie *Friendship*. I knew it, but now I was sure. I dialed up the young actor I'd spoken to at King's Road Café.

"Hello," he said.

"Clay. Hey it's Tim—the casting director. I talked to you the other day at King's Road. After your audition for *Friendship*."

"Yeah," with concern. "You were asking me about Suzanne Neal."

"Right. Have you heard about her?"

"Yeah, man, it's so crazy. We're all so freaked out about it."

"I'd like to talk to you about it."

"Really? Why?"

"Clay. I don't work at Raleigh Studios. And my name's not Tim. My name is John. John Darvelle. I'm a detective. Of the private variety. I had met Suzanne prior to her murder. So now I'm looking into it to try and find out what happened."

Quickly, "What? You're a detective?"

"Relax. Yes, I'm a detective."

"Listen, man. I don't know anything or anything."

People get strange when the heat is on. *I don't know anything or anything.* What?

"I know, you were her friend. I'm on your side. Everything's cool. I want to find out who did it. And I want to ask you some questions."

"Can't you talk to the cops or something?"

"Sure. And so can you. And you should. But I want to talk to you. Like I said, you were a friend of hers. You might be able to help me."

"Well . . . when?"

"As soon as possible."

"All right, yeah, I guess you can talk to me."

"Let's meet at King's Road again. I'll buy you lunch."

"Yeah, okay."

"In an hour. You'll be there?"

"Yeah, I guess. Yeah, I'll be there."

15

I was sitting in the restaurant when Clay ambled in. That's what he did, he ambled. His jolly, friendly countenance was still there sort of, but it was hidden underneath concern and fear. He'd tamed his Afro a bit. And he was wearing a stylish, slightly snug, ill-fitting blazer. It's like he had prepared for hipster court. I was sipping a cup of coffee.

"Hey, Clay."

"Hey, John." And then, "You know, I knew you weren't a casting director."

People always, *always*, tell me later they knew I was bullshitting them earlier. And those same people never, *never* question me in the moment.

"Right," I said flatly. And then, "Thanks for talking to me."

"Sure. I don't know what I can tell you that I didn't already tell you."

A waitress came by and Clay ordered a coffee.

I said, "Well maybe you're right. But let's try. Tell me something about Suzanne that's, I don't know, unusual."

"What do you mean?"

"Just tell me a story about her that you thought *defined* her in any way. Anything. Could be tiny."

He thought for a long time—which I also appreciated. "Man, Suzanne was a mystery. 'Member I told you, she was always friendly, always nice. But it was different coming from her. Like she was so nice to all these guys who weren't really in her league. It was cool. But the thing was, she had this *air* about her. Not like she thought was better than you. More like she was *actually* better than you, but she didn't ever want you to think that she thought that. And she probably *didn't* think that. It just *was*. She kind of seemed to sit on higher ground than us. Than everybody. But, still, she was like sweet to the core."

"Did she ever indicate to you that there was some trouble in her life?"

"Man, I didn't know her that well. Like I told you. Class, auditions, occasionally a bar."

"Okay, but think about those times. Did she ever indicate that there was or might be any trouble in her life?"

"Man. No. I don't think."

"Where else did you see her? You ever run into her randomly?"

"Um. Once, I think. At the Newsroom, in Santa Monica. She was having lunch with a friend, this girl Jenny who was like a news producer or something. She was cute too. Not like Suzanne. But I mean still pretty cute. A totally attractive girl, just not Suzanne level."

Clay was losing focus.

"So what happened when you ran into her?"

"Nothing much, man. I'm just trying to remember *anything*. But I do remember thinking it was kind of cool to be in the same place as her, but like a place she went in her *real* life. Not a place connected to, like, class or an audition or after-class drinks or whatever. You know what I mean? I felt cool that I was in the same place as Suzanne."

Hey, not everything you get in my business is earth-shattering. It's part of the job. Listening, oftentimes, to drivel.

The waitress came by and delivered Clay's coffee.

I switched gears. "Did you ever see Suzanne with Jimmy Yates?"

He laughed for some reason. "No. Why? Did she know him? Was she dating him? That guy owns this town."

"I don't know if she knew him. That's why I asked."

"I know Jimmy's married but it wouldn't surprise me in the least if he was into her. One time when we were out after class Will Percy came up and tried to pick her up. She politely declined."

Will Percy. Movie star. Not Jimmy Yates level, but pretty big. Comedy guy.

"Suzanne gave him some love, but in the end she politely blew him off. That made me feel good. Because it's like even movie stars get turned down, you know?"

"Yeah."

"It was kind of empowering. But believe it or not, I actually do okay with the ladies."

Not sure why he was telling me this.

"I know, I know, I'm not exactly ripped. With my hair, my shadow looks like two circles on top of each other. Like a freakin' snowman."

Ah, I see. He was setting himself up for his routine. It was mildly entertaining.

"What about smaller stuff, Clay? Anything she ever said to you, in class, whatever. Anything you ever heard about her that was odd, mysterious, interesting?"

"Hmm. Man, I wish I could help. I wish I could be like the guy in the movie that helps, but I just don't know what to tell you. I'm sorry."

L.A. *I wish I could be the guy in the movie who helps.* That's how people here think.

And then he said, "You know, one time she got dropped off at an audition and I was standing right there when she got out. And for some reason I looked into the passenger side window to see who she was with. It was like involuntary. You know, just general curiosity about anyone being *with* Suzanne. At first, I thought it was another girl because I got a quick glimpse of the driver's hair as they pulled in and it was long and blond. But anyway, so I looked in and it wasn't a girl. It was this wild-looking dude. Like a good-looking guy, cool-looking, but from like a seventies cop show or something. He had a beard and like I said long blond hair. He smiled, but it was a strange smile."

"And then?"

"Nothing, really. We just walked to our audition. But . . . Well, Suzanne made a joke, so it's probably nothing. But she did say: 'You weren't supposed to see that.' And then she laughed. Like she was making a joke about cheating on her boyfriend or something. But she was clearly kidding."

"She had a boyfriend?"

"No, that's not what I meant. I'm just saying the way she said, 'You weren't supposed to see that' was playful. Coy. You know? Like pretending the situation was something that it wasn't. You know, being funny. *You weren't supposed to see that.*"

"Right. But just to be clear: To your knowledge she didn't have a boyfriend."

"No. Not to my knowledge."

"And did you ask Suzanne who the guy was?"

"Yeah, I think I did. But it was totally casual. She just said he was a friend. And I said, you know, cool."

"And did you ever see the guy again?"

"No."

Afterward, outside. "Thanks, Clay. Thanks for talking to me."

He nodded. "Think the cops will call me?"

"No idea."

"What should I do if they do?"

"Talk to them. Answer their questions. Tell them everything you know."

He nodded again.

I said, "Hey, what kind of car did the dude with the long hair have? You remember?"

"Black Merc. Four doors. Fat. Loaded."

This time I was the one who nodded.

We shook hands and went our separate ways.

16

I got back in the Cobalt. Mountain Gray. Not fat. Skinny. Not loaded. Unloaded. Time to hit up another connection. His name is Jose Villareal. Real name: Joe Villareal. Of Mexican descent but one hundred percent American. Why did he go by Jose, then? Well, he told me why. He said girls liked Jose better so he changed it.

I told him: "Makes sense."

Jose's entire life centers around what will get him more girls. If he needs to change his name to get more girls, he does. If he thinks listening to some horrible band will get him more girls, he does. He'll cover himself in cologne. Wear cheesy designer clothes. Listen to talk radio deejays who dispense surefire tricks to pick up the babes.

And yet, he never has a girlfriend. You know people like that? You know people like that.

Jose's a tipster for the gossip rags and Web sites. His life is knowing where stars live, where they are going, where they are hiding out in times of trouble, and where they were last night. He doesn't take pictures really, he's not a photographer. He does sometimes, but rarely. He's just a tracker. That job exists. Can you believe that? Now. Before you pass judgment on Jose's profession—actually, go ahead and pass judgment, but let me tell you this. I'm okay with what he does. You know why? Because he helps me.

"Jose, it's John Darvelle."

"John Darvelle," he said, pretending to be glad to hear from me.

"Jose, how are the ladies treating you?"

"John, you have no idea."

"What's your latest tip for how to get them?"

"I'm thinking about adopting a baby. Girls love babies. Even ones that aren't theirs."

"Don't you think that's a little insensitive to the child? Wouldn't that be filed under: Doing Something for the Wrong Reason?"

"Hey, if it works I do it." And then, "I'm just fucking with you, John. Not even I would do that. Plus I'm too self-ish for a kid, you know that. Jose only cares about Jose."

Well, at least he can admit it. And, yes, he talks about himself in the third person from time to time.

He dropped the act. "What's up, John?"

"What do you know about Jimmy Yates?"

"Nothing. Clean. Nice too. Well, nice when the cameras are on. I've heard he can be a prick, but I'm not sure about that."

"Yeah? He's married, right?"

"Come on, John. I know you're a cool guy, I know you're off the grid and have all these crazy concepts like worshipping Mar Fucking Vista. And I know you don't watch TMZ and read *People* magazine like the rest of us. But you know Jimmy Yates is married. And you know who he's married to. She's a huge fucking star."

I did know that. I was hoping my question might trigger Jose to tell me something about Jimmy having marital problems.

"Oh yes, right. Leslie Aaron."

Beautiful woman. Big star. Not as big as Jimmy. He wouldn't like that. But big nonetheless.

"Yes," he said. "Leslie Aaron."

"And they're one of those annoying happy couples in Hollywood, right?"

"They stay out of the rags. But like I said, I've heard he was a prick. And I've heard he's got a wandering eye too. But that's super down low. Like suggest it and get sued down low. No one's ever reported it."

Jose's tone shifted to one of professional interest. He inserted a little charm into his tone. "Why do you ask, amigo?"

"I can't tell you. You'll tell your contacts."

"Yeah, you're right. I would. It's called My Fucking Job."

"Tell me this. Where does Yates live?"

"Now that I can tell you. But which house? He's got a few."

"All of the ones in L.A."

"Just two here. Beach compound in Malibu and the main house in the Sades."

Jose meant: Pacific Palisades.

He gave me both addresses. And then he said, "You know, John. You helped me out once big-time. But when does that run out? When do you have to start paying me for info like everybody else does?"

"Tell you what. You want to go to a taping of *Sally and Ally*? Might be some babes there."

Sitcom about college girls. Gary directs a ton of them.

"Oh god, yes," Jose said in a slightly disturbing way.

"Done," I said. "Your pants are still on, right?"

"Not for long."

Jesus. I hung up.

I drove to Jimmy Yates's house. The Sades had become the most chic address in L.A. Spielberg lives there. Hanks lives there. Jimmy Yates and Leslie Aaron live there. The elite. Beverly Hills still had cachet, for sure, but it was a little too old-school Hollywood, too old fogey. Larry King. Shit, Arthur Vonz. And a lot of it was nouveau tacky. Lots of those plastic surgery freaks walking around with orange-colored skin and cream-colored Bentleys. Hancock Park still had class, still had a little bit of a chic thing happening. Old mansions, traditional suburban layouts, "nice" people whose children went East for school. People who understand that going to boarding school doesn't mean you're a problem child. But Hancock Park lacked that California pizzazz. It was inland, boring, East Coast-y.

But the Sades. The Pacific Palisades had it all. It was

in the hills, in the mountains, *and* near the beach. So the houses crested canyons but also had ocean views. Yeah, I know, views. And rather than the somewhat claustrophobic quality of the Hollywood Hills, it felt open and free because all you had to do was look to the west and there was the Pacific.

Now don't get me wrong. In my opinion, it was still too inaccessible. You're still looking at an ordeal to get to, say, Venice. You're still locked into a corner of L.A. Sure, you can drop down to the PCH easily, but what does that get you? It gets you an enormous hassle. And to go east, to Hollywood, you've really only got one option: Sunset. Which for massive sections is a huge drag. I mean, let's be honest, I would not live there.

Look, the Sades is *just* west of Brentwood. Right? And fuck Brentwood. But the people who did choose the Sades? Who had the dough to choose the Sades? Who didn't have to leave their house during the hours that most people operate? It was the promised land of L.A., for sure.

I found Jimmy Yates's house. It was in the nicest section of the Pacific Palisades—The Huntington. That was what the neighborhood *within* the neighborhood was called. The Huntington. See, once you got to the Sades, you still weren't quite *there* yet. There was still room to grow. You had to step up the down payment just a little bit more to get to The Huntington.

Jimmy Yates had clearly done just that. I was outside his colossal house now. More specifically, I was outside of, you guessed it, his big old gate. Another goddamn gate. Ten yards away from it, off to the side of the road, listening to Dinosaur Jr.'s *You're Living All Over Me*.

Nothing happened for an hour. And then something did. Jimmy Yates himself appeared. Slid out a little iron door next to his big iron gate. He probably could see my car but he probably couldn't see me. The Cobalt didn't seem to cause any alarm in him. In his eyes I was a maid or a worker or a servant of some kind tending to one of the mansions on the street.

I was tucked under a tree, a shadow covering the Cobalt's windshield. Yates was walking toward me and he wasn't alone. He was walking a real-life bloodhound, the dog attached to Yates by one of those retractable leashes. The dog marched along inspecting everything, his DNA, his biology, rearing its head. The dog was looking for action. Just like me.

The dog had a nice shiny coat. Big old ears. A face with character.

Jimmy Yates wore weekend celebrity gear. Four-hundred-dollar faded jeans—faded is back—a long-sleeved T-shirt with a short-sleeved T-shirt over it, baseball hat, beard.

I thought, I wonder if that beard is detachable? And he just puts it on during the weekends to look casual and celebrity-like. He and the dog marched toward me. They were getting pretty close. They'd be able to see me soon, even with my trusty shadow hiding me.

Hmm. Not the best place to talk to him. All he has to do is tell me to fuck off, then go back behind his gate. It's better to confront unsuspecting people in public. They just naturally don't want to make a scene. But I was about to open my door and get out anyway, didn't have much choice, when they flipped a U-ey and starting heading back home. Not a very long walk. The bloodhound's face revealed some misery. He clearly wanted to keep going. You could just feel the pent-up energy. I thought, well, maybe Jimmy has something else to do. Or maybe he's just an egotistical movie star who only has time for himself and doesn't really even like the dog. Too bad if that's the case. Because that dog is tremendous, that's just simply not in question.

So. Had I missed my chance? Should I have just gotten out even though it wasn't the greatest location to ask him a few questions? Didn't think so. And, thankfully, I was right.

Five minutes later, Jimmy Yates came out of his driveway, driving this time, not the Maserati I'd seen him in before, but a black Chevy SUV with tinted windows. He drove right past me. I could see him behind the tint. I didn't like him. I'm not sure why, but I just didn't like him. I picked him up. He went to Sunset, then down to the PCH, then into Santa Monica, to Fred Segal. Fred Segal. Fancy hip clothing store that housed various boutiques and designers within it. Also had a café or two where you could get a twenty-dollar turkey sandwich or, you know, some wheatgrass. He went into one of the restaurants. I waited outside. Six minutes later he came out holding a big smoothie and sat at one of the outside tables. Three tables away from where I sat.

Stars drink a lot of smoothies.

That's a fact.

I got up and joined him at his table. Sat right down. He looked initially startled, then suddenly calm.

"Can I help you?" he said.

He was an interesting-looking, okay handsome, guy. Skinny. These guys are always really skinny in person.

"I hope so," I said.

"What, you want an autograph?" He slurped, showing me some smoothie in his mouth, displaying he could give two shits about me.

"No, I don't want you to write your name on a piece of paper and give it to me. I have no idea why anyone would want that."

He smirked and said, "Then, what's up?"

"My name is John Darvelle. I'm a private detective. I want to know why you were in Suzanne Neal's building three days ago."

Casually, too casually, he said, "How do you know where I was three days ago? Are you following me?"

He didn't say what a lot of people would have said. *Who is Suzanne Neal?* He deftly avoided telling a lie if he did in fact know her. Clever.

"What were you doing, Jimmy?"

He gave me a big I-have-no-idea-what-you're-talking-about smirk and said, "I think you should leave me alone."

"You went into her condo on Ocean Avenue three days ago. I saw you. You parked your Maserati in front of her building and went inside."

He pulled out his phone.

"Let me know if you want me to call the police," he said.

"Be my guest. I'm sure they've already talked to you."

"Actually I don't want the cops here. TMZ is probably watching all of this. What do you want?"

"Suzanne Neal is dead. But I bet you already know that."

"I don't know what you're doing. And I don't know why you're pestering me. But I'm leaving."

"Did you know Suzanne Neal, Jimmy?"

He looked at me, standing now, but didn't say anything.

I said, "She's dead. Why don't you help me find out what happened?"

He turned to leave. But before he did he shot me one more look. For a second an emotion ran across his eyes—sorrow. He began walking away.

"Just answer this, Jimmy. Did you know Suzanne Neal?"

He turned back to me. "Quit following me. Whatever you think happened didn't happen. I didn't have anything to do with anyone dying."

He was pretty smooth, not really saying anything. But then he went off script for a beat, usually not smart for an actor, and said, "I swear."

"You swear? What are we, in fifth grade?"

But I was glad he said it, because it was emotional. It was an accident. Unintentional. And that's a good thing in my line.

"Pretty clever how you never actually answered anything, Jimmy. I'll be seeing you again, pal."

He shot me another look. This time he looked annoyed. But still hurt. He hopped in his SUV and stomped on the gas. My blood was pumping. I was revved up. I hadn't had a game plan with Jimmy. I was just harassing him a bit. But I got what I wanted. He knows something. He must.

I stormed into one of the Fred Segal clothing boutiques and looked around. I saw a shirt I liked. I'm six-one, two-hundred. So I grabbed an extra large and went into a dressing room to try it on. I couldn't get the buttons to meet each other in the middle. I literally could not button it. I put my other shirt back on and exited the dressing room. I said to a beautiful saleslady, "Does this come in XXXXL?"

"No," she said vapidly. I don't think she knew I was being a smart ass.

"Is there anything bigger than this here?"

"That shirt is enormous. It's one of the biggest ones in the store."

"Who shops here? Like, skinny sixties rock stars? Do the surviving member of the Kinks frequent this establishment?"

"I don't know what you're talking about."

"How can this shirt be an extra large? It's literally tiny. It's not even an extra small."

She looked at me blankly. I didn't think this woman had ever smiled.

"Do you want to buy it or not?"

"No. But how much is it?"

She looked at the price. "Six hundred and twelve bucks. It's on sale."

"Well, that's six hundred bucks I won't have to spend. Say, is there a Marshall's around here?"

"What's that?"

"I've got to go."

17

I drove up to Mulholland, to the house in the Hollywood Hills where Suzanne Neal went right before she went back to her condo and was taken from the planet by gunshot. On the way up I called Linda Robbie, gave her the address, and asked her who lived in the big, and of course gated, Hollywood Hills spread.

Now at the house, sitting outside the gate, across and down the street a bit, my cell buzzed, startling me, even though I knew the call was coming. That ever happened to you? That's happened to you. A few sexual references and a proposal or two later, I got the name of the person who lived in this big hilltop estate. A man named Richard Neese.

Time to sign off with Linda. Thank you, beautiful. Yes, yes, we'll take off our clothes together one of these days.

Jeez, who knows, maybe we would.

I waited outside, staring at the big gate for a long time. This being the gate with the absurd ironwork. Lines and bars and some pretentious misguided attempt at some kind of art I guessed. All in the name of a gate. Day turned into night. Night that was eventually dark enough so that I could sneak in.

So I did.

Down a bit from the chaos of metal that was the gate, the impediment to entrance was simply a brick wall, which I easily climbed up and jumped over. On the grounds now. It was big and beautiful and California-y. Very different from the Vonz estate. Less of an artistic eye at work. Less manicured. More pure California mystery and beauty. Big sprawling trees. Exotic flowers. And a big Spanish-style mansion. The grounds, the house, had a moody, trippy feel. There was some furniture inside covered in red velvet—I was sure of it.

I made my way through the dark trees and shadows around to the back of the house. There was a big rectangular pool that had little gargoyle statues standing guard on each corner. Two of the four of them were looking at me. They were.

I stood at the back corner of the house. Glued to the Spanish stucco, I stretched my neck to look into the window nearest me. And I saw something that actually made me think I might be getting somewhere. There was a man sitting on the floor Indian-style, the lotus position. He wore sort of a tunic, had long blond hair and a brown beard. The man Clay Blevins had described to me? No doubt. His eyes were half closed. He was smoking a joint and drinking a glass of wine. Music was playing, some trippy combination of Gregorian chant and seventies-style guitar rock.

I could hear it through the windows. I liked it.

A woman entered. She was topless and wearing a sarong. This is how these people lived. Jesus. What had I done wrong to not be one of these people? My god, she was beautiful. Thin, darkly complexioned, Kate Jackson–style, with big, full, real breasts. She walked smoothly, gracefully, like a model on a runway, and sat behind the bearded dude. She started giving him a massage. I thought two things. One: How does this long-haired blond douchebag fit into my story? And two: How do I get one of those massages?

I pulled my head away from the window. I stood now again stuck to the side of the house, hidden in the shadows, and thought for a second. I looked at the pool, the gargoyles, then thought about the parts of the *inside* of the house I'd been able to see. It was California mystery combined with bad Victorian that was clearly expensive, but lacked real taste, lacked a sophisticated eye, betrayed an attempt at class by way of money and gaudy antique-looking crap. It was an attempt at superiority through mimicking what might have been in the house of Spanish or even English royalty in the 16- or 1700s. But even then that look didn't work and reeked of desperation. This attempt I had just seen was a failed one. And yes, there was some red velvet.

Moving on. I thought: The two inside aren't going anywhere. So, I moved sideways into the darkness of the trees, back to the side of the house, back to the shadows.

I got to the wall and got out of there, up and over and

into the Cobalt. I went back to my house in Mar Vista. I sat in my living room Indian-style and put on some groovy music. I didn't have any weed but I wished I did. I waited for a really hot babe in a sarong to come out and massage my back. It didn't happen.

So I got up, grabbed a Bud Light, and went outside on my back deck. Three beers later, I went in, took a long, hot shower, and went to bed. At 5 a.m., I popped out of bed, before my alarm went off, showered again, dressed, got back in the Cobalt, and drove back to Neese's.

Outside, ready to follow anyone who left the compound.

The girl left at around 8:30 a.m. Silver Audi A4. They probably went to bed early. Post-sex. All high and shit. Yes, jealous. I followed her down the little mountain, into Beverly Hills, to a high-end condo on Burton Way.

She pulled the A4 into a garage, parked. I parked illegally right in front of her building. She walked out of the garage and headed toward the front entrance to the condo.

I got out of the Cobalt, stood up next to it. "Excuse me," I said.

She stopped walking, looked over at me with fiery, but not worried, eyes. "Yes?"

She wasn't afraid of a stranger. Lots of beautiful women have this thing where they won't make eye contact with any stranger no matter how nice or approachable or normal he may be. And when they do, their expression suggests: Get away from me or I'll Mace you and I also just hate you in general.

But not this one. She looked right at me.

I walked over to her. "My name is John Darvelle. I'm

a private investigator. I'm looking into the murder of a woman named Suzanne Neal. Do you know who that is?"

"No," she said. And left it at that. No fumbling. No additional words.

"Really? Well how about Richard Neese? Do you know who that is?"

"Yes, I know Richard."

"Well, Suzanne Neal, the woman I just mentioned, went to Richard's house the night she was killed. That was three nights ago. Do you know why she might have done that? Why she might have visited Richard?"

"How would I know the answer to that? Richard knows a lot of people in this town. Excuse me, I need to go."

She headed for her door.

"Why does Richard know so many people in this town?"

She turned back to look at me. Cold but confident eyes. "Why don't you ask him," she said. And slipped into her condo.

I thought: Maybe I will.

I moved the Cobalt across the street and down a bit, then stayed put. I could see the woman moving around behind the blinds in the front right bottom condo. After about an hour she left, but I stayed. Until the mail got delivered. About an hour later. The mailman distributed the mail into the eight various boxes of the condo's mailbox bank. Once he was a couple buildings down, I found the box for the woman's condo, picked the lock, then opened it up and looked at the name on her mail. Rebecca Heath. Another name I'd need to add to my always evolving case notes.

18

All right. What did I know so far? The night Suzanne was killed she visited the house of Richard Neese, then came home to her condo, then was out on her balcony with a man, then later that night got murdered. Earlier that day she may or may not have been visited by Jimmy Yates, world-famous actor. I was betting yes. And, of course, the world-famous director Arthur Vonz was trying to contact her right at this same time.

She definitely had Arthur's heart in her hands. Did she have Jimmy Yates's? The man on her balcony's? Richard Neese's?

Hmm.

Also, upon looking into Richard Neese, I discovered

that another beautiful woman was a part of his world and thus a part of my story: Rebecca Heath.

Hmm.

And there was something about Richard Neese. The way Clay Blevins described him. The way Rebecca Heath seemed to be serving him. Was he some kind of boss to these lovely ladies? Maybe. Maybe. But why did I *feel* there was something else happening here.

Hmm.

My cell rang. Startling me again. Does your cell startle you like mine does? Damn. Is there a nonstartle setting? I looked at my phone. Unidentified. Oh well. Got to take a risk or two in life.

"John Darvelle," I said.

"Darvelle?" said a sort-of-familiar voice.

"Yes."

"This is Detective Mike Ott, LAPD. You remember me?"

"Nope," I lied.

"Too bad. I'd like you to come down here anyway. I want to talk to you."

Normally I'd give him more trouble. Make him all but force me to come down. But I really didn't want him, or any of them, too much in my business right now. And I was curious about what Ott wanted.

"When?"

"Oh," Ott said. "Now. Or five minutes ago."

"Fine," I said. "I'll head down."

"I'll be here."

"Oh, sir?" I said sarcastically. "What was your name again? Who do I ask for?"

"Ott, Darvelle. You know who I am. We met—"

"Sorry, I really don't care. I'll see you soon."

I hung up on him.

Next thing I knew I was in downtown L.A., at LAPD headquarters. Now, if you last as a P.I. in this town, in any town, for more than five years you *will* interact with the cops of said town. It just happens. You'll be in the same places. You'll be looking into the same things. You might even need each other from time to time. It's very hard to get them to respect you. You have to convince them over time that you're in it for the right reasons—just like you do with all your connections. You have to show them that you have a clue about what you're doing. You have to help them out a time or two and not make too big a deal out of it. But, listen. You must not give them too much respect. You start kissing their asses and they'll flick you away like a fly. They'll go out of their way to make your life suck.

But even when they do respect you, it's always a dance. Because ultimately they don't want to admit a private guy can do a good investigation. That being said, smart cops know that sometimes the private guys can do more than they can because the private guys aren't nearly as tied up with legal red tape. Jump over Neese's wall without a shitload of documents proving it made sense to do it? A cop will rarely do that. Too much risk. Too much to lose.

I knew the reason I was down at LAPD was because they wanted to know what I knew. But here's where it gets tricky. You can't bend to them too much, you can't always give them everything you know, just because they're cops. I'm not saying break the law. I'm saying there are times when *your* investigation comes first. And telling them too much will not just screw you, it'll screw the investigation. Because a lot of cops don't know what they're doing. And even more cops are often so tied up with the aforementioned red tape that they simply can't get to the bottom of things in as effective a way as you can. Period.

Now, as I've mentioned, I've been at it a good while in this town, and I've interacted, and worked with, a bunch of guys on the force. This guy, Mike Ott, we'd seen each other around. We were actually in the same meeting once—I was giving the cops some information I had on an L.A. lawyer suspected of killing his wife. As for today, I'm sure he'd asked around about me before I got there and had probably gotten a decent report. I'd helped out the dudes down there. A few times. But right now? Ott wasn't walking the floor trying to find out more about me, or double-checking that I was indeed a good investigator and maybe even a good guy. Nope. He wasn't doing that. Instead, he was right in my face. I was in a chair in front of his desk and he was sitting, not behind his desk, but *on* his desk right in front of me.

"Darvelle. A couple of the guys down here know you, said you were a good guy."

"I am a good guy."

He gave me a long cop look. And didn't take that line any further.

"Why are you looking into the murder of Suzanne Neal?"

"Who?" I said.

His expression didn't change. He was literally stone-faced. I never could figure out how these cops did that. I've told you already I've spotted waves of emotion or guilt or suspicion or *something* move across people's eyes, people's faces. None of that with Ott.

"Suzanne Neal," he said.

"Why do you think that I'm looking into the murder of . . . what was her name again?"

He gave me an I-know-what-you're-doing smirk. "I'm a cop and I'm looking into the murder and through my looking into it I found out that you're looking into it."

I thought: Jimmy Yates got questioned based on my call, then told the cops: "Hey, I wasn't even there, I don't know anything, but some P.I. named John Darvelle came up to me on the street."

I looked at Ott looking at me. He had a creased-up face that you get from smoking way too much. But sort of a handsome guy in an old-school, conservative-looking, tough-guy way. Big head of graying hair. Not losing it at all. At all. Even into his fifties. Yes, I was jealous. Also, very dry skin. His face was made of old, uncared-for leather. The dude needed some moisturizer.

"Well," I said. "If I were looking into the murder of a girl it'd be because I like to find out who did it when someone gets killed. Don't you? I think it's only fair."

"Who are you working for?"

"Now? Well, I always try to keep a lot of cases going."

Basically true. Also, I wasn't working for anyone. I was working for me. But more important, I'd already reported to the cops everything—well, almost everything—I knew at the time of the murder, because I *wanted* them to know anything that might help them. But since then, I'd begun to put a few things in motion so I could find out more. But, as I mentioned a minute ago, I didn't want Ott or anyone else to screw it up.

He laughed. "See, my thing is, if you're looking into this on behalf of someone, then that someone might know something that could help me."

"She doesn't," I said.

"She?"

"He."

"You not providing me information could be getting in the way of the case, which is illegal."

"I know the law."

"Really?"

"Sort of."

"Somebody called the police station the day after the murder and told us a bunch of information relating to the case."

"Would you mind passing that stuff on to me; it could be helpful."

"Was it you?"

"Huh?"

"You heard me."

"No, it wasn't me. If I knew a bunch about the case then I wouldn't be looking into it. Even though I'm not necessarily looking into it."

"That makes no sense."

"It makes some sense."

"Listen, Darvelle. I have a question for you."

Here it comes. He's going to ask me about Jimmy Yates. These guys are too predictable.

"Do you know what a Pipe Girl is?"

And . . . I was wrong. Totally. Which happens from time to time.

"A Pipe Girl? No, I don't. I really don't."

"You've never heard the term 'Pipe Girl'?"

I couldn't even rib him on this one. I could only tell him the truth. "No, I haven't."

Ott stared at me. His face was totally still, like a statue of a guy with a creased face and really good hair. He was trying to read me.

He finally said, "I think you're looking into the Suzanne Neal case. And I think you should tell me something."

"Okay, I'll tell you something. You need to moisturize. Your skin is incredibly dry."

He looked at me. He looked through me. I thought he was going to shoot me.

19

Four hours later I was sitting outside Richard Neese's house again, same spot I had while waiting for Rebecca Heath to exit. Waiting. Waiting again. My cell rang. Didn't startle me this time. Linda Robbie.

"Hey Linda."

"So I couldn't stay out of your business. This Richard Neese guy is a house flipper. But unlike most of them he doesn't appear to be a charlatan. He actually makes sales. Most people say they flip, but they don't actually flip. Like ever. Neese does. He makes sales. Makes money. Buys big, sought-after mansions, and other properties, corporate properties too, and either fixes them up or finds people who are willing to buy. He's made a lot of money over the past few years. A friend of mine sold a property for him."

"What else does he do? You have any idea?"

"My girlfriend didn't know anything. She did say he was attractive. In sort of an eighties way."

"Thanks, Linda. I gotta hop."

"I know where I'd like you to hop."

"Hey, you know, what? That actually sort of makes sense. I'm impressed."

"Are you going to reward me for it?"

Linda is nothing if not persistent.

I laughed. "I've gotta go."

We hung up. I sat there thinking about what to do. Now, I told you why being a private cop is sometimes advantageous. Because you can, you know, break the law on occasion to find out what you need to find out. But sometimes it leaves you without a move. I can't surf the police databases at will. I can't always get the information that already exists because I can't always get a cop to give me a favor. That's why I do a lot of waiting. I put on some Shane McGowan, *The Snake*. I listened to "Victoria" seven times in a row, then let the CD play.

I didn't have to wait too long for my next move to come to me. A car, a fat, black Merc four-door, as Clay Blevins might describe it, pulled out of the hideous crisscrossy steel gates.

I picked it up.

He drove east on Mulholland, stayed up top, cresting the canyon, then went right onto Nichols Canyon and headed down toward Hollywood. In a very hip part of the Hills now. Mansions and bungalows glued onto the side of Mount Groovy. The black Merc twisted down through the Hills. I stayed on the car pretty close. No need to hide the tail too much. I was just heading down the mountain, just like him. The Merc and I came up on a line of cars parked on one side of the tight canyon road. After twenty, thirty cars, there was a temporary valet stand in front of the entrance to a house. Were we going to a party? I love parties.

Neese pulled the Merc up to the valet and stopped. I zoomed on by, passing more parked cars, nice cars, on the other side of the stand. I slowed way down and watched him in my rearview getting out. Jeans and a T-shirt and that horrible, long, thick, flowing blond hair. I called Linda. Pick up, babe. I just talked to you. Pick up. She did.

"Is this my reward call?"

"I need something quick. Who lives at 6483 Nichols Canyon. As quick as you can."

We hung up. I parked way, way down the street, beyond where the valets were putting cars. Then: Cell. Linda.

"You got it?"

"Someone named Nick Blankenship."

"Shit, really?"

"Yep. Who is he?"

Nick Blankenship was a big rock star. And a good one. Lead singer of the band the Slobs. Good, inventive records. I really liked them. Had a record of theirs in the Cobalt as we spoke.

I told Linda who he was and then, "Thanks for such quick help. I may just drive over after this and have sex with you."

I hung up before she could accept my offer.

I looked in my trunk and pulled out a shirt that I had bought, believe it or not, at Fred Segal a few years earlier. I had found one in my size and spent a chunk of a case payment on it. It was the shirt I wore to stuff like this, made by a company called Scotch and Soda. It was black, a nice cut of black, and all over it were skulls and crossbones of different sizes and colors. It was a party shirt and, now that I had it on, I was ready for a Hollywood Fucking Party.

I walked back up to the valet stand and the entrance to the party. The valets were busy parking people's expensive cars, and there was a beefy doorman standing in front of a little stone alcove and, surprise surprise, another gate. This one was modest and little and only stood two, maybe three feet tall. Something that anyone, anywhere would have as the official entrance to a yard or courtyard area outside a front door. It was painted black and looked to be made of steel, but it was Nick Blankenship's version of a white picket fence. I already liked him, now I liked him more.

He had a reasonable freaking gate.

I barely looked at the doorman, just began walking right by him. He got in my way and said, "Excuse me. Are you on the list?"

"Do I need to be?"

"Yes."

"I'm in the band."

"Nick's band?"

"No, my band, that Nick's in."

The guy looked at me like: *Maybe.*

"I'm Freddy Wheeler. Dude. Move."

He slowly stepped aside. I pulled a fifty out of my wallet and handed it to him and laughed. "You're just doing your job, I get it."

I walked in. Amazing how easy it is. If you're ever in L.A. and you need to get into a party, try it. You can say almost anything. I've said I was Peter Fonda, Alexander Payne, Thom Yorke. Occasionally I get caught. Mostly I don't. By the way, Thom with an H. Not great.

I walked through the courtyard, through the front door, then into the party. Another amazing house in the Hills. There are so many of them. It was decorated in an unfortunate style. Minimalist, Philippe Starck–type junk. A rock star who knew how to write music but didn't know what to do with a house. All white and black. Leather and chrome everywhere. Some bad, expensive art. You know? You know.

Good party though. Attractive people everywhere, loud music, a wild feel. I walked out back. Big, well-manicured yard with a view into a deeper section of the canyon. Pretty trees and flowers. And, of course, a big old pool. At this level, you had to have a big old pool. Blankenship had hired some beautiful women, beautiful topless women, to swim around the pool dressed as mermaids. They would get out, sit on the edge, dive back in, frolic around. I watched them for a long, long time. I just couldn't help it. I like mermaids. I really do.

As I watched the mermaids, I was popping back and forth to the bar. Yes, they had Bud and Coors Light. Rock stars know how to drink. They don't know how to decorate their houses sometimes, but they know how to drink. I was starting to catch a buzz. I was starting to feel like I'd really been invited to this party. Shit, I was starting to have fun.

Then: I saw Neese appear at the outside bar that I'd been hitting. I peeled myself away from the mermaids and walked over.

"How's it going?"

He looked at me. "Good, man, you?"

"Good. Just looking at the mermaids. I'm going to go back to looking at the mermaids after I get another drink."

"Can't say I blame you," he said, on autopilot.

"I'm John," I said.

"Richard."

"So, you know Nick?"

"Yeah. Old friend."

"Cool." Long, awkward pause. "So what do you do?"

He looked at me. A little suspicion, a little disgust. "I smoke grass at Hollywood parties."

"Yeah? It would be nice to do that, then look at the mermaids some more."

No reaction. "Well, why don't you come with me, John."

I grabbed another Coors Light and followed Richard through the party. We weaved around past the pool, then went into the pool house, which sat directly across the pool from the main house. Then: Down some stairs into a basement that had been designed, it appeared to me, specifically for one purpose. TO SMOKE A TON OF WEED IN.

This room Nick Blankenship could handle. There were beads hanging. Big leather chairs. Big colorful carpets. A massive wall-sized black and white photograph of Led Zepp performing live. And the acoustics. *The acoustics.* The room had been created to blast loud music in. I loved it down here. The music playing now, the music *blasting* now: The Guess Who. "Laughing." Nick was a modern rocker with an appreciation for good songwriting.

Nick wasn't around, but there were a few other grass smokers in the room, some musician types. Skinny jeans.

Skinny bodies. Dyed black hair. And, of course, some attractive ladies fluttering about.

We stood in a circle in the middle of the room. Five of us. Me, Neese, two other guys, one girl. Neese produced a joint and fired it up. We all started taking hits, making random small talk.

A guy said: "I needed this."

Another guy said: "See you all tomorrow."

Laughter from the crowd.

The girl said to me, "Are you a musician?"

I said, "No. I'm a karate instructor."

Everyone seemed to think that was funny. Except for Neese. His smile was big, but it was totally full of suspicion.

Let me tell you something: The weed that's out there these days is strong. With all these dispensaries and people racing to get your business legally, it has made the weed potent. Potent. I was really high. I was on another planet. I mean, it looked like the guy next to me was wearing a black mesh tank top and blue eyeliner. Wait, that was actually true. But I was having a tough time remembering my act, remembering why I was there. What my plans were to get more information. Instead I was just smiling and saying to the new beautiful waif next to me: "This song is fucking great."

And it was. But, you know, keep your eye on the prize, Darvelle. Somebody in our ever-shifting circle produced a fresh, just-cracked half gallon of Jack Daniel's and passed it around. I know, I know, the case, but it looked good. I took a big, burning swig and then out of nowhere, surprising myself, I yelled: "Yeeeeeees!"

I positioned myself next to Neese and focused. Focused hard. Brought myself back down, which, with practice, you can do. "So what do you do besides smoking weed at Hollywood parties?"

With that suspicious smile: "Why are you so curious about what I do?"

With a confident frown I said, "Aren't you curious about what people do? Let me tell you, I don't care if you're a big Hollywood producer or a carpenter or a karate instructor like me, I just like talking to people about what they do. It's interesting to me how someone decides to spend their time on the planet."

"Yeah," Neese said, buying it. "That makes sense."

"So what do you do?"

"Mostly real estate. That's how I made most of my money. Flipping houses at first, then building them and selling them. Nowadays, I invest my money in places I think it'll grow."

"Cool," was all I could come up with.

Then a kind of intensity fell over him. I looked at him. And the weed in my brain made his inner person, his inner person that he tried to hide, appear before my eyes. This man was bad. I could see it in his black eyes.

He took a big hit off the joint and said, "You're not a karate instructor."

"Oh, but I am," I said. And then I screamed, screamed, "Hi-ya!"

The room looked over and gave me a round of applause. It was getting nutty down here. Wild. Trippy.

Neese said, "So if I took a swing at you out of nowhere you'd be able to deal with it?"

I looked right at him. "Yes. For sure."

"I don't believe you."

I think I was as high as I'd ever been. The weed was adding to, was twisting into a new shape, my picture of Neese. This man had black eyes, yes, but he had a black heart too. I could see it. I could see it through his chest. A black heart pumping in his body sending purple-black blood to his veins. He couldn't hide it from me in this moment. He was a bad guy and I was going to find out just exactly how bad.

Richard Neese was my story.

I thought he might go for it, take his shot, but instead he gave me his shitty smile and turned away from me, offering the joint to one of the girls, and offering me his back. He then drifted farther into the room, mixing in with the smoke and the loud music and the wild-eyed, whacked-out crowd.

I said to no one in particular, "I'm going to go look at the mermaids."

I left the basement. I went back upstairs. I went to the bar and did another shot of Jack, and drank a Coors Light. I took a breath. Calmed down. I wasn't exactly sure what to do now. And not just because I was unbelievably high and now pretty damn drunk.

So I just started to enjoy the party.

I don't get invited to these things much, occasionally with Gary Delmore, so why not, right? I checked out the mermaids again. This time, I sat in a poolside lounge chair and quietly observed them, my eyes opening and closing slowly, on the verge of some kind of dope-induced sleep. In my dreamlike, bent state of mind, they appeared, for flashes, to be actual mermaids. I watched them slithering in and out of the water, gliding through the pool, sitting on the edge, the water dripping down their naked bodies. One of them, posing and pensive, looked over at me, held me for a moment with her eyes, then gracefully reentered the water and vanished. I said out loud, involuntarily, "Come back."

All right, it was time to move on. I got up, drank a couple more beers. Chatted with some partygoers.

And let the time start to slide by.

I made my way to a dance room inside the house. I looked at my watch. Shit, it was midnight now. In the room, it was dark with flashing strobe lights. And the music was loud, and no more Guess Who. It was deejayed techno, dance, pop, hip-hop, whatever. One of the rockers from downstairs in the Weed Room appeared in front of me holding up the Jack bottle and smiling maniacally. One of the skinny guys in the skinny jeans. I hit it again, then hit it again, then hit the dance floor. Moved my way into a throng of Hollywood Hipsters. I was feeling good. I was feeling *great*. The case was lingering in my head, but really I was loose, lanky, free, feeling it. I was dancing with a beautiful girl, a sexy blonde.

She said to me, "I like your shirt."

But I didn't answer. I just kept busting out moves. Moves I didn't know I had. And I'm not talking about the Robot and the Lawn Mover. I'm talking way, way more advanced. I was popping my head back and forth to the beat. I was moving my shoulders. I was moving my hands around in front of my face in intricate, nonsensical patterns. I shook. I jived. I shived. I stood on one leg and just shook the other one as hard as I could. I caught a glimpse of the blonde looking at me with an almost concerned expression.

Then: I found myself in a corner, I'd lost the blonde, and I was simply doing deep knee bends over and over facing the wall.

I had lost my mind.

I spun around and the blonde appeared again, right in front of me. She was right up in my face. I grabbed the back of her head and kissed her. Softly. For a long, long time. Her mouth tasted like Jack Daniel's. Her mouth tasted like heaven.

She looked at me. Then she came at me and put her face right in my face, ready for more. I kissed her again.

Then, over the music, she kind of screamed, "Who do you know here?"

What a terrible question. I didn't answer. I just moved back to the center of the dance floor, leaving her in the flashing, strobing darkness. My moves turned more hippy-dippy. I had my eyes closed and was rolling my head around in circles. I had crazy thoughts ramming around in my mind. Visions from the case I was pursuing. I tracked it in my head from beginning to now. Every step of the way as my head went round and round. It calmed me down, brought me back to the planet.

I was ready to leave the dance floor. So I did that thing where you head off a dance floor, and at first you're still dancing, and then you move into kind of a half dance as you get closer to the edge of the dance floor. Then, when you get to the edge you're kind of barely dancing, but you still are pulling moves just a little bit. You're doing like a dance walk. And then suddenly you are just walking. It's an odd thing, that move. It's a really horrible thing to witness someone do.

I was thinking about it, now just off the dance floor, now just walking like a normal person. When a large man in a black suit appeared in front of me. I tried to squeeze by him, but he intentionally moved in front of me.

I felt something coming.

That something was his fist. He took a big, but quick, swing at me. I blocked it, twisted his arm around, struck him once in the kidney, then tripped him and slammed his face into the hard wood of the floor. I put my knee in the middle of his back. Hard. Some of the dancers noticed and looked over. Some didn't. I looked around, one way, then another. And I caught Neese in the next room by himself, looking right at me.

I was looking at Neese when a fist popped me in the side of the head.

"Owwww," I said, as I went down. I tried to hang on to the position I had on the first guy but just couldn't.

The guy who hit me, Black Suit Number Two, helped the first guy up. Through the haze of the booze, weed, and the fist to my head, I recognized Black Suit Number Two as the guy I'd initially bullshitted to get in. I pointed at him nonsensically. And then a third dude in a black suit appeared. I stood up. Now guys One, Two, and Three were standing in front of me.

The first guy, the one I had taken down, looked at me, furious. The two other guys stared at me. They wanted me to come at them. And I wanted to. I really did.

But this wasn't the time to put all my chips in. To go for it.

Black Suit Number Two said to me, "You need to leave. You weren't invited to this party."

The left side of my head hurt. Burned. My left ear rang. I said to him, "Okay. Let's go."

Black Suit Number Two grabbed my arm and began walking me out. We walked right by Neese, whose black eyes were still on me.

I said to him, "Did I pass the test, Chief?"

He said, "Not really. You pretty much lost that fight."

Okay. He had a point.

The Black Suits took me out onto the street, a bit down from the valet stand.

Black Suit Number Two: "Don't come back."

I said, "Tell Nick I'll see him at rehearsal. I have a few ideas I think we can work on."

"What?"

"You know, because I had initially said that I was in the band."

He looked at me blankly.

"Never mind."

I started walking toward the Cobalt. I found it, got in. I drove six blocks away, away from the party, away from the long line of cars. I parked, put my seat in full recline, and closed my eyes. I was drunk. I was high. I was wiped out. I crashed for three hours or so. I woke up, 3, 4 a.m., cranked up the Cobalt, went home, went to bed.

20

The next morning I went to my office and sat at my desk. I was just thinking, looking over my notes, looking at the pictures of a dead Suzanne Neal. I was tired. I was hungover. The pictures of Suzanne were particularly affecting. Gruesome.

And just sad.

I looked at her two tattoos. The rose, which looked like a rose, and the pyramid, which looked like this:

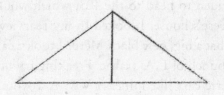

I snapped a picture of the pyramid with my phone, then got in my Cobalt and headed to Neese's. Yep, I was going to sit out there and wait again. I parked farther away from his house this time, but close enough that I still had a good line on his gate. Two hours later, the black Merc came out.

I picked him up. He drove to Rebecca Heath's apartment in Beverly Hills. I pictured her topless in that sarong. Oh yes. She came out of her apartment and got in his car. Man, she was sexy. Involuntarily, my mouth twitched a little bit watching her cross the condo's front lawn. That model walk, the one I'd seen her exhibit in Neese's house.

I was excited to see where this was going to take me. But Rebecca got out of the Merc ten minutes later and walked back inside. Then Neese pulled off.

And so did I. A few cars back from Neese, but right on him. At the La Cienega and Olympic intersection I got very unlucky. It happens. Neese went through the intersection, and headed south down La Cienega toward the 10 Freeway. Right then a traffic cop pulled up, signaled with his hands for all traffic to stay put, then turned off the traffic light, walked into the intersection, and started directing traffic himself.

Don't know why this happened. They were fixing something or something. I lost Neese. Three, four minutes later I went through the intersection taking the route Neese took. Nothing. I made it to the 10, took it west, nothing. Then I decided to head to the 405, which would take me *back* to Neese's house. I looked in my rearview and saw, wait, was that a big, new black Merc? I took a careful look. No, just a bunch of L.A. traffic. Freaking hallucinating. A sea of generic cars like mine. A VW. A Toyota. A Kia. A

Honda. A Veedub-ota-ia-onda. They're all the same. And then, wait, yes, Neese *was* behind me. He had picked *me* up picking *him* up and now he was behind me. Right behind me. Well played, Neese. Truth is, I didn't beat myself up about getting made. I wasn't being too discreet. I didn't care if he made me. I wanted it. And I got it. And now, friends, I knew Neese wanted to talk again. Well, well, so does Darvelle. When I got to the 405, I took it to Venice Boulevard, then made my way to Venice Beach, then to the Venice Pier parking lot. I paid, parked, walked onto the pier. I knew Neese was behind me but I didn't look.

It was cloudy at the beach. Some might call it depressing. But it actually gave the beach character. It was gray and cool and not what you envisioned the California beach to be. A melancholic, substantive vibe. Even the guy I saw Rollerblading down the boardwalk in a tight Speedo with a parrot on his shoulder and a Walkman from 1983 seemed less absurd, less cartoony, more understandable, more just a guy doing his thing.

The waves were big, crashing into and underneath the pier. I walked all the way out to the end, took a long, dramatic look at the ocean, then turned around. Neese, his long, horrible hair flowing in the wind, was twenty yards away, heading toward me. I gave him a big wave. He got to me and said with whatever the opposite of a smile is, "Nice to see you."

"Really? You really feel that way?"

"What do you want? And who are you?"

He wasn't mincing words. And I wasn't going to either. "I want to know how you knew Suzanne Neal. What your relationship was. I want to know why she's dead. I want to know if anything you know can help me find out who killed her. Comprende?"

I have no idea why I said, "Comprende?"

If I'd caught him off guard by going right to Suzanne Neal, by intimating that I already knew for sure that he knew her, he didn't show it. He was cop-level stoic.

"Why do you think I know *anything* about what you're talking about?"

I looked at him. I saw his black heart again. Without the aid of very potent marijuana. Neese was telling me through his performance that he was a serious guy. But I already knew that.

He continued, "Before you answer that, who the fuck are you?"

"My name is John Darvelle. I'm a detective."

"Who hired you?"

"I'm working for myself."

"Bullshit."

"Suzanne Neal is dead. And she went to your house the night she died. I saw her."

He looked at me. I could see possibilities, options, decisions moving across his coal eyes.

He said, "You don't know who you're fucking with."

He was right. I didn't. But I also really didn't care that much. I'd been in trouble before. That's the beautiful part of having experience *in any field*. It relaxes you. Some.

I said, "You're rich. You hang out with beautiful women. And you're involved in my story. And I want you to know something. I will find out what you know."

He began to speak. This time with less edge, with more California charm and even an intelligence I hadn't yet seen.

"Listen, Kung Fu. I know you're tough. But I don't know why Suzanne got killed. You want the truth? I'm sad. I'm really sad. Suzanne was beautiful. And I don't mean the way she looked. I mean in here."

He pointed to his heart.

He continued. "I'd love to continue telling you about my feelings for Suzanne. But instead I'm just going to tell you to leave me the fuck alone."

At that moment I knew *we* weren't alone. He had a couple guys either on the pier or in the parking lot. I knew it. I *felt* it. I wondered if they'd make a move on me right out here in public. I didn't look around. I just looked at Neese.

"Look, Neese. Let's suppose you're telling the truth. Then you've got nothing to hide. So give me something you know about Suzanne Neal."

He rediscovered his prior tone. "I know she was an actress who I occasionally slept with who got killed a few nights ago."

"You *occasionally* slept with her, huh? I've noticed you've got other beautiful women in your life as well. They tend to hang around you."

"Yeah. Sue me."

I wasn't going to full-on accuse him of anything I thought he *might* be involved with. Not this guy. Not yet, not now. Later maybe, probably, but not now. I simply needed more information. My story was only just unfolding. But I did want to ask him something else. See if I could get anything, even just a reaction, on something I was curious about. I pulled out my phone, and opened up the picture of Suzanne's tattoo pyramid.

"I want to show you something."

He stared at me, expressionless.

It then occurred to me that saying, "I want to show you something" on the Venice Pier had probably been said a time or two. But with very, very different results.

I showed Neese the picture.

"Suzanne's tattoo," Neese said.

"What is it? Why did she get a pyramid tattoo?"

Neese's face twisted into a smile. He laughed; it seemed real. It was real. "Come on, Darvelle. What does it mean? *Nothing*. Just like all of them. Maybe she got it in college when she was studying ancient fucking Egypt. I don't fucking know. She had a rose as well. Why aren't you showing me that one?" He laughed again. "Jesus, man, I was beginning to think you were good."

I looked at him. Then I looked around at the pier, at the parking lot, to see if I could make his goons. Hard to tell out here. As diverse a crowd as you could find, maybe anywhere.

"I'll be seeing you, Neese."

I turned and walked away.

"Darvelle," he said. And I turned around.

The levity was gone.

"Let this one go."

I looked at him and told him something with my expression: Not going to happen.

I turned and walked back to the Cobalt. All the way down the pier without turning around. I could feel Neese's eyes on me the whole way.

21

Home. Called Arthur Vonz, not there, left message. Then: Long run around lovely Mar Vista followed by a swim in my pool. Now: Sitting out in the sun, drying off, thinking, thinking. My cell rang, I was ready for it.

"Arthur," I said.

"John, how are you doing?"

Vonz sounded pleasantly surprised.

"Well. Listen. I want to talk to you. Not on the phone. Can we set up a time?"

"Yeah, of course. What's up?"

"I'll tell you when I see you. When are you free?"

"Uh . . . today, now. I'm at my offices. On the Paramount lot. Come on over. I'm in and out of meetings, but we'll make time. Just give them my production company name at the gate. Sparrow Productions. Security will have a pass for you and'll give you directions to my bungalows."

We hung up. I drove over to Paramount Pictures. On Melrose, deep in Hollywood. The legendary studio that produced *Chinatown* and *The Godfather* and *Starlight*. Another big security gate. Another impediment to entrance. But this time I had ammunition. I was here to see Arthur Vonz. The Arthur Vonz. The security guard—smiling, inviting, polite—pointed and said, "Park over there." And then he handed me a little map and pointed out exactly where to go.

On the lot. Some big stages, some big, bland buildings, some California bungalows tucked under trees. The suits sitting in their fourth-floor offices, the artists, directors, writers, producers working out of the charming, and private, bungalows that dotted the lot.

I wound my way through the lot toward Vonz's. It really did still have some of that old-school Hollywood magic. Like, a piece of the lot was built to look like a section of New York City. You're walking along and suddenly you're in front of the façade of a New York deli. That looked *real*. I caught a couple actors walking around in costume. Cop show. At least I thought they were actors. Yeah, for sure. Too good-looking. Too much positivity, and eagerness, in their eyes.

I was toward the back of the lot, the big buildings and stages giving way now to the bungalows. I was ducking under trees, navigating between little buildings, walking across little yards lined with verdant green foliage, with bright California flowers. It was quiet, peaceful, a nice place for a director to decide what movie to shoot next.

The Vonz bungalow, a tan stucco building underneath the shade of trees with a charming little sidewalk leading you to it. Some benches outside, out front, for people to sit on and chat. I walked into the building. There were three secretaries working the phones. Behind them, there were three offices I could see inhabited by two women and one man. All on the phone. One of the secretaries motioned for me to sit down on the nice leather couch, but before I could, a door at the end of the hall opened and there was Vonz. He was with a tallish bald man whom I instantly liked.

"John, welcome," Vonz said, and smiled.

Vonz had the dashing thing going. White pants, blazer, some reading specs sitting on the end of his nose.

We shook.

"You ever see the movie *Saturn Rain*?"

Sounds like a space movie, but it's not. It's a movie about a Vegas stripper.

"Yeah, sure. I loved it."

"This guy right here wrote it. Bruce Parrish."

I shook his hand.

"Nice to meet you," I said.

"Yeah, you too," he said.

Vonz said to me, "Bruce's writing a script for us." Then to Bruce, "See you in a couple weeks."

"Yes you will," Parrish said, and he disappeared out the door.

Vonz ushered me into his office. Surprisingly simple. Not decorated with the flair of his house or his home office. A big nice desk with some chairs in front of it, posters of his movies on the walls, some stylish couches, and a sitting area off to one side. Vonz sat behind his desk. I sat in front of it. Vonz pushed a button on his desk and the door shut behind me.

"That's what you get when you win a couple Academy Awards, huh?"

Vonz smiled. "So, what's going on?"

"I couldn't let the Suzanne thing go," I said. "I'm looking into it. I thought I'd tell you what I've found out so far."

Vonz didn't respond verbally, but he did with his body language. He leaned forward and an intensity came over him.

I told him what I knew, what had happened. Without any conjecture. As I told him his face grew tired. But when I finished talking he said, "Wow. Good. Thank you for coming by. I'm glad. I'm glad you're looking into it."

He thought for a moment. He spun his chair around and looked at the wall behind him for a bit, then spun back to look at me. "I know what it's like to not be able to let something go. And to pursue it on your own. My Amazon picture. We were just about to shoot and I just didn't feel I was ready. I felt something was missing with respect to my knowledge of the subject. I couldn't let it go. So I went, on my own dime, and lived with the tribe we depicted in the film. I held up the production to do it. Nobody could really understand why I was doing it. We had done so much preparation. But *I* needed to do it. So I understand why you looked into it on your own. Because *you* needed to do it. But, bottom line, you got on this case because of me. Not to mention, I want to know what happened too. It's a long-winded way of saying: I'll pay you for your time."

"You want to pay me, okay. I'll bill you. But not for the past week, that was on me. From now on."

He nodded.

"I'm going to read your letter."

He nodded.

"And I also want to ask you something."

He nodded again.

"Was Suzanne a prostitute? Did you pay her for sex?"

He looked at me for a long time and then curiously started laughing. But it wasn't a laugh you get from a good joke or from someone tickling your feet with a feather. It was a laugh of shame.

"What's so funny?"

"That's what you think it all means, that she was a prostitute?"

"Have you ever heard the term I mentioned? Pipe Girl?"

"No, is that a term for prostitute?"

"I don't know. I thought you might know."

He shook his head.

I said, "Well, whether or not it means prostitute, Suzanne potentially being one would have occurred to me either way. It already had when Ott asked me if *I'd* ever heard the term. Look, I don't know exactly what is happening and I could definitely be wrong."

"If Suzanne was a prostitute, I didn't know about it. And that was never a part of our relationship. There was never any talk of a financial arrangement. Did I take her on vacation, yes. Did I buy her things, did I pay for things, yes. But it wasn't any different from how I've treated any woman I've ever dated, and that includes my wife. And Suzanne never asked, even a little bit, for anything. Like I said, what I felt with Suzanne was love."

I looked at Vonz. I believed him. That he had no clue whether or not Suzanne was a girl for hire. And that he loved her. I know, I know, it doesn't mean Suzanne wasn't a pro. She didn't *seem* like one though. To Vonz. To me either. Was she? We'll see. Yes, we'll see.

"Jesus," he said. "I guess it makes sense. Nice place. A few men in her life. And a dangerous guy up on Mulholland who seems to associate with very attractive women."

"Yeah," I said. "But there's a missing piece to this puzzle. It's not that simple. I know it. I can feel it."

I told Vonz I'd keep him posted. Well, now that he was paying me it was part of the job. I walked out of his office, through the reception area, then opened the exit door. And who did I bump into? Mr. Man-Child himself. Mountcastle. He was paler and blobbier than ever, still dressed like a schoolboy. And right now, covered in sweat, holding a bunch of scripts that said "Property of Paramount Pictures" on the front.

I didn't say anything to him. But I didn't let him come in the door. I made him back away and let me out first. He moved away deftly; the freak was still light on his feet. But he *did* move away, and let me come through. Small victories, people. Small victories.

22

There was a guy I needed to talk to. His name was Marlon Pucci. Marlon was a New York City mob guy who had gotten out of the business by the skin of his teeth and had moved to Oceanside, California, just north of Carlsbad, to retire. His mob name was Marlon the Marlin. Why? Because his claim to fame was that he killed a guy once and took the body way out in the middle of the Atlantic Ocean to dump it. So, thus, the seafaring nickname. Look, I didn't make it up. It doesn't really make sense. It's not like Marlon was some waterman. He was a New York mobster who hung around a pool hall in polyester pants and pleather blazers.

But the thing is, he sort of started becoming his nickname. Retrofitting. Even before he moved to Oceanside, back in New York, he started talking about retiring on a boat, about the freedom the sea offered. He even got an anchor tattoo on his left forearm. His friends would say: "Marlon, you know nothing about the ocean, fishing, boats, anything. You've been out in the ocean literally one time, and it wasn't to enjoy the fucking freedom of the sea. It was to dump a dead body so you didn't go to prison. What are you talking about?"

And Marlon would say, "Yeah, well, nobody knows anything about anything. I'm Marlon the Marlin. So fuck you. I'm retiring on a boat."

He had a point.

So these days he lives on a sailboat in a nice little marina in Oceanside with his wife, Fran. I don't think they've ever taken the boat out into the Pacific. They've never put the sails up. They just live on it happily in the marina. They have drinks in the evening. They watch the sunsets. Occasionally, they leave the boat and hit the bars and restaurants of Oceanside.

Marlon had hired me once a few years ago. He'd found a little trouble in his new trouble-free life. Well, his wife had found some trouble anyway. They had called me. I drove down. And Marlon was straight with me. Told me he'd had a criminal past, had served time even, but that he was done with that now. And that his wife needed some help. Her son from her first marriage was missing. I gathered quickly that it was an addiction thing, and that he owed some people some money. I tracked him down, living in a disgusting house in L.A., out of his mind on meth. I brought him to Fran. She wept when she saw him. So did

Marlon. They straightened out his debts for him and the kid, Robert, cleaned up for bit. These days, I believe he still has some problems. But Robert keeps in touch with them and he hasn't gotten into money trouble with bad people again. And most important, Fran knows where he is.

And Marlon? He still answers my call when I have a question for him—because I'd helped out his lady.

Marlon the Marlin is in fact straight up now. Out of the crime game completely. But like all these guys, he's still got his ear to the ground. And like most of these guys, he likes to gossip. And he knows what's up, even in L.A. That's why I took the 405 South, to the 5 South, to the Tamarack exit to Carlsbad. Then up the PCH a bit to the coastal California town of Oceanside. Shops, restaurants, blondes in bikinis. All set on a hill funneling down to the Pacific. So charming, so California, so I think I'm going to move here when I retire and live on a boat like Marlon the Marlin.

I pulled into the Oceanside Marina, parked, walked down the docks, and found Marlon's beautiful forty-five-foot sailboat. It was 2 p.m. Marlon was sitting on the boat, shorts, no shirt, boat shoes, enjoying the sun, having a cold beer. In that moment I thought: Marlon was getting the last laugh. He couldn't sail, he didn't know anything about boats, didn't know anything about the sea. But who cares? Look at the guy. Happy as a clam. And decidedly, one hundred percent Marlon the Marlin.

"John, my boy, welcome aboard."

I smiled, hopped on the boat, sat down, was immediately handed a cold Coors Light. Yep, another thing this former murderer got right. Marlon was a deep tan. And he had become kind of a fat skinny guy. Or a skinny fat guy. No, he was a fat skinny guy. Skinny bird legs, ropy arms, a little old man gut. But I could tell looking at him that he was still strong. And when you looked into his dark eyes, mostly they were friendly, but every so often you could see a flare of history and suspicion and darkness and toughness that comes only from firsthand experience. He had a little bit of Neese in his eyes. You better be really careful if you decide to fuck with Marlon Pucci. Chips down, he'd abandon the trouble-free life and cut your throat in a second.

But right now? He was smiling, nice as hell, happy. And I noticed he'd gotten a mermaid tattoo on his right shoulder. All right by me. I like mermaids. You already know that.

"What can I do for you, John?"

"I have a question for you."

He made his hand into a little handgun, moved his eyebrows up and down, pulled the thumb trigger, and said, "Shoot."

And then: "Hi, John."

Fran had emerged from the living quarters of the sailboat. She was absurdly tan, wearing a sort of nightgown slash caftan slash dress. She wore three or four bracelets and two or three necklaces and some big, bright red earrings. And she still had the curly, frizzy blond hair. She was carrying a very large cocktail with an enormous amount of ice.

I stood up. "Hi, Fran."

"Sweetie. How are you?"

She squeezed my arm. "Mmm. You're still in good shape, I see."

"Well, you know, I have to be for my business."

"Take your shirt off, get some sun," she said with a salacious flair.

"Jesus, Fran," Marlon said with a shit-eating grin. "What do you want to do, make a porno?"

I said, "Well, we are on a boat in a marina. Seems like a lot of them are indeed on boats in marinas."

Marlon ignored me and said to Fran, smiling, eyebrows raised. "One of those pornos where the old fart gets the young stud to come over and take care of his wife. I sit over and here and watch in a captain's hat while this guy goes to town."

Fran howled with laughter. She and Marlon still had some pop. "Let's do it!"

"Get out of here," he said. "Go to the store. Me and John gotta talk."

"I'm getting wine, a couple jugs of rosé."

"Sure, sugar, whatever. Get me some beer too. And some Mount Gay."

He turned to me. "Mount Gay and tonic. That's what us boat people like."

I nodded. Fran grabbed my arm again. "Great to see you, John."

"You too, Fran."

She looked at Marlon. "You *are* going to take care of me later. Go ahead and take your Cialis now."

A shark smile appeared on the Marlin. "I already took it. Took two. Now get out of here."

Fran headed off toward the parking lot. Her nightgown dress thing flowing behind her like a cape, like a superhero. *Alcoholic Mobster Wife Woman to the rescue!*

Marlon turned to me, took a big sip of his beer. "Your question?"

"Do you know the name Richard Neese?"

Marlon deflated a little bit. He didn't know Neese. And he did not like moments that suggested that he was no longer in the know.

He said, "No. Who is he?"

"I'm trying to figure that out. How 'bout this. Have you ever heard the term 'Pipe Girl'? As it might pertain, I suppose, to criminal activity?"

Marlon smiled, then laughed. He had something on this one. And he couldn't hide that he appreciated still having some skinny.

He downplayed his excitement and said, "Yeah. Sure. I've heard the term."

"What does it mean?"

"Well, it's mostly a rumor as I've always understood it. But . . ." He leaned toward me just a bit. A mobster shooting the shit with his boys. "Apparently, out here in L.A., a guy decided to do the girl-for-hire thing in a new way. Oldest profession in the world, but with a new twist."

"Okay. What kind of twist?"

"Well, it's an interesting idea as I understand it, and I don't know too much. Nobody does. It's a rumor. You just hear little edges of it, always a little bit different from what you heard before. But it's like this. What if you could hire a girl, a beautiful girl, top fucking shelf, do whatever you needed to do, whenever you wanted, get your rocks off, get her rocks off, whatever. But, but. Here's the twist. The girl comes with a *guarantee* that she'll never tell anyone. Like, she won't tell her girlfriends. She won't fall in love with you and tell your fucking wife. She won't write it on her goddamn Facebook page. And she'll never, ever go to the press. The only people who will ever know are you, her, and whoever's running the ring."

The Marlin was getting into it. Excited to be imparting this privileged information to me. I didn't say anything. I just sat there waiting for more.

"Now, we're in L.A. right. Or you are, I'm on a boat, you know what I'm fucking saying. But the idea is, let's say a guy is married and is sick of screwing his old lady. Well, he gets one of these Pipe Girls so he can have his jollies and know, I mean *know*, she'll never say anything and fuck up his marriage. Or, even better, a famous guy gets one of these girls and he knows she won't go to the press and fuck up his fifty-million-dollar-a-year career. Like, lots of these famous pricks get pros. And it's all fine and dandy for a while. But then they always, *always* get screwed. And not screwed like a cock in a pussy. Screwed like the famous person moves on from the pro, the pro cashes in by going to the *National* Fucking *Enquirer*. And then all hell breaks loose. And the guy's whole life goes down the toilet. You know what I'm saying? So just imagine if silence was guaranteed. *Guaranteed*. Imagine what people with money would pay. We're talking a hundred grand a weekend."

"And the name?" I said. "Pipe Girl?" I thought I knew the answer, but I wanted to hear him tell me.

"Right. The name. Pipe Girl. Well, you know what a pipe dream is, right? Is a dream that's never going to happen, because it's too ridiculous, it's too perfect. Well, so is a beautiful ten who will give you everything you want and never tell anyone."

"Right," I said. "It's a good name for the service."

I thought for a second and said, "But here's the problem. Here's why I don't think it can be real. How do you do it? At the end of the day, how do you control who opens their mouth? It's the one thing no one's ever figured out—in any field. What, you hire some trustworthy prostitutes? You make them *promise* not to tell? Come on."

Marlon looked at me. And that flash of darkness crossed his eyes like a wave. The hardened criminal appeared inside him for just a second. And he leaned in toward me just a little more. "Well, John, first, you appeal to the self-interest of the girls. You pay them very well. Change-your-life money. John my boy, self-interest is how you persuade people to do things. But the second thing is how you really make it work. And that's the other thing about the Pipe Girl rumor. And that is this: If you're a Pipe Girl and you talk, you die."

I laughed. "Okay. It's interesting. But let's deconstruct this a bit, Marlon. Say a girl goes to the press. You know, performs her services on one of these guys, then goes to the press. And then gets killed. The guy she ratted on will immediately get looked into. Her murder will be heavily investigated, especially if the guy has some notoriety. And so on. It's a house of cards that you can't control."

He looked at me and let out a booming laugh. "Don't be naïve, boy. When there's big money involved *anything* is possible. Look, you choose the girls very, very carefully. You make it very clear to them what they are getting into. And, like I said, you make them rich. Not fucking stripper, porno actress, Bunny Ranch money. Not decent condo in the Valley and low-end Mercedes rich. Money to live on for life. Okay? And like I said, you make it very, very clear that if any information leaks *ever*, they will not be pleased with the consequences. And, listen, John, if a girl does talk, you know how easy it is to cover up a fucking murder if you're good? All right, hypothetical. Girl bangs celeb. Girl talks. Girl gets whacked. Cops look into it. Here's what you do. You frame the murder on some no-name, low-rent pimp that's already in business, invent a drug history for the girl, some mental illness, get the celeb to say, 'I have no idea what she's talking about, I've never seen her.' Get the actual pimp, the guy who actually did it, to say, 'Yeah, I knew her, but I'm a businessman, this is ridiculous.' That's if the real pimp ever even gets questioned. Which is probably not going to happen. And then? Then it's over, son. Over. Done. Finito. The cops are moving on. And the truth is, if that *were* to happen, that *one* death makes every other girl in the ring shut up forever. That one murder seals your fucking business plan."

I said, with very little confidence in my voice, "Well, what if one of the guys talks?"

Marlon laughed for thirty seconds straight. He had tears welling up in his eyes. "I know *you know* how stupid that question is. But I'll answer it anyway. Guys don't talk. Period. And even if they did, what, tell a friend, tell the press, what difference would it make? Ever? The girls would deny it. Then the ringmaster would put a gun to the guy's head. Johnny, there's no scenario where the guy would tell. The guys you pick for this kind of thing, shelling out the dough to protect their life and whatnot, these aren't the guys that are going to talk. Or cooperate on some kind of sting or something. Give me a fucking break."

He paused to laugh again, then said, "What if the guy talks. That's funny."

Marlon the Marlin finished his beer and sat back for a moment.

"Sounds like you know a lot about this. Have put some thought into it."

"Shit. We used to talk about it a lot. Look, I'm making it sound like no big deal, like it would be ridiculously easy. Truth is, it would be tough to do. Quality control is always very hard I don't care if you're selling fucking widgets. But it *is* possible. That is for sure. When I heard about this going on out here, you know, from these California guys, I told my boys back in the city. And we laughed about it. But we liked it. As a business. As a business model. You know that saying, 'It's just crazy enough to be true'? That's what the Pipe Girls are. Crazy enough to be true."

"Well," I said. "I would agree with the crazy part. It just seems like there are a lot of holes. Beyond the quality control. Beyond getting the girls to be quiet. You think there's a market out there for people to pay 100K or whatever to get laid? I mean, look, these guys can sneak around if they're careful. Go to Vegas. Get a pro. Get a rub and tug. Or do what most people do. Jerk off, go for a run, and move on."

Marlon smiled at me, a twinkle now is his hardened eyes. That's the thing about these mob guys. A lot of them are charming bastards. "Look, John, you're a good guy. You're a smart guy. I know you're just keeping the conversation going so I'll keep telling you what I know. You're good at that. But I bet you right now you're saying, 'Yeah, I can see the market. I can see the business model working.' Look, in this country, in this puritanical fucking country, how many rich guys have you seen throw two, three, four *hundred million dollars* down the drain because they were banging the nanny or the maid or the masseuse? I'm not talking throwing their money down the drain willingly. I'm not talking paying the other woman to keep her temporarily quiet. I'm talking about losing everything, all of their money, their entire position in society, all of their endorsements, all of their movie deals, all of their whatever, because they just couldn't help themselves and they got caught. They just couldn't keep their dick in their pants and as a result it all goes away. Rich guys, celebs, politicians, athletes, judges, fucking presidents. They make the stupidest moves. Because they don't have a risk-free alternative. They do the dumbest things. And they lose fortunes, careers, legacies, everything. History, literally world history, goes down the drain. Pussy has more power than anything else on the planet. *Anything.* And these guys on TV say, 'Oh, so-and-so *wanted* to get caught, thought he was invincible, was crying out for help, is addicted to risk.' On and on. Bullshit and more bullshit. Look, wanting to get caught? Wanting to no longer be a congressman or a beloved movie star? Wanting to go on fucking *Leno* and grovel and apologize for a chance, *a chance*, to reenter the game at a much lower position? Wanting to run for office again someday and *lose*? That's true one out of every thousand times. Maybe. But most of these guys, they want a hot piece of ass to sit on their face, spin, and give them a nice massage afterward. And then they want to go back to making movies or making laws or making tons of fucking money running the world. And the truth is, most of these guys want to go back and hang out with their goddamn wife and family. They actually are pretty happy. They don't want to lose that either."

Okay, he had a point.

Marlon grabbed another beer out of the cooler sitting right next to him and popped it. He sat back, moved into a position more worthy of pontificating. "I always thought. If you could figure it out. You know, like I said, choose the right girls. Take care of business in the right way when you had to eliminate one of them. I thought, yeah, a very good idea, a very *big* idea. Do it right, and you could make fuck-you money. I often wondered if it was really going on out here. And if it was, could I take it back to the city. But I'm out of that whole business now, as you know. I'm done and I'm on my fucking boat."

"Let me ask you this, Marlon. Straight up. Do you think the Pipe Girls are real? I mean, you make a hell of an argument. Don't get me wrong. But do you really think they exist? Right now, in present-day L.A.? Or, like you said, do you think it's just a rumor?"

"Well, John, by the very definition of the business plan, very few people would know about it. And those who do know, the girls and the carefully selected clients, don't talk about it. I mean, the system is designed to be silent. To be air-fucking-tight. Right? So how would anyone outside of that small circle know? You know? The very fact that there's a rumor means the system is breaking down. Which means the Pipe Girls probably don't exist."

"Okay. So you think it's bullshit?"

He took a big gulp of his new, fresh cold beer. And his tired, tan face stretched into an enormous grin. "Oh no. I think it's true. Rumors are always true, boy."

23

Well, I wanted to talk to Jimmy Yates again. See if Mr. Superstar could tell me anything more than he did when he was petulantly sipping a smoothie at Fred Segal. I didn't like that guy. Yeah, I wanted to talk to him again. I wanted to punch him too. I'd definitely do the former, hopefully the latter.

But I needed just to think a little bit. You have to do that sometimes in life. You just have to *think*. From Marlon the Marlin's I drove just slightly south back to Carlsbad and swung a right off the PCH into the Tamarack beach parking lot. I have to tell you, this part of the country, yes, it has that Southern California magic that L.A. has, but the glow here is even more present. It's otherworldly, other-planetary almost. These little seaside towns built in succession between San Diego and L.A., one two three four. Del Mar. Carlsbad. Oceanside. Encinitas. All right next to, right on top of, beautiful, uncrowded, dramatic stretches of beach, of ocean. Not the insanity of L.A. and not the vapidity of San Diego. Something else. Total Southern California for sure, but almost small-town America too, only right on the Pacific. With hills and cliffs and verdant, bright California flora. You almost can't believe these little towns exist. Almost can't believe they haven't *become* San Diego or Los Angeles themselves. No, they had stayed pretty small. Had kept their personality. Their charm. The hills tumbling down to white sand, and in the afternoon, almost purple sand. And big green waves rolling in right at you. And the sky, the sky that as the day gets older becomes burnt orange and purple and wispy-white with clouds. And a feeling that as you watch the sun slide behind the horizon you too might get sucked into wherever the orange ball was going. I'm telling you. Gorgeous. Mesmerizing. Bewitching.

Right now? Four-thirty on a Wednesday. The sun starting to set. The air starting to cool. That orange glow starting to appear above the ocean. That purplish-pink look to the sand.

The beachside parking lot I pulled into was pretty empty. A few surfers in the break gliding around on waves, a few surfers in the lot changing into board shorts or back into street clothes.

And me sitting in my Cobalt trying to figure out what to make of all this stuff.

I thought: Maybe it would ease my mind to get out in the ocean. From inside the Cobalt, it looked so refreshing, rejuvenating, cleansing. There was a surfboard rental shack in front of me and to the left. And I had a bathing suit in my trunk. I got out, got the suit, got back in my car. Then I took my pants, shoes, socks, and underwear off, about to put my bathing suit on. For a few seconds I was the guy in the public beach parking lot with a shirt on and no pants, sitting in his car looking down at his dick. Yep, to anyone else I was a twisted pervert sitting in a shitty little car half naked. I thought: Jeez. I should start furiously masturbating just to fully complete the story. Don't worry, I didn't do it. Instead, I quickly put my suit on, got out, walked over to the surfboard rental shack. Then rented what the tan, probably high guy told me was a "fun shape" board. Paid, went back to my car, hid my keys, removed my shirt, walked down to the break.

I had surfed a couple times in my days in L.A., could paddle the board, could sit on it out in the water like you see people do. Could I actually ride a wave? Not really. I waited for a lull in the waves and plunged in. Man, cold. But I was right. After a minute, it felt amazing. It really did. I paddled out to where some of the other surfers were.

A few waves came rolling in. Excitement shot through me as they moved toward me. I turned the board toward the shore and paddled as hard as I possibly could. The waves just seemed to rise and fall underneath me and then go away toward shore. Usually with a surfer on them making it look so annoyingly easy.

And then: A big one. I was going to catch this if it killed me. Now, right now, it was on top of me. I didn't really have to paddle this time. This one just took me. I was now going what felt like a million miles an hour down the face of a moving monster. For a second, for one second, I felt a freedom I've never felt before. Okay, Darvelle, time to hop up on your feet. I sprang up. And then I defied, I think, the laws of physics. I was instantly thrown forward. The board went one way, I went the other. Then I started half somersaulting, half cartwheeling *across* the face of this wave. I was a disaster in a bathing suit. And then, whoaaaaaaa. I went way up, then way down. Thump. On the ocean floor. I literally didn't know which way was up. I'd been under for a few seconds, it felt like a few years, when I started spastically writhing and struggling to get to the surface, to get some air. Finally, finally, finally, through no actions of my own I popped up out of the water.

"Huuuuuuuuuhh," I gasped, filling my lungs. Holy shit. I was almost at the beach, way in from where I had fallen. I was looking toward the shore, when I instinctively jerked around to look out to sea. My fun shape board was coming at me. Fast. Right for my face. Which it hit. Right above my left eye. I thought I'd known pain in my life. I was wrong.

Less than ten minutes after I had paddled out I was back in the Cobalt. I had a golf ball on my head now. It was big and I could already see it turning black and purple.

But something had happened out there. Despite my total inability to ride a wave, something, yes, something was now occurring to me.

I pulled out my phone and opened the picture of the

pyramid on Suzanne Neal's ankle. And I looked at it. Again, this is it:

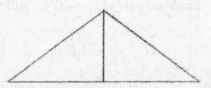

I turned it ninety degrees to the right. Like this:

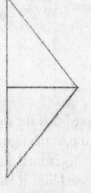

And then I began to deconstruct it. And instead of seeing it as one shape, I began to see it as two shapes *within* one shape. The first one was this:

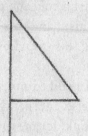

It was a P. An abstract P.

And the second shape was indeed the whole figure, but it was in my mind one part of two. It was still this:

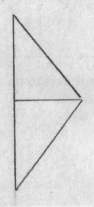

Only now I realized that the top right line, the one that goes from the very top of the figure down and to the right to connect with the horizontal line, doesn't actually connect with the horizontal line. It almost does, but it doesn't. And so this figure was a G. An abstract G.

PG.

Pipe Girl. I thought: Oh man, really? Was that crazy story Marlon the Marlin told me true? Or am I making this up, am I seeing this P and this G because I *want* it to be true? Am I turning this stupid pyramid into something that's not really there?

And that's when I realized my surfing injury had rattled loose something else, another thought that had been in my head waiting, I think, for me to find it.

I cranked up the Cobalt and drove up the 5 to the 405 to the Mulholland exit to Neese's house. And I sat there looking at his horrible gate. The one I'd looked at so many times. With the crisscrossy metal copper design. And in that design, hidden amid all the other horizontal and vertical lines, was the same pyramid a dead Suzanne Neal had on her ankle.

24

So the pyramid was in Neese's fence, right in plain sight—if you looked really closely. But, right now, it wasn't Neese who I wanted to talk to. I needed someone weaker. So it was back over to the Sades, to Jimmy Yates's place. Without much waiting at all, Jimmy's SUV pulled out of his gate. He wasn't in the same SUV as the last time I tailed him. Now he was in one of those boxy, silver, war-style Mercedes SUVs.

What a joke.

He started heading down Sunset, toward Hollywood. I figured, here we go, back to go get another goddamn smoothie. But nope. It wasn't smoothie time. It looked like he was going to Riviera Country Club. A really beautiful and challenging golf course spread out right in the Sades. A private club, but also the location of the L.A. Open.

Yep, Riviera. He pulled onto the property. I did too. The lot was pretty full—good. Jimmy maneuvered the top-heavy, boxy Merc into a spot between two cars—a tight squeeze. I quickly grabbed an end spot in a different row, away from him.

Out of the Cobalt and over to Jimmy's spot, fast. He was awkwardly getting out of his ridiculous SUV, pinned in a bit by the Lexus next to him. He slid out, then shut the door and turned around.

Turned around to face me. Right in his face.

"Hi, Jimmy, remember me?"

It was tight between the two cars. We were stuck in a little claustrophobic alley. And his tall, boxy car blocked us from the activity of the club. Perfect. And, shit, I just remembered, I had a big black bump on my head so I probably looked really crazy. Perfect-er.

"Yes, I do," he said. "Get out of my way."

"You're going to talk to me, Jimmy. Right now. And you're going to tell me more than you did last time."

"Actually right now I'm going to call the cops."

He produced his iPhone. You know, those phones that you can't type on or make calls on? I snatched it away.

"Give that back to me."

"Suzanne Neal was a Pipe Girl. You know that term? I think you do."

"I told you this the last time you stalked me, bud. I don't know what you're talking about."

"Next up, I'm going to Neese. The modern-day pimp. We'll see what Neese has to say about me knowing about you using his service."

"Do whatever you want, whoever that is."

And then he started screaming. It was actually a smart move.

He screamed, "Hey! This asshole . . ."

I grabbed his arm, yanked him toward me, twisted it, twisted his body around, and put him on the ground. Put his face in the cement. He had a good view of the undercarriage of his horrible SUV. I was wrenching his arm in a very painful way. I was just about to break it. This poor fuck was in agony.

"Stop screaming," I said.

He did. He was absolutely silent.

"You need to help me out, Jimmy. Suzanne was a pro, I know that. Neese was her pimp, I know that too. And you were using her. Right?"

I released some pressure. He looked back at me wild-eyed, hysterical.

"I could have you fucking killed," he whisper-screamed.

"Really," I said. "I could kill you right now."

I tweaked his arm and I could see tears sprout in his eyes.

He didn't say anything. This asshole was starting to impress me. Or maybe it was just Neese had told all these guys exactly how to behave. And they were terrified to disobey him. But I had a Plan B. Now, pressuring, bullying, kicking the shit out of someone to tell you something doesn't always work. That is for sure. But the times it does work is when you can really zero in what it is that person has to lose. Usually, that's family, friends, money. But I had a special case on my hands here. I had a star. This guy had the world kissing his ass day and night. He was on top. And, ask anybody, these guys will do anything, literally anything, to protect that. They'll protect it more viscerally than they'd protect their own family. Sad, but was I pretty sure of it.

"Jimmy. I have a friend named Jose Villareal. Works for the rags. I'm giving him this story right now. I'm telling him that you used Richard Neese's service to hire a prostitute and now she's dead. I don't even know the whole story yet, but I'm going to give it to him prematurely, because I know you're involved. I know for sure. It's going to ruin my case, but you know what else it's going to ruin? Your life. But it's worth it to me because Suzanne Neal is a corpse, and you don't give a shit. So, say good-bye to your perfect image."

It took him less than a second to say, "Don't do that."

"Then give me some information."

He took a deep breath. I released the pressure on his arm a little bit.

Jimmy Yates said, "I have never spoken about this to anyone. Yes, I used Richard's service. Okay. But that's all I know. Okay, I swear. Suzanne was who I got. That's who Richard gave me. She was really special actually."

Time to test him. "So you used a pro. Weren't you worried that she would talk? Or bribe you somehow?"

"That's the deal with Richard. The girls don't talk. And I'll tell you this: She never did. Never. Suzanne never said a word about it to anyone. Truth is, the only reason you even know about all this is because I got careless that day you caught me. I . . . I . . . I couldn't . . . I got . . . I got careless."

I looked at him, with half his face stuck to the cement. He hated, hated me having him in this position. I could see the disgust in his face. That some random P.I., that some *civilian*, was forcing him to say something he didn't want to say. He thought he was so special. His face simply betrayed it. He disgusted me.

"How did Neese make sure the girls didn't talk?"

With just the slightest letup on his arm he was already getting cocky again. "Dude. I don't know. Paid them well? Who the fuck knows? He just said, 'Trust me.' And he was right."

I grabbed the short hairs of his head, right above the back of his neck, and gave them a quick, hard twist. He shrieked.

"You were there the day she got killed, Jimmy. I don't know what you told the cops when they contacted you. I guess you lied to them and told them you didn't even know her. But you were there the day she got killed. So you know something about why she got killed. Either that or you killed her."

I yanked his arm.

"I didn't kill her. Jesus, how is this happening? Look, man, she told me she was going to quit. Does that help you?"

I just looked at him. And I thought: Hmm. Maybe that does help me. I let up on his arm a bit.

"How did you meet Richard Neese?"

Jimmy looked back at me, but I could see he was looking sort of behind me. I turned around to see a security guard looking at us, angling his head to see us better, approaching from about twenty feet away.

"Everything all right back here? Jimmy, that you?"

I let go of Jimmy's arm, then helped him up. We both stood looking at the guard, who was now just beyond Jimmy's SUV and the Lexus.

"Everything's fine," I said. "This gentleman, well, let's be honest, Jimmy Yates, tripped getting out of his car. And I came over to help."

The security guard grabbed his walkie and said, "Backup. South parking lot. Silver Mercedes SUV. Just beyond the sidewalk to the pro shop."

Guess Mr. Security Guard read the situation right. Not bad. Or maybe he saw in Jimmy's eyes that he was in pain, and wanted to kill me.

But Jimmy didn't say anything. He was frozen. Still paralyzed over whether or not I was going to the rags.

I said, "Well, while the backup comes I think I'm going to leave. Excuse me."

I began walking out of the little alley. The security guard stepped forward and got in my way, trapping me. This was not good. I had just gotten some info, I wanted out of there. Jimmy was frozen. Not sure whether to help me or say nothing.

This is what's known as a jam.

So: I made a move for the security guy's throat. He went to block me with both hands. Bad move. Rookie move. I grabbed his gun out of its holster, cocked it, and pointed it at his face. He got really, really scared.

"Get out of my way."

He backed up. His heart in his throat. I walked out. Walked over and got in the Cobalt. Then pulled it around to Jimmy's car, where he and the security guard now stood. I got back out of the Cobalt, walked over, and handed the security guy his gun back. Then I looked at Jimmy and said, "I know you're a good actor, but you better not be lying."

Back in the Cobalt and out of there.

25

Folks, I now knew some stuff. But I also *didn't* know some stuff. I was pretty convinced that Neese ran a prostitution ring with a high-concept twist, but I didn't have anything on the murder. Neese popped Suzanne because she broke the rule and talked? Maybe. But maybe not. There was also Jimmy Yates. And the dude on her balcony the night she got killed. And the information that Jimmy had passed on—that Suzanne had told him she was going to quit.

There was more to know, plain and simple. There were more *possibilities*. And if I wasn't careful here, it could all go away. Like Marlon the Marlin said. I go to the cops, the cops go to Neese, then everyone lawyers up and shuts up. And maybe we get Neese on some pimp charges, but Suzanne is still dead, and no one goes down.

I needed to examine some possibilities. I needed to think hard.

I thought: A hike. In the mountains. Clear my head. Walk and talk. Talk to myself, that is.

Another real bonus about L.A. You had the beach and the weather and the Hollywood scene if that was your thing. But there were also mountains right there on the coast. And I'm not talking about the various hills where people lived. I'm talking real mountains that were uninhabited and beautiful. With long, steep trails, with real nature, with beautiful trees and—true story—mountain lions. Mountain lions, walking around the hills of Los Angeles. No, not walking. Slinking, poking, sliding around the hills of Los Angeles. Deftly. Mysteriously. Gracefully. I love the big cats.

I headed toward the range that sat right on the coast. The Santa Monica Mountains. I was already pretty close; they bordered the freaking Sades, for chrissakes.

I was now entering a more difficult, delicate, and potentially violent section of the case, so I want to tell you about somebody that's very important in my life. Just a quick aside; it won't take too long. I want to tell you now, because I was thinking about him at this moment in the story. I think about him, his influence, when the heat gets turned up.

I grew up in the San Fernando Valley. The Valley, as most people know it. The part of L.A. that gets made fun of. And not because superficial movie stars are walking around bathed in attention and vanity. No. The opposite. Because it's considered lame. Ordinary. Suburban. Tacky. The stepchild of Los Angeles.

Truthfully, an unfair stereotype. The Valley has beautiful sections. And I'll tell you this: It's grounded in a reality that the rest of L.A. isn't. It *is* really, really hot in the summer though. Whatever shit it gets for that it deserves.

My family was normal, from the outside. Mom, Dad, brother. When we were kids, my mom stayed home and took care of me and my brother, and my dad was an accountant for a tire company. A good man. A guy who sat in his chair at night and watched TV and said things to me and my brother, with a vacant but sweet look, like: "Everything okay at school?"

I loved him. He's dead now. He had a heart attack. He never seemed particularly stressed or unhealthy but he had a heart attack anyway. As a dad, he was who he was and I got that. And so did my brother. My mother? She was more of the firecracker type. Tough. Downright ruthless sometimes. She had to be, I suppose. To make sure my bro and I turned out okay. I never saw her fight with my father, but I never saw her really connect with him either. But let's get back to my father. Did *we* connect? Well, not really. I respected him. So did my brother. He went to work and did what he had to do to make life okay for the rest of us. But, truthfully, he seemed a little paralyzed. Sweet, always sweet and nice. But just a little sad. And not quite *there* with the rest of us. I don't know if he wanted to be out there doing other things, pursuing other dreams, or another life altogether. I really don't know. But if I had to guess I'd say no. It was more like he was just stuck in the wrong universe.

Enter our neighbor. A man named Jim Douglas.

Jim Douglas was a major force in my life. He was married to a woman named Candy and they had four daughters whom they loved and raised and parented beautifully. I'm still in touch with all of them to this day. Jim was a career military guy. He had been in Vietnam, a Green Beret. He had another color associated with him too. Black. Jim and Candy and their kids are black. But Jim's skin wasn't the only thing that was black. His belt was black too. He was a serious badass karate master. A black belt and a champion.

As much as Jim loved his daughters, he wanted a son. And me? Jim was the kind of guy that I was desperate to be around. At first, he just stepped in where my dad wasn't so proficient. Taught me how to throw a football. Taught me how to shift my weight when hitting a baseball. My dad wasn't threatened—something I later realized was really admirable. My dad *liked* that I was excited to hang with Jim. He liked that I was learning the things that I innately was interested in. Like sports. And camping. And how to really hurt a guy if you ever had to get in a fight.

Yes, Jim taught me how to fight. Not at first. Not for years. But eventually. I was about thirteen and I was at his house and I remember him sitting in a big recliner, drinking scotch. He filled up the chair totally. Jim was a big man. About five-eleven, pretty tall, but thick and strong and kind of stocky-looking when he stood up despite his height. In later years he sported one of those cement-hard guts. I hope I have one of those one day. What is the deal with those things? You have a gut, sometimes a big one like Jim's, but it's hard as steel. So you're not really fat I don't think. Anyway, that night, I remember vividly he wore a red, totally unbroken-in baseball hat with some kind of army logo on the front. The hat was enormous.

Just a giant, flat front and a flat, uncurved bill. Like he had intentionally not broken it in all. Lee Trevino–style. I could tell you an entire story about the size and crispness of that hat.

He said, "Sit down, John." And then he said, "John, you're going to have to fight sometimes. Now, don't start fights. And once I teach you how to fight that doesn't mean you should find stupid reasons to practice either. You know what I'm saying? Make up stuff like you had to get in this fight or that fight. And another thing. Once I teach you to fight, don't get sucked into cleaning up other people's messes either. Some guy you know cops a bunch of attitude to some other guy, then wants you to clean up his mess? No, that's not what I'm talking about. I'm just saying there are times you're going to need to know what to do. There are times when fighting is the *right* answer. And when you feel like that is happening, you just have to ask yourself one question. One simple question. Is now the time? And if the answer is yes, then do this. One: Commit yourself totally to the cause. Two: Aim your punches for the throat and the nose. And three: Finish the job and get out of there."

That was the introduction. He eventually taught me actual moves. He trained me. So I can fight karate-style or barroom-style. It's not perfect. And I'm not a black belt like Jim. But, boy, it comes in handy a lot in my business. Most people, even tough guys, don't really know *how* to fight. But even if they do, I always go back to another thing Jim said: "Technique isn't what it's all about. It's about commitment. Ask yourself that one question. Is now the time? If the answer is yes, then go for it completely. Completely. And you'll win over ninety percent of the time. Maybe more."

Another thing Jim taught me a couple years later was in his words, "The most important thing in life, really." Jim had a billiards room set up in his house. Wood-paneled walls. Pictures of him, his family, his army buddies. Jim and I were shooting pool. He wore a light blue terry-cloth shirt which looked amazing against his black skin.

I said, "What, Jim? What's the most important thing in life, really?"

He looked at me and he was very serious. His eyes betrayed intensity and experience and truth. "Loyalty. Loyalty is the *most* important thing in life. You know why? Because loyalty is hard. You'll see what I'm talking about when you get older. Life becomes grayer and more nuanced and the decisions you make get more and more difficult. It gets harder and harder to remain loyal to people. Listen, John. You're going to make a lot of friends in life. And you'll meet men and women who are charming and fun as shit and hilarious. All that stuff is *easy*. And none of it means dick compared to loyalty. Your friend who always makes you laugh? Who's always there for a good time? That's all fine and good, until he fucks your girlfriend. See? See what I'm saying? John, listen to me. Do you see what I'm saying? He ain't worth a shit compared to your friend who always has your back."

Which brings me to yet another thing that Jim taught me. It was right around the time of the loyalty lesson and Jim said it was connected. This time we were on a canoe trip. His wife and daughters and his brother, Otis, were with us too. But in our canoe it was just me up front, his daughter Shawna in the middle, and him in the back, in charge.

We were just paddling along, gliding down the river, and he said, "John, listen. Turn around and look at me and listen."

I turned around and stretched my neck to look around Shawna at Jim. Jim wore gray gym shorts, a necklace with a cross on it, and a bright orange life preserver. Also: Army-issue shades. These days he had the aforementioned gut, which, I'm proud to say, he had no shame about whatsoever. I was looking at him, waiting for him to speak. As he paddled along he was sweating profusely, which he also didn't appear to give a shit about.

He said, "John. Don't ever make your mind up about somebody until you see how they behave when the pressure's on."

Instinctively, I turned to look ahead and make sure we were still going in the right direction.

"Don't worry, I got the canoe. John. John. John, turn back around, son. Turn back around now."

I did.

He continued. "See, somebody might seem great, and then something happens that puts a little tension into the situation. Forces that person to make a *tough* decision. Will he or she keep their cool and do the right thing? Or will that person suddenly become *someone else*? A panicking, selfish fool? Now, it can work in the reverse too."

Jim was working the paddle, sweating, steering us down the river as he spoke.

He said, "John. John. John, look at me. See, somebody might not impress you at all. You know, in everyday life.

Might be a bump on a log. Or even a seemingly selfish cat who doesn't seem to understand the bigger picture. But then . . . then something heats up. I'm talking about anything. A guy being a jerk at a ball game. A car accident. A boss who doesn't treat his employees right. And that person who you thought was a nobody will stand up and handle it like a pro. Tell the guy at the ball game he needs to adjust his attitude. Get people to the hospital that need to be at the hospital. Tell the boss calmly that he can't treat people like that. Conversely, somebody who you'd *think* would handle pressure in just the right way, sometimes won't. Sometimes that person who fronts confidence, who fronts courage, will wilt like a flower that's been picked out of the ground. You see what I'm saying? John, do you see what I'm saying? When pressure enters into a situation, when the element of tension enters, that's when someone's true personality emerges. Remember that. Now turn around and paddle, help me steer a little, son. We're getting off course."

He chuckled at his little joke.

Back to the Santa Monica Mountains. Back to the story. See, it's times like these, when a case takes a turn, when I can feel the fire coming, that I think a lot about Jim. About Jim's advice.

And it comforts me.

So, my hike. I had decided to go on a hike to mull things over. To plan my next move. Here's what happened on that hike.

26

I pulled the Cobalt off Sunset onto a little road that would take me to a hike I knew and liked. I found the trailhead, parked, changed into some shorts and running shoes. No one around, I did it right out in the open. Didn't feel nearly as twisted as I had sitting at the surf break in a T-shirt and nothing else.

I headed up the trail. Look we're not talking Grizzly Adams here, there were old ladies who walked these trails, but it was nice. Outside. Sun. Fresh air. The intensity of L.A. no longer choking me.

I was winding my way up into the sky. Thinking. Thinking about some of the other maybes. Like, did Suzanne tell Neese that she was going to quit or wanted out, and he got pissed off and popped her because of that? Can't see it. Just doesn't seem like good business. There must be some turnover in his bizarre world. He must allow them to leave at some point. Well, maybe Suzanne told him she was going to quit, he put some pressure on her to stay because she's good for business, clearly that's true, and *then* she broke her promise and told someone else what she did for a living. Come on. No way. She's not a moron. See, that's what bothered me. That's why I wasn't in the Cobalt headed downtown to talk to Ott. There had to be more to the story. It was very likely in my mind that Neese had this twisted system set up, but that he *didn't* kill her. That maybe Jimmy Yates did. That maybe someone I hadn't met yet did.

I was making myself crazy. I simply needed more information. I was getting too theoretical here. Too far down a little path called Maybe Lane.

Thirty minutes later I was almost at the top of the trail. I looked behind me and saw the big mass of sea—the Pacific. The waves breaking on shore seemed tiny when set against the now blackish-looking monstrosity of water that stretched into infinity. That stretched all the way to that curved line that was the horizon. It felt haunting, powerful. When I looked the other way I could see all the way to downtown L.A., the buildings in a little cluster covered in haze. I was sweating, and even though I was telling myself not to, I was running through possibilities in my head.

There was a smaller, less traveled trail that intersected the main one I was on just beyond where I was standing. It went up, even higher, to the peak of the mountain. I took it. It wound around through some thicker brush and trees.

This trail was less maintained, less walked on, so there were bushes and vines haphazardly crossing it.

This trail had more mystery. More unknowns to it. It more represented what was going on in my head. Lots of variables, lots of strands and vines I just didn't quite understand yet. And few that seemed to sync up and connect for me.

I got to the top of this trail, as high as you could go on this hike. The space opened up and there was a sort of natural viewing area here. It was private, peaceful, quiet. I sat down on a big, smooth, warm rock. I looked down at the ground next to the trail. Twigs and brush and . . . something moving. I sat very still and watched as a snake, a California rattler, moved, unaware of me, from the brush bordering the trail to right *on* the trail. Slithering. Moving, *slanting*, sideways and forward at the same time.

It was frightening, I had never seen one before. But it was headed away from me, it appeared to be simply crossing the trail. I was very, very focused on it. Aware that if I moved, it might panic, turn around, and strike me.

I was frozen, but locked on it, until it disappeared into the brush on the other side of the trail. It was a relief that I could no longer see it. The old ostrich mentality. You know, I can't see it so I must be safe. When I finally stopped looking at the area where the rattler had been I was hit with a presence around me. I jerked my head up and to the left. Two men were standing above me. One guy had his arms at his sides. He was big, muscular, with a pockmarked face and black hair. His black hair had one of those white streaks in it. Skunklike. But not dyed. The guy didn't put it there. It was natural. Caused by a birthmark, I think. I'd seen one before. Just a two- or three-inch white streak amid a shock of black. The other guy was big too. But bald, shaved clean. He was holding a crowbar. Old school.

This was going to get very ugly.

In my mind, my chances appeared. They raced by. I had no gun. Nowhere really to go. There were cliffs and precipices all around. Crowbar Guy reared it back. But it was White Streak who punched me hard, hard in the jaw.

I was down on the ground. And instinctively I looked for the snake. Where was that slithering menace? Another thing out to get me. Crowbar Guy brought the steel tool up high and swung downward hard, right at my head. Okay, these guys were not fucking around.

I dodged it.

White Streak was now in front of me. I kicked him in the balls. I didn't get a direct hit, maybe the side of one ball, but enough to neutralize him for a few seconds.

I got to my feet. Crowbar Guy had it up again and it was coming down at my head a second time. I moved but it caught me in the shoulder. I punched him in the throat. Got him, he was down, the crowbar out of his hands lying on the trail. I went for the crowbar, get the weapon out of there, but didn't get to it. White Streak punched me hard in the ear. A flash of red light exploded in front of my eyes, and I heard a piercing ringing that I knew wasn't there.

I turned to face White Streak. I went for his nose with a right, but he blocked it. I kicked him in the nuts again, full contact, then tagged him in his left eye with my left fist.

I was jacked up, folks, I was all in.

White Streak was standing there, open, open for the kill. I went for his nose again, but he moved just slightly. I got him in the side of the face, but hard, very hard. But he didn't go down.

I turned around. Crowbar Guy was crawling toward the crowbar. He grabbed it. I stomped on his wrist, may have broken it. The crowbar was set free. Myopically I went for it, leaned down to grab it. I was on it, it was in my hands, when a foot collided with the back of my spine. I shot forward, landed on the brush, landed on, I think, a cactus, whose spines, thirty, forty of them, went into my stomach. I was stuck to the earth essentially.

Down on my stomach, I still had the crowbar. I couldn't do anything with it from my position, and I didn't want them to get their hands on it, so I threw it over the side of the trail. It disappeared over the edge. It was twenty yards away now, down the canyon, out of the picture. I turned over, pulled myself off the cactus. White Streak, who had kicked me in the spine, stood over me. I grabbed a tennis ball–sized rock and threw it at his face. I caught him in the same eye I'd punched him in. Bright blood splattered in the air and formed a red mini firework in the sky. I got up, spines sticking out of me, and stood in front of both of them. Jim would tell me to get out of there, this one wasn't winnable, but I wanted more.

I was going to go at Crowbar Guy, who was now crowbarless. And whose right wrist hung at his side, lifeless, at a strange, unsettling angle.

White Streak turned around, then back, and now held a gun pointed at my face. It was wrapped in a navy blue towel to silence the blast. I could just see the barrel sticking out the end. There was a calm over both of them. I thought: These guys are killers. Their orders? Kick the shit out of me, then end it, end me. Was this where it was going to be? Here on a side trail in the Santa Monica Mountains? With a silhouetted hawk overhead? With snakes and scorpions hiding in the brush beside me?

White Streak kept the gun on me. Crowbar Guy took two big, fast steps and kicked me hard in the chest. I went down, backward. My head banged against the hard sand. It was a dull, deep thud. Now dizzy, bleary, disoriented, staring skyward at the sun. The two men were hard to see, the sun was blinding me. I looked over to my left. And that's when I saw the rattler. He was hidden in the brush but his face was inches from mine. Inches. I looked right at the creature's diamond-shaped head, but mostly at the two dots that were his black, soulless, indifferent eyes. His eyes were the same, *the same*, as the eyes of Richard Neese. The snake's head was frozen, perfectly still, but his neck was coiled, cocked, ready to strike.

Crowbar Guy grabbed my shirt with his good hand, lifted me up, pushed me against the rock I'd been sitting on when they appeared. White Streak pointed the gun right between my eyes. Crowbar Guy looked at the gun, then at White Streak.

All he had to do was pull the trigger. If I went for the gun, he could pull it. If I just sat here, he could pull it. A rock and a hard place—with my life on the line. I was scared, I was very, very scared. My body tingled and a wave of blood rushed through me, my insides, on their own, preparing for something big. And then I had an oddly rational thought. *John, you have a choice. Would you rather die scared or die strong?* And I said to myself: *Fuck it. Let's do it.* And I sat up as straight as I could and looked right into the barrel, into that oily, black circle of death. My conscious mind, my subconscious mind, every part of me knew I had maybe one second left. Images began to appear in my mind. Quickly, but each one clear and searing and vivid. A dog I had as a child running to me across our lawn. My brother and me on a roller coaster, looking at each other as we roared down a deep drop. My mother hugging me and putting her cheek against mine and her hand on the back of my head. And then my father, sitting in his chair in a light blue dress shirt, giving me a tender but heartbreaking smile. And then one final image. It was a giant white oblong balloon sitting, floating, on top of a placid, blue, sun-dappled body of water. It was so beautiful. It was so peaceful. I waited for the bang.

It didn't happen. White Streak didn't pull the trigger. Instead, he first punched me in the face in the same exact spot the surfboard had hit, right above my left eye. A flash of pain went through my body. I felt the pain collect in my spine. Then he leaned down, picked up a rock, held his hand high in the air—pronouncing that it was coming—and struck me on the skull. My head jerked back and I could feel cool air hit the wound on my now opened cranium. Hot blood trickled down my face.

Then, the barrel of the gun was right in front of me again, but it was Crowbar Guy who said, "You know Richard Neese?"

I almost imperceptibly nodded.

He said, "No, you don't. You think you do, but you

don't. Trust me, you don't. Stop doing what you're doing."

They walked away, down the trail. I heard twigs snap, and muttering as they faded away.

I sat, my back against that same rock. Some blood had found its way into my mouth. I looked out into the canyon and said to no one in particular, "No."

27

had shut my eyes, and fallen asleep. Not a smart thing to do with a head injury. But I didn't drift off into the infinite of some kind of coma. Instead I just opened my eyes, hours later, no longer sitting up against the rock, but instead lying on the now cool dirt of the trail.

My friend the rattlesnake was nowhere around. At least I didn't think so. It was dark out. And beautiful. Moonlight dappling the brush and the trail. And a quiet you almost never hear in L.A.

I got to my feet. The world moved and shifted and finally settled before me. I pulled the remaining cactus spines out of my stomach and started down the trail. Taking it slow, pondering where I was with this thing yet again. Neese's boys were sent to rough me up, so I would stop looking into his ring. But he didn't send them to kill me. Too risky right now. He doesn't know enough about what I know, what I might have told, and who I might have told.

I stumbled down the trail, the sky spotted with stars, the moon out, full, hanging over me, its doppelgänger looked to be sitting right in the ocean, right *on* the ocean.

I made it to my car. I got in. Looked at myself. The spot above my left eye was more swollen than ever and cut too. Looked like I'd need stitches. The swelling caused my left eye to sit slightly closed. I felt the back of my head where the guy had put the rock. Yep, a second golf ball on my head, and lots of dried blood there too. I'd need stitches there as well. Jesus, my head was covered in massive bloody bumps.

I drove to Santa Monica Medical Center. It was a strange, surreal drive down a dark PCH. I was woozy, disoriented, and I had to put an exhausting amount of energy into focusing. Into not crashing my car and dying. At the medical center, they took me right in. As part of a continuous haze, I was behind those swinging doors, then in a chair, then down a hall and into a bed. I had a nurse over me, cleaning, looking at me, concern in her eyes. She was probably thirty, Mexican I'd guess, dark hair, dark eyes, soft features.

She was beautiful.

Her soft touch as she examined me and cleaned my wounds, sadly, was almost worth getting the shit kicked out of me. She was very lightly rubbing my face and head with cotton balls soaked in alcohol. At a few points her face was right up near mine. Her lips right in line with my lips. I almost kissed her. I was opening and closing my eyes. And the comfort I felt with the nurse, and the relief that

I was getting the attention I needed, caused me to close my eyes and drift away. In and out of sleep—at one point I saw a doctor with a needle and thread, repairing me like a goddamn sweater. But the nurse still looked on behind him. And then at some point, blackness and deep, uninterrupted sleep.

I woke up alone in a hospital room. Sun streaming in. I looked at my watch: 7 a.m. The nurse from the previous night walked in.

"Good morning," she said.

"Good morning."

"You feel okay? You were pretty banged up."

Man, I was right, she was beautiful.

"I feel okay."

And I did. I felt okay.

"You're still here? How long is your shift?"

She narrowed her eyes and gave me a sly smile. "Oh, I'll do anything to make sure my patients get better." And then she laughed at her own playful bravado. "I went home. For like eight hours. Now I'm back."

I felt my face above my left eye.

"Stitches there," she said. "Just a couple. But about ten more in your head."

The doctor walked in. I vaguely recognized him from the previous night.

"Mr. Darvelle, you've got a couple deep cuts. One on your face, one on your head." Long pause. Then: "Head injuries are dangerous. What happened?"

Everything he said was very matter-of-fact. Almost no emotion attached to his comments. Judgment, but not much emotion.

"I was hiking, slipped and fell, tumbled down the side of the gulch, rocks banged me up."

He didn't believe me. No way. But he was too much of a pro, or maybe too tired, to get into it. "Get some rest. Keep the cuts clean. Nancy, give him cleaning instructions, please. And tell him when he needs to come back to get the stitches taken out."

The doctor looked at both my cuts quickly, then flipped around and exited the room. Nancy did as told and gave me cleaning instructions. Then she told me to get dressed and she too left.

I got up, put my shorts and T-shirt back on, not sure how they got off, and walked out of the room. Nancy was there waiting.

"Do you play Ping-Pong, Nancy?"

"Oh yeah," she said. "I'm excellent."

Then she looked at me. "All those scrapes and bumps on your head. That's nothing compared to what I'd do to you if we ever played Ping-Pong."

I was in love with her.

I left the hospital, got in my Cobalt, and sat there for a moment. Then I got back out, walked back in the hospital. Nancy was still in the waiting room. I motioned for her to come over to me.

"Nancy, I might need to call you with questions about my injuries."

"You can call the center. The nurse on call will answer any questions you might have."

"Well, maybe I want to call you and ask you to play Ping-Pong sometime."

She looked at me. Made me wait for what seemed like

an interminable amount of time. Then she forked over the digits.

I was beat to shit. I was in a wild, concussive fog. And I still had lots of unanswered questions about the case. But I did have the phone number of a nurse named Nancy Alvarez.

28

I was back at my desk, the big slider open, by 9:30 a.m. You know, I actually felt better. I'd taken some blows. But I actually felt good. Like Vonz's movie *Starlight*, my perspective had been changed. I was now looking at the world through a swollen left eye and a throbbing, pounding, unrelenting headache. But I did have a new idea, and I needed to call Clay Blevins to act on it. And I had made a new decision: Do nothing else on this case without my gun. I'm talking, don't take a shower without my gun. Which is fine. I should have been operating that way already.

Before I called Clay, I opened up my desk drawer and pulled out the letter Vonz had written to Suzanne. The letter I'd never opened. I sliced it open with a pocketknife, unfolded it, and looked at it.

It read:

Suzanne. I miss you. I want to see you. Call me, Suzanne. I have to talk to you, to tell you something I never had the courage to tell you before. But if you don't call me, I want you to know that you changed my life forever. It wasn't just your beauty, your smile, your light. You unlocked something in me that I'd hidden away out of fear. And I'm forever grateful. Call me, Suzanne.

Love, Arthur

You know, not much. I was sorry I'd read it in a way. Invaded the privacy of it. I was a bit embarrassed by it. By my intrusion *and* by the content of the letter. Vonz's writing, it was nice, direct, sincere, but to a third party this kind of stuff almost always comes across as cheesy. Sentimental. Prosaic. Vonz probably wouldn't let lines like that in one of his movies. But apparently in his life a little sentimentality was okay. Which I have to say I respect. But, still, reading it gave me the willies a bit. Sentimentality, to people outside the immediate communication, never quite works. It feels *gross*. Suzanne probably wouldn't have thought so though. Suzanne was *in* the immediate conversation. She probably would have liked it. I put the letter in my drawer and called Clay Blevins.

"Clay, it's John Darvelle."

"Did I help?"

That's what people always wanted to know. People. We're simple. Did I help? Did I contribute? Am I important and worthy?

That's all we care about.

"Yes," I said. "But I need to talk to you again."

I drove to Clay's apartment in Los Feliz. Los Feliz is way east. East of Hollywood, east of Hancock Park. A neighborhood that for years was inhabited by poor people, fringe characters, even small-time criminals. But as the nice, gentrified areas of L.A. got more and more full of people, prices went up and people went looking for new places to live. Not everybody could handle Los Feliz and Silverlake, but the artists could. So the two neighborhoods became artist communities of sorts. And the posers followed soon after. What are you going to do? It happens. These days, these hoods could be described simply as: Hipsterville. Cooler than cool. Radder than rad.

Drowning in irony.

As I pulled onto Vermont, the main drag through Los Feliz, I saw residents, young residents, bopping down the streets. Wearing: Polyester pants, cheap dress shoes, old cardigans, and plaid blazers. Smoking: Old-school pipes and cigarettes out of long extensions.

I saw a guy wearing a brown three-piece suit with a pocket watch. He was probably twenty-three. I pictured a giant, pencil-thin mustache walking down the street with a cane, wearing some seventies sunglasses. I have no idea why.

Los Feliz did still have some genuine charm. Old Spanish-style California buildings. Funky hills and undulations to the landscape. Palm trees somehow right in the medians of the roads. And lots of classic old bars, some of which were frequented by real Los Angelenos.

Clay lived in an eight-plex, one street off Vermont. A mistake of a building built in the sixties or seventies. He opened the door, let me in. Bad carpet, popcorn ceiling. Strange, as one of the reasons this area became chic was because of the old-school Spanish buildings built with big rooms, high ceilings, interesting archways, and hardwood floors.

Not this place. This place could have been in a lower-class neighborhood in Phoenix. The place was fairly trashed, looked like he had a roommate who wasn't around. I saw a couple pizza boxes next to the garbage in the kitchen. Inexplicably, there was an Eddie Rabbit poster on the wall, Eddie looking pensive and serious.

Clay was all smiles as he welcomed me in, but then he took in my battered face and his smile went to a frown. I pressed on. "Clay, your memory of the blond dude in the Mercedes was very helpful."

"Excuse me? Excuse me?"

"Yeah, what?"

"Um. What happened to your face?"

"I fell, hiking."

He laughed. But it was a laugh diluted with fear. It was a laugh that said: Are the guys who did that to *you* going to come after *me*?

"Don't worry, Clay. No one is going to come after you. Now, I want to ask you something."

"Yeah?" he said in an unsure way.

"When we were first talking you said you ran into Suzanne once when she was with a friend."

"I did? No, Suzanne was a total babe! You know how it goes with totally hot babes. They don't have any friends."

I laughed. Often true. Not totally true. But in L.A. it could be very true. Some beautiful girl with a lost soul, always, always pursued by some rich guy, then never fosters any friendships—or much of a personality, for that matter.

But I didn't get that vibe from Suzanne.

Or, wait. Had her beauty and charm just created that illusion? Caused me to give her this magical *real* quality that she didn't even have? Could be. Ever seen a guy who's really pussy-whipped, even though the girl is just terrible? You ever see that? You've seen that. It's a horrible, horrible sight. Just horrible. It's like an actual sickness that you just have to wait for him to heal from. Like he's got the flu or something.

"I'm kidding, man," Clay said. Even though he seemed a bit scared, Clay still busted out a routine or two to keep his acting chops sharp. *Hey, you know what I've noticed? Hot girls don't have friends.*

I admired it.

"Yeah, Jenny," Clay continued. "Jenny was her name. Jenny Bickford. At the Newsroom Café. That's who she was with that time I ran into her."

Jenny. I hadn't written down the name. It happens from time to time.

"She's a news producer or something. That's what you said."

"Yeah. And cute too. Not like Suzanne. Not like I'd let a guy punch me in the face twenty-five times straight if that meant I got to bang her."

Here we go.

He continued, "But pretty. Real. Come to think of it, in

that moment, I kind of had a crush on her. I kind of have a crush on every girl though."

I knew the feeling.

And then Clay said, "Hey, you want to smoke some weed?"

"I have to run."

"This shit is good."

"I believe it. The *shit* these days appears to be quite good."

"Ohhh, yeah."

I was about to leave, but I had another question for Clay.

"So, what do you do when you get high, Clay?"

"What do you mean?"

"I mean, you're going to smoke some weed when I leave and then what are you going to do?"

"Sit here."

"That's it?"

"That's it."

I split.

29

Called Ken Booth. I could hear him not smiling or producing any emotion whatsoever over the phone. He found Jenny Bickford quickly. She was a TV producer for a company that produced reality shows and talk shows. She too worked on the Raleigh Studios lot, but the Manhattan Beach location, not the Hollywood location. Damn. I was way east. I now had to go way west, then way south.

So I busted over to the 10, then hit the 405 South, got off on Rosecrans, headed west to Manhattan Beach. Most people say, "Manhattan Beach isn't really L.A." The knock being that it's white-bread, homogenized, Orange County–ish. Full of rich, douchebag USC graduates who party hard, and do Jell-O shots, and pump iron, and have really good bodies and really bad haircuts. That, and successful, rich white people. All that is true. But the thing is, it's beautiful, on a really nice stretch of beach. And the girls there, the women there, aren't part of the Hollywood scene. They aren't heroin chic with smug attitudes and empty bank accounts. Instead, they're healthy, and they have jobs during the week. And on the weekends, they wear bikinis all day and smile a lot and play beach volleyball. I heard Shaq lived down here when he played for the Lakers. You know why? You know why?

Because Shaq is smart.

I wasn't going to make it all the way down to the beach. Raleigh Studios Manhattan was closer to the 405. I pulled up to the security gate, and, good news, Ken had actually gotten me a lot pass too. Ken, that's what I was saying about him. He acts like a friend, he does nice gestures like that. But he never gives any indication that we're buddies. He didn't even tell me about the lot pass. I just got there and discovered it. Hey, man, I'll take it.

I pulled on the lot. Newer than the Hollywood location. And a lot less activity. They used to film some of *CSI: Miami* here, I knew that. A lot of people don't like that particular *CSI*. Think Caruso is a joke. I will ask you to look at Caruso in a different way.

As a total genius.

I'm serious. I like his mannered, ridiculous, over-the-top vibe. But let's get back to the story. I'd gotten directions from the gate guard for the building of Pacific Productions, the company Jenny worked for. In the lobby there were big posters of all the shows Pacific Productions produced. Some dumb reality shows, *Moving Back In with Mom*. Seriously. That's a show they produced. I know, I want to see it too. But they also made a few decent, reasonably intelligent talk shows. *The Danny Baker Show.* Actually liked that one. Sort of a West Coast *Charlie Rose.*

At reception, the freaked-out receptionist—my face was a bit of a train wreck—told me to sit and wait while she got Jenny. After five minutes and three small installments of cold water out of a little paper cup, Jenny appeared. Clay was right. Jenny was cute. The kind of woman people refer to as the "marrying type." Which is an annoying and patronizing term. But she was indeed the marrying type. That's how I would probably describe her.

Except there was nothing bland or common about her. She had mystery to her. Black-rimmed glasses, soft brown eyes, and a slight upturn to her mouth at the corners.

I stood as she approached, and we both instinctively moved away from the seating area where I had been to another one a little farther away from the receptionist's desk. We landed on a black leather couch.

"Hello. How can I help you?" she said.

"My name is John Darvelle. I'm a private detective. I'm looking into the murder of your friend Suzanne Neal, and I'd like to ask you some questions."

She looked at me. I could tell she was processing the cut above my left eye and my lumpy, bumpy, stitched-up head. "Okay. This is a little . . . surprising. Who . . . who are you working for?"

"Myself."

She didn't press it.

"I've already talked to the police."

"Good. I hope they figure it out. I bet they won't. But I hope they do. Can I ask you a few questions?"

"Let's go outside on the lot."

We walked out of the building, out onto the lot, back out into the sun. It wasn't the Hollywood Raleigh in terms of activity, and it sure as hell wasn't the Paramount lot in terms of glamour and history. There was no New York street here. This lot was quiet, clean, new. Big white buildings and stages. I guessed there was some filming going on somewhere but it didn't seem like it. Peaceful almost. No Hollywood tension. And you could smell the ocean. Which is always nice.

We walked sort of aimlessly around. "So, what do you mean you're working for yourself? No one hired you?"

Shit.

"I knew Suzanne. I met her just before she was killed. And I'm a detective. So, I'm giving it a look."

She looked at me. "What happened to your face?"

I looked at her with total seriousness, "I cut myself shaving."

"You shave the area above your eye?"

"Yes."

She looked at me skeptically. But we continued walking around the generic, sparkling clean lot, and she didn't seem to have an issue with resuming our chat. I said, "So, how'd you meet Suzanne?"

"I met her at an industry function. A party for *The Danny Baker Show*. I think it was celebrating the one thousandth episode or something."

"Why was she there? Who was she with?"

"I really don't know. Girls like Suzanne can go to any party they want. And she knew Danny somehow. We met in the line at the bar, and she was one of those people who you like immediately. Well, you knew her. You know what I mean?"

"Yeah."

"We had fun that night." She laughed at the memory. "Definitely had a few drinks. And we stayed in touch."

"Did you know that Suzanne had a relationship with Jimmy Yates?"

"What? The movie star?"

"Yes."

"No, I didn't."

It seemed like she was telling the truth. Because she was surprised, but not *that* surprised. Like, surprised that it was such a big star but also, yeah, Suzanne was a babe, we're in L.A., shit happens.

"Did you ever go to Suzanne's condo in Santa Monica?"

"Yes."

"How did she buy that, do you know?"

I was testing her. Did she *really* know Suzanne? Had Suzanne told her the truth? Which if Marlon the Marlin was correct would be a conversation she would die for if Neese found out. Jenny looked at me with her soft brown eyes. They had feeling in them.

"I don't know," Jenny said. "I was a friend, but she didn't tell me everything. Like how she bought that place. Family money, I don't know. Suzanne was so . . . warm, in a way. But she had a secretive side. She could engage you and keep you away at the same time, if that makes sense."

I was going in. "Did you ever think some rich L.A. guy was keeping her comfortable? You know, like a Jimmy Yates? Somebody like that?"

After a pause. "Yeah, it occurred to me. But I never

thought about it that much. We were friends, but you know, it's not like we talked every day. I didn't really care about where she got her money. I didn't *want* to give it that much consideration. We just had fun sometimes. Then I'd come back to work on Monday and I wouldn't really think about it."

"Did you ever think she might be a prostitute?"

Jenny stopped walking. "What? No. No way. She didn't have to do that. If Suzanne was going to sell her soul she could have just married somebody. Believe me, she had plenty of opportunities. Like I said, maybe she had some help or whatever. But an actual prostitute? No. Not possible."

"Who else did she date? I told you about Jimmy Yates. Who are these opportunities you are talking about? Can you think of anyone specifically?"

She paused, briefly, and then said, "She told me went on some dates with Arthur Vonz, the director."

"Well, he could certainly afford to buy her a place I would imagine. Or help her out."

"Yeah. I guess. Listen," she said. "I didn't even tell the police that. Maybe it's no big deal. Suzanne went out with guys all the time. I didn't give them a list of every guy she ever went out with. They didn't ask. They didn't ask me that much really. More just had I talked to Suzanne lately, did she mention being afraid of anyone, did she have enemies, that kind of thing."

"It's okay. You answered their questions. But those are some good ones. *Did* she ever mention any enemies? Being afraid of anyone? Scared of what might happen?"

"No, she didn't. Which is what I told them."

I looked at her. *The marrying type.* She was really pretty. She, like Suzanne, had a specialness about her. A quality that made *you* feel good. That made you want to get to know her more, know more about her.

I said, "Thanks for talking to me, Jenny."

She said, without any smile at all, "You might want to be more careful next time you shave."

30

So. Suzanne's friend didn't know too much, or she wasn't telling me if she did. That's the thing. If the girls aren't allowed to reveal that they are Pipe Girls, then if, if they had ever said anything to a friend, like Jenny Bickford, then the friend sure as shit wouldn't admit to knowing it either. She'd be afraid for *her* life. Especially if the girl who told her was now in a drawer at the morgue.

Yet, she had been honest with me about Arthur Vonz. She had parted with something that was probably told to her in confidence. Something that she didn't know I knew. So she had *tried* to help me. I think. Maybe Lane. Parked there again. Guessing at stuff. Yeah, guessing at stuff. But I'm a good guesser.

Back at my desk in my office. Toast had popped by,

which always made me happy. I held him for a moment. Pet him. Talked to him a bit. Then I put him right up on my desk, where he quickly let the eyelids drop.

I jumped online and looked at some photos of Danny Baker. At social events. At news events. Stills of him interviewing guests on his show. He had the anchorman face, only a little more tired-looking than most. But he had that classic, handsome, timeless look, but with a touch of California. He was tan, with stylish hair that was just beginning to go gray. And was just a bit longer than your average talk-show anchorman type.

I read up on him. It was easy to find articles all over the Web. And it was easy to find out where this "shameless workaholic" had lunch every day. At a modest little deli in Beverly Hills. Larry King–style. His production offices were in Manhattan Beach, but he taped his show every day in a modest, nondescript building in Beverly Hills. Thus the daily lunch spot.

In the Cobalt, on the road, at the deli.

I ordered the "famous" tuna sandwich, sat down at a corner table with a red and white checked plastic tablecloth, and waited. Damn, the tuna *was* good. I asked one of the people who worked there why it was so good. She smiled and said, "We put little bread crumbs in it. That's the secret. But don't tell anyone."

And then, there was Danny Baker. Just like all the articles said. It's amazing how many of us are creatures of habit. Myself included. I liked to drink three to four cold, cheap American beers at night and then play a few games of Ping-Pong. Danny Baker liked to come to this little deli and have lunch before heading off to interview dignitaries, politicians, artists, and experts.

He went through the little line, said some pleasantries to the people behind the counter who recognized him, then went outside and sat down at one of the little tables right on Beverly Drive. He got right to work on his, yep, you guessed it, tuna sandwich.

He was midbite when I emerged from inside and sat down at his table right across from him. And then, there I was staring at this face I'd seen a million times on TV. The handsome anchorman face, with the tired lines and the longish hair. Just long enough that you'd go: His hair is kind of long for someone who's interviewed the president many times. But it's not so long that you'd go: Were you ever in Whitesnake?

I said, "Don't worry, I'm not a paparazzo, or some crazy fan. I like your show though. Really one of the best shows on TV."

I was confusing him a bit—intentionally. You have to. It tends to scare people, catches them off guard. I *do* like his show, quite a bit. That part wasn't gamesmanship.

I continued, "I have some information that I think you'll find interesting."

He was calm. So if he *was* a little caught off guard he wasn't showing it much. Which annoyed me.

He said, "Is this a tip? Are you a source?"

He took a sip of his icy brown beverage.

"Diet Coke?" I said.

He nodded and frowned a bit, showing a fair amount of confusion.

"I love Diet Coke." And then, "Am I a source? Well, sort of, in that I have a story for you."

Now he was nodding, the frown replaced with an engaged look. He eyed me like I was one of his guests. Interested. Or really good at faking it.

I continued, "It's a story about you, in fact."

A little shift in his eyes and in his body language. Maybe he was starting to tense up. I was now less annoyed.

"I'm not sure I follow you," he said.

It really seemed like I was on his show. Sitting across from him. Sitting across from a now leaning-in, more-interested-than-ever Danny Baker.

I thought for a moment, here on *The Danny Baker Show*. I decided to throw out a guess. A dangerous guess. But like I said, I'm a good guesser.

I said, "I know about you and one of the Pipe Girls. Suzanne Neal. Now, what I don't know is how often you, let's say, got together with her. And another thing I don't know is if you know that she is dead."

His face went white. Adrenaline coursing through his veins—for sure. His whole appearance now *different*. Another astonishing transformation as white-hot thoughts about his career being forever changed or over, about what kind of trouble he might be in, about how his life might never be the same, all at once ramming around in his brain.

Folks, I think my guess was right.

He started to get up and said, "I'm going to the bathroom."

"Sit down."

He did.

"Why are you going to the bathroom?"

"I thought I was about to throw up."

"Do you still think that?"

He didn't say anything.

"Take a sip of your refreshing, crisp Diet Coke."

He did. And then he sat there again. Some color came back to his face. But his mouth hung open just a bit. He looked like he had been stunned, shocked, unplugged.

"Okay," he said. "What do you . . . What do you want to talk about?"

"Did you know she was dead?"

"Yes. I did. Listen, can we go somewhere else? I come here every day. And . . ."

"I get it. Let's get in my car."

The Cobalt was less than ten yards away. We threw out our lunches and walked over to the Cobalt. He got to the passenger side door and hesitated.

I said, "Get in. We'll just drive to the park a couple blocks away."

He nodded and got in. I headed to a small public park at the intersection of Santa Monica and Rodeo Drive, less than a three-minute drive. I parked in some shade.

"Do you want to get out?"

Danny shook his head. And then: "Who are you?"

"My name is John Darvelle. I'm a detective."

I told him I was private, but that the cops were also investigating the case. I told him I was helping them out. Which, in my own way, was true. But also remember: Just the mention of the actual cops was sure to throw him off a bit, to tighten up that sphincter just a touch.

I said, "How did you know Suzanne?"

He took a breath. "I met her at an industry party. She

was there with . . . you know, I don't know who she was there with. It doesn't matter. She was a beautiful, charming girl. We ended up having some mutual friends and over the years I got to know her a bit. Never that well. But I did consider her a friend. I don't know what happened at the deli. But suddenly the fact that she's *dead* just hit me. Oh man. But . . . but . . . what were you saying, Pipe Girl? What is that?"

Okay. Okay. I saw what was happening. Danny wanted to get away from his local deli so he could lie to me. Because he wasn't sure how I would react, better go someplace private.

Yes. Danny Baker hadn't admitted anything to me yet. He had reacted in a way that said a lot, but he hadn't actually *said* anything. He'd only told me that he knew Suzanne Neal and that he knew she was dead.

Hmm. So what was *I* going to do? I was almost certain, no, I was certain, he was a Pipe Girl customer. But the question was: Was now the time to Jimmy Yates him? To force him to tell me he had used a prostitute? To force him to tell me what he knew about Richard Neese?

Wasn't Danny Baker simply going to tell me the exact same thing that Jimmy Yates had? What was I going to get out of that? More confirmation that Richard Neese ran a ring?

Here I was again.

I needed something that related to the *killing*.

Shit, I had jumped the gun. I had gotten too excited and had prematurely confronted Danny Baker.

I cut the interview.

But I did have one question. "Danny, when was the last time you saw Suzanne?"

"When was the last time?" he repeated.

Jesus. Lying, for sure. I mean, repeating the question? Classic.

"Two months ago. At a premiere party. I think."

I looked at him for a long time, then said, "Okay."

I asked for his number. He gave it to me without hesitation. *Yeah, of course, nothing to hide, call me if you need to, no problem.* I drove him back to the deli. He took a deep breath as he was getting out of my car. And this time he looked at me. And he said, "I hope I helped. And that you, or the cops, or whoever gets to the bottom of this."

But his eyes said, "I know a lot more than I'm telling you."

I went back to my office. Okay. Neese is a bad guy. That is for sure. Neese runs a ring. Neese may enforce his ring's special qualities through murder. Probably does.

Okay.

So here were the questions.

Did Suzanne tell someone, or threaten to tell someone, that she was a Pipe Girl?

Did Suzanne tell Neese she was hanging it up, and *that* somehow led to her murder?

Was one of the men who used the Pipe Girl service somehow responsible for Suzanne's death?

Those were the questions.

But Neese. Neese was at the center of this story. His form of punishment for squealing was at the center of this story. But I needed something more than a rumor from a guy on a boat named Marlon the Marlin.

That's when Jenny Bickford called me.

"Hi, Jenny," I said.

"Hi," she said.

"What's happening?"

"Well, I thought of something that might help you."

31

Now, people of the story. I'm a private detective. I bullshit people a lot. And I try to *detect* bullshit a lot. This, whatever it was about to be, felt like something she wanted to tell me before and didn't. And that usually means it's worth looking into.

"Great," I said. "Thanks for calling. What's up?"

"Well, this may not help," sounding very casual. Just so casual. "But Suzanne has . . . Suzanne has this friend who you may want to talk to."

"Okay. What's her name?"

"Her name is Allison Tarber. And the reason I think she might be helpful is . . . Well, you're a man, so this might not make sense."

"Try me."

"Well, you know when you have a good friend who has a good friend but you and the *other* friend don't ever really connect?"

"Sure. I know when that happens."

"Well, that's the way this is. The three of us were only together a few times, but I just remember that when I was around them it felt like they were in on an inside joke that I wasn't a part of. That they had another kind of relationship. You know what I'm saying? You know that feeling?"

Yeah I knew that feeling. Everyone knows that feeling. It's a terrible feeling.

I said, "Yeah. Like maybe this girl Allison has a nice apartment somewhere that someone might have bought her?"

Jenny didn't respond. She just said. "I don't know about that. I'm just saying maybe she knows something, or knew a side of Suzanne that I didn't. I don't know. Just thought it was something that might help you."

I thought about Jenny. There was a sincerity to her that you don't see that often anymore. Like she couldn't help being a good person.

I love people like that.

"Do you know how to contact Allison? Know where she lives? Where she's from?"

"I really don't. You know, we never connected. Like, as friends. But also literally—we never got together or anything. It's funny, I think I remember her being from Alaska. I don't know if that helps."

"It helps. Thanks, Jenny. Call me if anything else pops into your head. Or for anything you might need."

Long pause. "Yeah, okay, John."

Normally I might have been discouraged by this. You could look at it like it was a trail up a different mountain—a trail taking me further away from the epicenter of my story. My case getting diluted. But I had to try. Because I had to get to the *murder*. And, what else did I have right at this moment?

Right. There was that.

Before I called Ken Booth to see if maybe she was an actress, or called Larry Frenette to see if he could look through the paper's computer, or called Linda Robbie to see if this Allison Tarber had any high-dollar real estate in her name, I decided to do a little amateur-level looking around. Facebook. Google. The way normal people all over the place investigate each other these days.

Facebook. Nothing that looked promising. Google. A few matches but quite frankly none of them looked like I assumed Allison Tarber should look. Because, like you, I'd assumed she was another Pipe Girl. Like Suzanne Neal. And the cool-under-pressure, steely-eyed Rebecca Heath.

Then I tried: Allison Tarber, Los Angeles. And less than a second later I was looking at a link that would take me to an *L.A. Times* newspaper headline. I clicked on the link. And here's what the headline said: "Hiker in Santa Monica Canyon Falls to Death."

Hey, Jenny Bickford. Yeah. Looks like this *might* help. Because Allison Tarber is, you know, dead.

There was a brief article dating back just over a year. And a picture next to it of a very young and very pretty girl. The picture looked like a headshot. Probably was.

I read the article. It was simple, factual. It said that Los Angeles resident Allison Tarber, an aspiring actress, was hiking in the Santa Monica Mountains, slipped near the top of the trail she was hiking on, and fell about fifty feet into the canyon, hitting her head fatally on the way down.

She had been hiking very near where I'd almost done my last hike ever. Where I'd gotten the shit kicked out of me by two mouth breathers. Where I'd been face-to-face with a black-eyed rattler.

The article didn't indicate any foul play, any investigation at all. It was pure information.

It was cold-feeling. Clinical. Heartless.

So instead of now going to Ken Booth or Larry Frenette or Linda Robbie, it was back to Elliot Watt. Back to drawers of the dead. Back to the morgue.

I called Elliot. He wasn't glad to hear from me. He didn't say, "Hey, John! What's up, homey?! How's the Darv doing? Yeah, come on by!"

However, because it was an old case, with no heat on it, he didn't give me too much attitude. Not a single put-upon sigh. Not a single guilt-trippy speech. He just said, in a flat, bored tone, "Yeah, come by and I'll give you the file."

I got to the morgue. Quiet that day. Elliot was sitting behind his desk, hollow-eyed, blue veins showing beneath his clammy alabaster skin. He was reading *Popular Mechanics.*

"*Popular Mechanics*, huh? What *is* that magazine, Elliot?"

He looked at me with disgust. "Darvelle, what does that even mean?"

"I just mean, I bet if you asked twenty people what the content of *Popular Mechanics* is, like what a typical article might be about, nineteen of them would have no clue and the one who did know would be some kind of criminal or degenerate or twisted basement-dwelling weirdo who's like forty-eight and lives with his mom."

He said, "I'm sorry, didn't you come here to ask for *my* help? To have *me* do you a favor? And your way of buttering me up is to blatantly insult me? Yeah, that makes sense. That makes a lot of sense, John."

"Right. You have a point. You absolutely have a point. But, seriously. What are you reading? I mean, what article are you reading right now? What's it about?"

He looked at me, fed up. His big blue bug eyes were half closed. And he conveyed a mixture of boredom, exhaustion, and confusion. He said, "I'm reading an article about a new kind of self-inflating tire."

"Why?" I yelled. "Why would you read that?"

He didn't respond. He just put the magazine down, then picked up the case file and autopsy reports for Allison Tarber.

"Here you go," he said.

"Is this my copy?"

"Yeah, but it's quiet today. And nobody cares about this case. You can read it here if you want to, in case you have any questions for me."

See, I told you. Elliot Watt's cool. Good guy. Wants to help. Fighting the good fight. He's in the you-scratch-my-back, I'll-scratch-your-back ring of trust—you already know that. But here's why, specifically, he helps me out. Because one time I helped him in a way that he seems to really appreciate. He came to me some years ago and said, in his words, "I have a favor of the large variety to ask."

Elliot had this girlfriend. Tracy. I'd met her randomly once. Ran into Elliot and her at a movie theater in Culver City. This girl was very attractive. I know, hard to believe. Now, she was of the goth, pale-skinned, tattoo-on-her-back-of-a-snarling-rabid-hyena variety, but she was legitimately, objectively attractive. Elliot broke up with her because he said she was, again his words, "Fucking nuts, John. Fucking nuts." So, after he broke up with her, she wouldn't let it go. Called him and texted him constantly. Stalked him. And eventually threatened to kill him. Now, it sounds maybe even kind of amusing. But as I learned through a quick investigation, Elliot was right about this girl. She was mentally tweaked. And she hated Elliot for leaving her.

Obviously, Tracy didn't kill Elliot. But she did get a friend of hers named Ollie to further harass him and beat him up. Ollie was tough and mean and he loved Tracy. So he'd take his anger out on anyone she asked him to. Ollie kicked the shit out of Elliot. And afterward, hung around his house and neighborhood and, anytime he had the chance, antagonized him and terrorized him and pushed him around and scared him. Ollie was like a schoolyard bully, but in adult life. And much, much more dangerous.

So, I have this friend who I'll tell you about at another time in more detail. His name is Clete. That's actually his name. Clete. He's from Arkansas. He's six-four and wiry-strong. He has probably five percent body fat. Maybe less. He's the toughest person I've ever met. Once I was at his house, and he was on the roof of it, actually leaning off the roof of it, to reach over and saw a dead limb off a tree that bordered the house. He slipped and fell, and on the way down crashed very hard into several branches and brick window ledges and then THUMPED on the ground. He got right up, unscathed. He had no injuries. He literally was not hurt at all.

I said, "You all right, dude?"

And he said, "Yep."

And walked into his house.

Anyway, Clete and I went and found Ollie and, mostly with Clete's unique use of force, we quickly fixed the Elliot Watt situation.

Ollie walks the earth these days with a scared look in his eye—not to mention a permanent twitch.

Elliot never heard from Ollie, or Tracy, again.

But let's get back to the story.

I sat down in Elliot's bleak morgue office and looked at the Allison Tarber case files. The "case" never became a case. Nobody ever suspected anything. It was just a really bad accident that resulted in a really bad head wound that resulted in the worst news there is.

A young person dying.

I looked at the pictures of the corpse. Another dead, naked, and, before the fall, beautiful young woman. Half her head was caved in. And she had cuts and bruises and slices and gashes down the left side of her body. The other side of her, the right side, was surprisingly unharmed. Amazing in a way—the randomness of a violent fall.

Elliot peered at me from behind his *Popular Mechanics*. He had a look in his eye that said: Would you like my opinion?

So maybe that's why he'd told me to stick around. Not

necessarily out of the goodness of his heart. More: I've got a POV on this. I thought, hey, whatever, once again, I'll take it.

"Yes?" I said to him.

"What?" he said coyly.

"Do you have some thoughts on this? What does the expert say?"

He walked over to me and his demeanor changed from twisted, pale *Popular Mechanics* reader to twisted, weird, but highly confident professional.

"Well, this girl was obviously very banged up. The head injuries killed her almost certainly. Actually the head injuries did kill her."

"Okay."

"Look, I took a look at this file before you came over. I'm not going to ask why you're looking into this girl, or how it might be related to the other girl, I'm just going to tell you what I thought back when she first came in. Basically it's like this: I always look very carefully at the bodies, because I do my job unbelievably well."

He said this with no irony. Which I appreciated. False modesty is so boring.

He continued. "Basically I wasn't just being a nice guy when I said stick around here to read the report."

I didn't mention that that had occurred to me. I just listened. Sometimes that's best.

Elliot continued, "Because I want to tell you what I found, that nobody at the time seemed to think was important or even necessarily accurate. In fact, my boss wouldn't let me put it into the report because he said it was just a theory. And theories don't fly here because then the cops spend all this money looking into something that may not even be real when they should be doing other things. You get my fucking drift?"

"I do," I said. "Let's hear it. What is it?"

"So I found this one cut right on her left front hip. A gash really. A small chunk of her body missing."

He pointed to the picture. The cut he showed me was just inside her left hip bone. In a sort of sexy area of the female body. It looked to me a whole lot like all the other cuts on the left side of her body. Indistinguishable from the others as far as I could tell.

Elliot continued, "See, this cut just wasn't consistent with the rest of her injuries. Now, she had slices and gashes and tears all over her body from falling down into that goddamn gulch. Why people like to hike is beyond my ability to comprehend, by the way. It's like, walking around on a trail at ten thousand feet with scorpions and mountain lions and cliffs that you can fall all off everywhere. It's like, are you stupid?"

I thought, not to mention rattlesnakes and subhuman guys who want to kill you.

"But, anyway," Elliot said. "This cut, this one right here that I'm showing you, was too clean. It was like the fall didn't cause it. It was like she'd been stabbed with a knife that had a very sharp but not serrated edge. Now, I couldn't, can't, prove this and you *could* possibly come to the conclusion that it was just a weird, knifelike rock that stabbed her and took out a chunk of her. That *is* possible in that it's not *impossible*. But it seemed to me like she had been cut prior to her fall."

"What do you mean? What are you saying?"

Sometimes my questions weren't exactly genius.

"I'm saying one way to look at this is that someone cut her before she fell off the cliff. And that someone wisely thought that falling hundreds of feet down a canyon bouncing off rocks and trees would both kill her and cover up the cut. Which for all intents and purposes it did. Not even my boss bought my theory. Which is why I said it *could* have been a one-in-a-million cut that sliced out a section of her body perfectly. It's just doubtful. Or let me put it to you better, John: It didn't happen. Now, why cut her here? What would that really do other than hurt like a motherfucker? No clue. Seems pretty random. Maybe somebody trying to scare her by stabbing her in a pretty, you know, private area. No clue."

I looked at him. Then I looked at the pictures again. Then said, "Thank you for your professional opinion, my friend."

He nodded. "You bet."

He put his nose back in *Popular Mechanics*.

I grabbed my copies of the reports and left.

32

I went to a bar in Culver City near my office, called Ford's Filling Station. Nice place, dark wood, brass touches, big windows. It was four-thirty. Probably the best time to go to a bar. The day still has promise, yet, at this time of year anyway, the light is dimming. The sun is low. The rays slanting into windows. And usually, bars aren't too crowded at this hour. And that was true here. Just a few people chatting. Some good jazz playing. Mellow and relaxing. I ordered a cold Budweiser.

"Sorry, only big domestic we have is PBR."

PBR. The beer places like this offer strictly to be ironic. I don't drink it on principal.

The bartender said, "We've got a nice honey wheat you might like. It's really popular. Really robust flavor."

I closed my eyes, pinched the bridge of my nose, and sighed.

Then, without speaking, I methodically got up and, my face paralyzed in a trancelike annoyed smile, walked out of the bar. I went left and staggered into a restaurant a couple doors down. It was California fusion or something. I beelined it to the bar.

"Bud, Bud Light, something like that."

"We have Amstel Light and Heineken."

I stared straight ahead and blinked a few times. I then closed my eyes and pointed my head toward the floor for about forty-five seconds. When I looked up, the bartender was still waiting for me to order. I shook my head disgustedly, got up, and left.

I skulked up the street to a rough-looking dive I'd seen a lot but had never been into. Mary's. I walked in. "Bud please."

"You bet."

"Thank god."

"Huh?"

"Nothing. Also, a shot of Jack."

The bartender nodded, and brought both back instantly.

I took a sip of the beer; it was freezing. I nailed the shot; it was warm and delicious. Is it that difficult? Honey wheat? What? I marveled at how good the beer and the shot were, both individually and as a combination. I finished the beer, got another round; this one I took a little easier. I looked around the bar. A dive. But great. Possessing fully that late-afternoon calm-before-the-storm vibe.

I sipped the second shot and took a nice, relaxed pull of the cold beer. Oftentimes on a case you have to reset. You begin to get more and more information and if you follow everything you suddenly find yourself too far away from the center. From the eye. You begin to start processing all these possibilities, too many to control, and *way* too many to all be true.

So: Was Allison Tarber a Pipe Girl? Think so, don't you? And the cut that Elliot Watt pointed out? What was that? Well, maybe it was *her* tattoo. Maybe it was *her* PG symbol cut out of her before she got pushed over a cliff by Neese or one of those baboons I ran into in the very same canyon.

Maybe because of the way they had decided to rid the world of Allison Tarber, banging her off rocks filled with sharp edges, they could go one step further to dodge suspicion by removing her Pipe Girl stamp.

So: Did Jenny know that Tarber was dead? Did she know that Tarber and Suzanne were in the same business? And if so, doesn't that mean that someone broke *the promise* and told her the big secret?

And: If Tarber was indeed one of Neese's girls, whether or not Jenny Bickford knew, does that connect her to Suzanne Neal? Does that help me put Suzanne's murder on Neese?

Well, sure. Because it was another girl in his ring who was now dead. It makes the notion, the silly notion of his business plan, seem not so crazy. And, shit, maybe Allison Tarber was the one who died to make the whole thing work. That's what Marlon the Marlin had said. Kill one of them and the rest of them shut up forever.

I left Mary's, went back to my office, called Jenny Bickford. It was 6 p.m. I sat at my desk, listening to her cell phone ring.

"Hello," she said.

"Hi, Jenny. It's John Darvelle."

"Yeah, it said so on my phone."

She sounded nervous. She kept talking.

"But I still always just say hello rather than just start right into a conversation, you know?"

She laughed. Sweetly. Awkwardly.

"Yeah. Listen. I'd like to talk to you again. In person."

"Sure, I guess, yeah. Hey, did that Allison Tarber thing help?"

She wasn't a good liar. Which to me is a good quality. A good thing.

"Maybe. I really don't know yet."

"Well, it's Friday, so Monday I guess?"

"I was hoping for tonight."

"I'm about to leave for the day."

"Where do you live?"

"Santa Monica."

"How about coming by my office? It's in Culver City, and from Manhattan Beach you can hop right off the freeway."

"Well . . . I was going to go home."

"It's not too far out of your way. Please. Come by."

"Okay. Culver City? Where exactly?"

I told her.

"Okay. Okay. Give me about an hour."

One hour later, she came peering around the corner of my big, and still open, sliding door. It was almost dark now. The last bit of light hanging in the air. The streetlights just coming on, giving the lot in front of my ware-house a yellow glow.

Her face, then her body appeared in the doorway. I could see vulnerability on her face. She couldn't hide that was she was hiding something. And she couldn't hide that she knew we were about to talk about it.

"Hi," she said, arms crossed.

"Hi. Come in. Have a seat."

She did, at one of the chairs in front of my desk.

"Thanks for telling me about Allison Tarber. I looked into it."

"Yeah, what did you find out?"

"I found out that Allison is dead."

This time Jenny didn't feign massive surprise.

"I knew that. I thought . . . I thought . . . that might help you. I'm not sure why."

I got up and walked over to the slider. Appearing to be trapped in thought, pondering the great questions of the case. But that's not what I was doing. What I was doing was scanning the lot. Looking for the two guys who had remodeled my face. Nothing. Nobody. Hadn't seen those two since. My thought was: They and Neese don't know what I'm up to *exactly*. So they're probably waiting to see what I do next. Waiting to see if I was going to cause any more trouble. Which I was.

But, at this point, I had to do whatever I was going to do *fast*. Or else I would surely hear from them again. And soon.

I thought: Are they out there? Are they watching? Just. Don't. Know.

I thought about shutting the slider. No. Leave it open. Business as usual.

I walked back over to my desk, sat down, and said to Jenny, "Jenny, I believe Suzanne was a prostitute. A special kind of prostitute called a Pipe Girl."

Jenny was about to speak.

"Hang on," I said. "If you're a Pipe Girl, you make a lot of money. Much more than the regular kind of prostitute. However, the catch is, if you tell anyone, *anyone*, what you do, outside of the pimp for lack of a better word, and the customer of course, you are killed. That's what it means to be a Pipe Girl. That's the deal you make to become a Pipe Girl. It's a prostitution system meant to totally protect the customer by guaranteeing that the use of the service will never, ever get out. I know, it sounds absurd. How many holes can you see in this business plan, right? But take all the problems out of the equation for a moment and you can see genius in the idea. Which is: Imagine the money you could make if you were able to provide rich men with beautiful women who would never say a word."

Jenny looked at me. Not nodding, but indicating somehow that she wanted me to continue.

"Jenny, Suzanne told you she was a Pipe Girl, didn't she?"

She said, very calm now, "I can't talk about this, John."

"I think you can. And I think you should. Did she tell you she was a Pipe Girl?"

Quickly. "Yes."

So there it was. Suzanne had told. Had done the thing she was forbidden to do.

Jenny continued. "But, I have to tell you this. I'm the

only person she ever told. I'm close to positive of that. And I know her . . . boss, or whatever you want to call him, didn't know she had told me. So that's not why she . . . got . . . killed."

"How do you know?"

"I'm just sure of it. Suzanne and I had gone out the night she told me. We had dinner. And too many drinks. And she came back to my apartment to spend the night. You know, so she didn't have to drive. We were drunk. We were very drunk. And she told me she had to tell me something. And she did. In a very straightforward way she told me the arrangement she was in. And it was like this huge relief for her. I've never seen anything like it. Her telling me was like this catharsis. She began to cry. To sob. And she hugged me, for a long time. But then . . . the next morning I woke up and she was already awake, sitting in my kitchen. And she was so serious. No, she was scared. She was scared. That's what it was. And she told me that she'd never told anyone that. And then she apologized to me for telling me. And I remember saying: It's okay. And then she explained why she was apologizing. She said that I couldn't repeat it ever. Ever. To anyone. Because if anyone ever found out she could be in danger. That's what she said, that she could be in danger. She had a look in her eye that I've never seen anyone have. So intense. So focused. I said, of course, Suzanne, I'll never say a word. And then she just kept saying that she was sorry. So sorry. But, but, the truth is, I never did repeat it. Not even back to Suzanne. We never once spoke about it again. It truly was like it had never happened. And so . . . And so . . ."

"And so what?"

"And so that can't be why she was killed. Because it's like she never told me. It really is like she never told me."

I was thinking: Maybe she told Neese she told you. Doubtful. I mean, why would she do that? But maybe.

Jenny said, "I think you should talk to Danny. Danny Baker."

"I did."

Without really hearing me she said, "He loved her. But she loved him too. That was the thing. Lots of people fell for Suzanne, but with Danny, she loved him too."

A man appeared in my doorway.

Jenny sensed it, jerked around, saw the man, and froze. She looked back at me. True fear in her eyes. But there was nothing to be afraid of. It was Jim Douglas. I had asked him to come, and he had showed up right on time. As always.

He walked in. He was wearing a maroon leisure suit. And not in an ironic way. He was really wearing it—wearing it with pride. Also: Leather dress boots with a zipper up the inside ankle. He had big glasses on that tinted automatically when you entered the sun. They were at about a quarter tint, having adjusted to the light in my space. He had a freshly lit Benson & Hedges 100 sticking out of his mouth. It slanted across his face and popped against his black skin.

"Hi, Jim," I said.

He smiled.

I walked over and gave him a hug.

I introduced him to Jenny. She got up and he walked over and shook her hand.

I said to Jenny. "Jenny, this story is coming to an end. Now, I don't think you're in danger. Especially if what you told me is true. And I believe it is. But I want to make sure you're safe. If you want to take your story to the police, you can. But I wouldn't. Not yet. Just go home for the weekend. Stay home, or around your house, all weekend. Jim here is my very old friend and mentor. You won't know he's watching you. But you will be very safe. Nothing, *nothing* will happen to you when you're on Jim's watch. Right, Jim?"

"That's right, boss."

"Jim, how long is that cigarette? Is it a 120? Or is it a 130?"

"They don't make 130s, my boy."

"What's it like? Is it good? Describe it to me."

He took a drag and blew two plumes of bluish-white smoke out his nose.

"Listen. Is it good? Yeah, it is. Is it making me tingle all over? Well, yeah. But don't start again. Okay. Don't start. They kill you. I'm just lucky."

I looked at Jenny. "Not even cigarettes can kill this guy."

She didn't react. She just said, "Where are you going?"

"I'm going to visit Danny Baker."

33

I got Jose Villareal to tell me Danny's address, then made it to his house in forty minutes. Not terrible for a Friday night. These days the Friday five o'clock traffic lasts until nine, sometimes ten. That's not a joke. But tonight I got a bit of break and cruised relatively unscathed into Hancock Park. We've talked about this neighborhood. It's nice. And I'm noticing now, quiet on a Friday night. Nice dark streets, the houses set back on big lawns.

Danny's house was one of those houses in nice neighborhoods where the whole property sits up on a little hill about four feet from the sidewalk. Just a little hill. You just have to walk up a small little embankment from the sidewalk in front of it, three, four feet, to get *up* to the yard. Not sure why they do that. It makes the whole structure maybe just a touch more grand. It's like the house is wearing heels for a night out on the town.

I sat right in front of his house in the Cobalt. Again, to passersby I was the maid or the employee. Yeah, I was the help in the beat-up Tercel with the blue body and the brown replacement door sitting in front of a Hancock Park mansion. Except I was in a Cobalt. And the Cobalt was in top shape. And I wasn't a maid. I was a P.I. that was about to see just what Danny Baker knew.

Would Danny be home? We'll see. Looking at 9 p.m. on a Friday. Maybe. Real professionals don't go out on Friday night. They chill. Wind down from the week. Then hit it Saturday and even Sunday. So maybe he was home. And why was now the time to see what Danny knew, as opposed to before at the park by the deli? Because now *I* knew more. I had more, so I could use it to push him further. To push him to the limit. If he knew more than Jimmy Yates, I thought now was the time to pull it out of him.

I dialed him up. Ring. Ring. Ring. And then he answered. And he wasn't coy like he didn't have caller ID, didn't know who I was.

"The detective calls."

"Hi, Danny."

"What can I do for you?"

"I want to talk to you some more about Suzanne Neal. I don't think you've been totally forthcoming with me. And I need you to be."

"I'm not sure what you mean."

"Listen, Danny. I will make you tell me the truth. Whether you like it or not."

I was surprised at my tone. Surprised that my heart was beating as hard as it was. But I thought about Jim Douglas, the lessons he'd taught me. I was committed to this one. I was all in. If I threw a punch it would be at the throat.

"Hang on a second," he said. "I need to walk outside. Going to go out on the balcony . . . Hang on . . ."

I thought: Maybe for some privacy from his wife? Can't say I blame him, given the circumstances.

I heard him, fumbling in his house, heading toward the balcony. "Is your wife home?"

"Actually, no. Just going out to have a smoke before we get into this."

Through his phone, I heard a door open. But he didn't appear on the front doorstep or the front balcony that I was looking at through the Cobalt's windshield. So I exited the car, walked quickly down the little alley next to his house. Slid in the shadows next to some trees that created a wall between his house and his neighbor's. And now I was in Danny Baker's backyard. Beautiful backyard. Big, lit-up pool. Lots of well-groomed grass, hedges, flowers.

I looked at the back of the house. And there he was up on the balcony, looked to be off the bedroom, holding a smoke in one hand and his cell in the other.

"So," he said. "What do you want to talk about? What didn't I tell you?"

I looked at him up on the balcony, the light from inside the house behind him. He cast a shadow, big and mis-shapen, across the pool next to me. I looked at him stand-ing there, pulling on his smoke. His shirt was untucked, and he was barefoot. Relaxing on a Friday night. His hair was messed up, he wasn't sporting the ready-to-go-to-air

TV personality do. The light from the house put him in silhouette and it caught a curl in his hair that had been flattened out when I'd seen him in person. And then he moved his left hand and the light caught the face of his watch, and a quick little flash, a quick little sparkle, shot off his wrist.

And I knew the figure I was looking at was the figure who had come up behind Suzanne Neal the night she was murdered. Danny had told me he hadn't seen Suzanne in a while. I had suspected that he was lying—now I knew it for sure. Hadn't seen her? Danny had been in her apartment mere hours before she was killed. I'd come over here with the intention of using the new information I had to scare Danny into telling me something I didn't already know. But, without saying anything, I now had something that I didn't have before. And now, right now, Danny was going to tell me what he was doing, what exactly he was doing, at Suzanne's that fateful night.

I stepped out from the shadows and stood in front of the pool. I clicked off my phone and said, "Danny?"

"Jesus Christ!" he shrieked. "Jesus. My god, you scared me. What are you doing?"

"Come down here Danny. Let's talk."

"I'm calling the police. You're trespassing."

"Please do. I know the police well. I'm sure they'd love to know that you were in Suzanne Neal's apartment the night she died. Right before she died."

Danny looked at me. "I'll be down in a second."

And then: We were sitting by his pool at a lovely table under a parasol as if it were a beautiful, sunny afternoon. But it wasn't. It was dark. And it was about to get ugly.

"You were at Suzanne's the night she died. You know how I know that? Because I saw you."

Danny was being very calm. Putting on quite a show. He'd had an initial moment of panic when I'd hit him with the information. But on his way down the stairs and out the door he'd gotten his shit together.

He said, "What are you talking about? I already told you, yes, I knew her. But I hadn't seen her in a couple months. Much less the night she died."

"I saw you. You were on her balcony. You came up behind her and pulled her back into the apartment."

He said, part smart ass, part curious, "You were watching her apartment the night she died?"

"Yes, I was."

"One might ask why *you* were there."

"What happened, Danny? Tell me. You want me to pull you out of that chair and put your head in the pool until you think for sure you're going to die or you're already dead? We can do that if you want."

And I was getting there in my head. I was ready to pull a move like that. I needed some answers. I had to stop guessing about everything.

I had to release the stress.

This—this I knew to be true.

Danny looked at me, scared. He didn't say anything.

I pulled out my camera. And found the picture. The picture of him. I looked at it. Impossible to make out who it was up on that balcony but *I* knew it was him, and once I showed it to him, *he* would know it was him and with a little luck he wouldn't surmise that neither the police nor anybody else could really make out, for sure, who it was in the shot. I turned around my camera and showed him the picture.

"See that, Danny? That's you. With your arms wrapped around a woman who was a few hours away from being dead. Now, you want to talk to me? You want to tell me something."

"Why do you have a picture of that? How could you have known . . . Why were you looking into Suzanne?"

"Danny, did you kill Suzanne Neal?"

"What? What? I'm calling my lawyer."

Time for the Jimmy Yates treatment. Time to see if Danny Baker's vanity would control him.

"Danny, this picture is on the Web within the hour if you don't answer some questions."

He looked at me. Still. Silent. I had him—I thought.

"You knew Suzanne was a Pipe Girl and you used the service, yes?"

"I will never admit to talking to you."

"Yes or no?"

"Yes."

"Do you know what happens to a Pipe Girl if she reveals what she does or who her clients are?"

He didn't answer.

"Answer me, Danny."

He looked at me. A defeated energy overtook him. He said, "I think I do, yes."

"To your knowledge, did Suzanne tell someone she was a Pipe Girl? Did she break Neese's trust?"

"I don't think she did, John. I really don't."

I believed that he didn't know the truth—that Suzanne had slipped up with Jenny Bickford.

"Well if that's true, then Neese wouldn't kill her. But you? You were right there the night she went down. And you know what else I know? There was more between you and Suzanne than sex, Danny. Somebody's heart was involved. Hers, for sure. Yours? Well, probably. And when that's the case, murder becomes a lot more likely."

I stood up. I pulled Danny out of his chair and put him on the ground next to his pool. He looked scared. I wasn't sure that he did it. But I wasn't sure that he *didn't* do it either. I was about to put him in serious pain.

And then: He began to cry.

I hadn't done anything yet. Just scared him. But his tears weren't from physical pain. They were coming from somewhere else. They were coming from his heart. "What are you crying about, Danny?"

Through his tears he said, "Suzanne didn't tell anyone she was a Pipe Girl."

Jenny Bickford was quite possibly right on the money. Suzanne's secret appeared to be contained between the two of them, like it never happened.

"What are you talking about?"

Still on the ground, he sat up and leaned against an enormous clay pot that housed a plant. Rich people seem to have a lot of enormous clay pots.

"I think I really screwed up, John."

Now we were getting somewhere. "What do you mean?"

It started to rain. Lightly. An L.A. rain where it doesn't seem like it's ever really going to start, to fully break through, to dump down. A rain where it takes a while before you even realize you're getting wet.

We both moved back under the parasol, back to the chairs where we'd begun. Once again I was across a table from Danny Baker. But now he was on my show.

He said, "I mean, I made a mistake that I didn't know I was making. Suzanne loved me. And I her. And she was going to leave Neese, stop being a Pipe Girl, to be with me. But when she told Richard, well, he didn't want her to go. Obviously. She made him a lot of money. So he asked her not to make such a quick decision. And he's very persuasive. So Suzanne agreed to stay for a little longer, which I didn't like. I knew that his whole business was about the girls not telling anyone what they did. I just . . . I just didn't know the consequences of talking—at that point. I thought, na-ively, that Richard would just kick them out if he found out that they'd talked. So I told Richard that Suzanne had told someone what she did for a living. Even though she hadn't. I told him she told a friend of mine, a fellow journalist. I just made it up out of thin air. Right on the spot. But it *felt* very real. I said she'd done it accidentally-on-purpose. Over a dinner with too many drinks, she'd let it slip, be-cause she was upset about it. I said not to worry, it was an off-the-record conversation. I thought it was the perfect way to anger Richard because he was so proud of the con-trol he had over these women. I thought it would force his hand. Would get Suzanne fired. And then a few days later she gets shot. And I thought . . . And I thought in a horrible moment of realization *that's how* he ensures silence."

I could tell he was relieved to get it off his chest, to expose to *someone* the turmoil that was in his head.

So Danny Baker was there the night of the killing. But according to him, sitting defeated across from me, he didn't kill Suzanne. Instead he *got* her killed by inadvertently telling Richard Neese something that would trigger an automatic murder. But Danny Baker needed to tell me more. There were still gaps in his story, and, of course, in mine.

"So what were you doing there that night? Was it just a run-of-the-mill night between the two of you?"

"I was reassuring Suzanne that everything was going to be okay. I had told her what I'd done. And she had gone over to Richard's earlier in the night to try and clear up the situation. To try and tell Richard that I had made the whole thing up. That I was the one who had lied. That I had no idea what it really meant. Which, of course, I didn't. So she was scared. She said Richard believed her, but that you never knew with Richard. That she could be in real trouble and not even be aware of it."

Danny, his cheeks wet with tears, managed a laugh. "It's ironic, because it was the exact *wrong* thing for me to say to Richard. You know? I didn't know it, but I said the one thing that I shouldn't have. It's almost like divine intervention or something. Like, I just made up some random thing to try and help my situation, but it was the one thing that would ruin it forever. Like some kind of twisted fate. Do you believe in that stuff, John?"

"Yeah, I do."

His story tracked. I'd seen Suzanne go to Richard's house that night. And come back to her condo to be embraced by a man I now knew to be Danny Baker.

I looked at him. The handsome TV anchor shattered by shame. And now he was in a double jam, because, sure, no married public figure wants to be associated with a prostitution ring, but Danny Baker had a bigger problem on his hands. Was he a marked man? Was Richard Neese after him now too?

"Why would you leave Suzanne's house that night, Danny? Why would you leave if there was even a chance she was in danger?"

"She told me to. She was going to leave right after me. She said she knew where she could hide. Until she was sure Richard wasn't going to do anything crazy."

"Has Richard Neese ever threatened you?"

"He wasn't happy to see me the night I went over there."

"What do you mean?"

"Well, at first I just tried to persuade Richard to let Suzanne go. I even offered to pay him. Pay him a lot of money. And then when it wasn't working, I told him the lie—that Suzanne had told people what she did. Richard's tone instantly shifted. He almost calmed down. He very slowly and directly asked me what I was talking about. Once I finished telling him the story, he asked me if she had told others. I very cavalierly said I didn't know, I doubt it. Then, he quickly made me leave. And he said, very directly and calmly: Keep this to yourself, Danny. And he looked at me in a way. In a way that I definitely found frightening. And that's why I felt I had to tell Suzanne what I'd done."

"Danny, have you said anything about this to anyone?"

"Not until now. And it feels . . . good."

"Go back inside and don't say anything to anyone unless you feel your life is in danger. If you truly think you are in trouble call the cops. If you don't, if you don't, Danny, listen to me, keep your mouth shut."

He looked at me, confused, even desperate. I had no sympathy for him. I had disgust for him.

"For how long? How long until something's going to happen?"

"The weekend. This will be over before the weekend is."

He nodded and said, "Okay."

I walked back around his house, across the lawn, down the little hill, and got into the Cobalt. I cranked her up and drove back to my office.

34

So I thought: First, does it track? And then: Is it real—even if it does track? Hmm. Let's see. Maybe Neese flew off the handle. Maybe after Danny Baker talked to him he thought: At this point it doesn't matter if Suzanne talked, I'm not going to risk it. Yeah—maybe he was like Sam Spade at the end of *The Maltese Falcon*. Thinking: I don't know if what you're telling me is true or not, but I'm not going to be a sucker either way. So I have to assume the worst.

Or maybe Danny's performance triggered another kind of rage within Neese. And he was mad, whether or not she'd squealed, that Suzanne had fallen for a client. So the whole thing, in his eyes, was a big mess, a big mess that he needed to get rid of.

I didn't think Danny Baker had killed her. I didn't feel it. Truth is, I was closer than ever to putting the killing on Neese, for sure. Problem was, I still needed the proverbial smoking gun or there would always be at least a sliver of speculation.

And that's when I thought about it: *Yes, the gun.*

The gun.

The gun from my hike that day. The gun that Crowbar Guy and White Streak had held in my face. In that moment they had had a thought, a thought that maybe prevented them from killing me. Crowbar Guy had given White Streak a look. A look that I think said: Don't do it. Not now. And, possibly, yes, possibly, not with *that* gun.

Here's the thing. A lot of criminals, hit men, thugs aren't that smart. They're not exactly t-crossers, i-dotters. You know what I'm saying? So sitting there back at my office, back at my desk, looking out the slider into darkness, it occurred to me that maybe those two guys weren't sent to scare me, they were in fact sent to kill me. But they couldn't kill me because the gun they had was the same gun they, or Neese, had used to kill Suzanne.

And *that's* why they didn't pull the trigger that day. Shit, it was silenced by the towel and ready to go. They weren't screwing around. But just before trigger time they backed off.

See—it's very possible that Neese had them kill Suzanne, or he did it himself, then told them to get rid of the gun. But because they were lazy, or stupid, or both, they didn't do it. And then they got their next assignment, to kill me. But when it came time to do it they realized: We can't use this gun. The bullet will match the bullet that killed

Suzanne. And we don't know what this guy Darvelle has told the cops. Once the bullets match, they'll go straight to Neese and we'll all go to prison.

So instead of whacking me, he just whacks me on the head, and I don't die.

I called Marlon the Marlin.

"Hey, it's John Darvelle."

"I know who it is, pal. I've got caller ID. Just because I'm a seafaring gentleman doesn't mean I'm totally fucking out of it."

"Who is that?" I heard his wife scream.

"It's John Darvelle. Probably wants another favor."

Then to me, "You do want another favor, right, John?"

"Yeah, Marlon, I do."

"Hey, what did you ever find out about that thing we were talking about?"

These guys refer to everything as "things."

"I'll tell you later. But, for now, I need some help."

I described the two guys who had kicked the shit out of me and held me at gunpoint. And then I told Marlon I needed to know where the one with the white streak in his hair, the one who held the gun, hung out. Where I could find him.

"I need some time, kid. Could be an hour, could be a day. I'll get back to you."

"Thanks, Marlon. I'll be with my phone."

Turns out it was an hour. Because fifty-seven minutes later, he called me back.

"John, here's what I got."

"Great, what?"

"You ever heard of a place called Jumbo's Clown Room?"

I couldn't help but laugh. "Yeah, sure."

"I understand the gentleman with the white streak goes there quite a bit, lives in the neighborhood. His name by the way is Donny Greer."

"Marlon, you're the best. Thank you."

"So what is it, Jumbo's Clown Room? Sounds kind of twisted."

"It's a gentlemen's club of sorts."

"Oh yeah? Would I like it? Hot women?"

"I'm not exactly sure I'd describe it that way. Women, yes. Hot? Well, I guess that depends on your taste. I'll take you there sometime. But right now, I've got to go. Thank you again."

"You bet, kid. Just promise to tell me the whole story when you have it."

These guys always want the story. I can't blame them.

"Aye aye, Captain."

I hung up.

I drove to Hollywood. To Jumbo's Clown Room. Like I told Marlon, it's a gentlemen's club, a strip bar. Sort of. It's really just a dive bar deep in Hollywood where the owners decided, hey, let's bring a topless dancer out every now and then.

This isn't a high-level, high-dollar, Vegas-type operation. We're not talking a bunch of beautiful, manicured porn star–style women parading in and out, dancing around, molesting a golden pole in the middle of a big, lit-up stage. No. At Jumbo's there's a small stage, or really a flat, wide, wooden box raised about a foot, that sits opposite the little bar. And every so often, to the thrilling sounds of Foghat, Kiss, or Molly Hatchet a dancer comes out, rips her top off, and "dances." Sometimes the dancers are attractive in a rough-around-the-edges kind of way. And sometimes, well, they aren't.

Scars, botched tattoos, active pregnancies, and rashes absolutely do not get you banned from performing. On some nights, you'd think they were a requirement.

But don't get me wrong, it's a great place.

A random, wild, anything-goes spot. A fun, unexpected joint to sit and have a cocktail or seven in should you ever find yourself deep in Hollywood. I go there not infrequently. I like to take friends from out of town there especially. Every one of them, every last one of them, says to me afterward: We're going back there, right? I was in there once, by myself, having a beer, enjoying a considerably overweight dancer whose arm was in a sling, and the guy next to me was shirtless, wearing a purple wig and karate pants and licking his glass rather than drinking out of it. And no one gave him, or her for that matter, so much as a bemused glance. Including me.

That's a true story.

I parked on Hollywood Boulevard. I put a black trucker hat on and pulled it low. I walked in. It was late. And crowded. And a bartender I knew, Terry Forte, was working. Good. I tucked myself in at a table toward the back wall, away from the bar and the "stage." Terry didn't see me. Nobody did. I had a view of the whole place. I sat there, had a Bud and a shot, looked around for White Streak. No sign.

I watched a couple dancers. Marveled at a woman gyrating around to Deep Purple. Attractive but with a long scar on her leg. Looked like a knife or ax wound.

And then, Mr. White Streak walked in.

Marlon the Marlin. The guy is money in the bank.

White Streak snagged a seat at the end of the bar near the entrance. Almost as far away from me as possible.

I flagged my waitress.

"Yeah, sweetie?"

"Hey, babe. I'm friends with Terry, the bartender. I need to talk to him back by the bathrooms. Could you send him my way?"

I slipped her a twenty. "My name is John Darvelle."

She smiled and headed toward the bar. I slipped off my stool and walked over to the bathrooms in the back corner.

Forty-five seconds later Terry Forte came marching down toward me, big smile on his face. Terry is six-three, bald, and about forty pounds overweight. He has an unusual and intimidating physical presence. But being large and reasonably menacing and working the bar at a legendary L.A. establishment isn't what he's mainly known for. What he's mainly known for is his beard. A while back, Terry grew a long, ZZ Top–style beard. It came down past his chest, past his stomach, right to his belt. And then, and *then* he shaved all of it off except for one hair. So he has one three-foot-long hair that comes out of his chin. It blows in the breeze caused by his movement, it dances in the air in front of him when he walks, looking almost like a magic trick. Looking almost like it's *alive*. Terry protects it with his life so it doesn't accidentally get snagged on something and break off. And if you try to investigate it too closely or touch it he will fend you off with force. I've seen him level a guy with a fist to the center of the chest simply for moving in for too close of a look.

I would definitely not want to be around if someone accidentally politely touched it and ended up with it in his hand looking hopelessly at a furious, homicidal Terry Forte.

"Hey, Terry."

"Darvelle, how're you doing, buddy?"

"Great, we'll catch up another time."

He nodded and his face twisted into an expression of business.

"There's a guy at the end of your bar. He has a white streak in his hair, like a birthmark."

"Yeah, I've seen him a bunch. He comes in."

"Yeah, listen. I need him to be hammered tonight. Blotto."

"Shouldn't be a problem."

I gave Terry a hundred-dollar bill and said, "I'll explain later. Gotta go."

"You got it, John."

I walked back into the main room. White Streak was still at the bar. Despite there being a dancer on stage, he was facing forward, staring straight into the mirror behind the bar, like people do. Drinking and staring. It's amazing how popular that is.

It was pretty crowded. I thought I could get out of there reasonably easily without him seeing me. I yanked the hat down even lower, and hugged the backside of the crowd around the bar. White Streak kept his position. It looked good for me.

And then it didn't.

It looked like White Streak was paying his bill, was going to get out of there. Yeah, he threw down some money, shifted in his seat, started to get up. If he turned around now, right now, he'd make me. I was stuck right behind him basically. With the stage blocking me on the left, and people in front and back of me.

Fuck. Don't turn around, White Streak. Don't turn around.

Terry appeared, magically, right in front of him, holding a shot of whiskey and wearing a big smile. White Streak took it, threw it back.

Terry stuck out his hand for White Streak to shake. White Streak took the bait. Big handshake for Terry.

He sat back down.

And I got out of there.

35

I sat in the Cobalt on Hollywood Boulevard across from, and with an eye on, the Clown Room. I looked around, taking in the happenings of east Hollywood Boulevard. It's not something most people ever do. Just sit in a bleak, but interesting and real, section of a town and just *watch*.

I do it a lot.

There was a little strip mall across from Jumbo's that had some junk stores and a Thai massage place called Nuch. Pronounced "nuke." I've been. It's good. And aboveboard, legit. No happy endings. So it's not perfect. But it's good.

And the people. Rough-looking characters just appearing from the side streets walking around. Not exactly homeless, but close, I think. Where did they come from? Where were they before they appeared out of nowhere slowly walking down the street? And where were they going?

I looked at the cars lining the street with mine. A real mix. Just like the crowd at Jumbo's. A jalopy. Then a Porsche. Then a Hummer.

A Hummer. Did those still even exist? Who would buy one of those? Who would want one of those? I actually knew a P.I. once who had one. One of those guys with a fancy car to complete the P.I. image. We talked about these guys. It makes absolutely no sense.

And then, two and a half hours later, White Streak stumbled out.

Stumbled. Literally stumbled.

He looked like a drunk guy in a movie where you say: No way is that guy *that* drunk. People can't get *that* drunk.

But White Streak was that drunk.

It was like he'd been drugged. Or hit in the head with a crowbar like he and his buddy had done to me. He was zigzagging down the sidewalk.

Good job, Terry. Well done. You one-hair-beard-having badass.

White Streak got in his car. This could be ugly. This could really not work out. This was a risk. Not just because my plan could end quickly and in a very messy fashion. But because someone else could get hurt. Or killed. Yeah, I know, obvious.

He cranked up his Tahoe and pulled out onto Hollywood Boulevard. People drive drunk in L.A. a lot. But not usually *this* drunk. White Streak was weaving something fierce. It was as if his truck was the drunk one now. I tailed him, right on him; he wouldn't notice, no way.

He didn't have far to go. About a mile west of the Clown Room. A building three blocks in from the Formosa Café to the south, three blocks in from a nicer stretch of Hollywood Boulevard. We're not talking an Arthur Vonz– or Richard Neese–level neighborhood, but a nice enough little area filled with decent, sometimes charming apartment buildings and houses. White Streak lived in a Spanish-style eight-plex with vines crawling up the white exterior. He somehow got the Tahoe into a garage that was attached to the building.

He stomped up a set of stairs in the front of the building and barreled into his apartment. This guy was hammered, shit-faced, trounced. He vanished into the apartment and slammed—slammed—the door shut.

I waited twenty minutes and then walked up to his door. I listened, carefully. No movement, nothing. I knocked very lightly. Again, nothing. He was passed out, had to be. The door was unlocked. I turned the knob and slowly, quietly, carefully walked in. He'd left a light on in the living room, which poured in a bit to the bedroom and the kitchen, but only a bit. I could just barely see the things that make a bedroom and the things that make a kitchen sitting beneath the darkness.

I pulled my gun, then moved quickly into the darkened kitchen. Then, from there, I could look more carefully at the expanse of the apartment. One bedroom. Living room. Kitchen with an alcove for a dining table. My eyes adjusting, I could now make out the shape of his legs on his bed. The rest of him was cut off by the bedroom door, by the angle from where I looked. He looked to be totally dressed. His legs weren't moving. They were totally, completely still. Dead. Yes, this man was properly tanked. I focused back on the main room. The apartment was quite nice. Well kept up, some nice, if generic, artwork on the wall. Amazing. This is how a hit man lives. He spends his days with another sub-mental hitting people in the side of the head and neck with a crowbar and then spends his evenings making sure that his lovely painting of a blue jay is sitting at just the right height above his charming sofa.

I checked the kitchen first. The drawers, under the sink, the cabinets. Nothing. I moved into the main room. Doubtful it would be here. I looked through all the drawers. In the sofa. Under the sofa. On top of some tall shelves. Nada. I checked the bathroom. Under the sink, the cabinets, tucked behind the toilet like in *The Godfather*. You'd be surprised. People copy that stuff.

But still, nothing.

Then I went in the bedroom. I was stepping very, very lightly. To my adjusted eyes, the bedroom had a dark gray glow. I could see White Streak's total form on the bed now. He was on his back lightly snoring and, other than his chest moving, he was still. Paralyzed. Cemented onto his bed. I looked in his closets. Drawers. Under his bed. This man was a bit of a minimalist, thankfully, but even without a lot of clutter I still couldn't find a hidden gun.

Shit, nothing.

The last place in the bedroom I looked was the bedside table, right next to White Streak's head. I slowly pulled the drawer open.

And: Nothing.

It was empty save for a nice-looking gold watch. I shut the drawer and looked over at the drunken man on the bed.

And then: He popped up, sat almost straight up, and looked directly at me.

I pointed my gun right at his face, right between his eyes.

We were both frozen. Him: glazed-looking, staring at the gun. Me: heart pounding, looking at a man with the barrel of a gun three inches away from his face.

I did not know where this was going to go.

And then: He went right back down, just like he had popped up. The man was still asleep. He'd never woken up. He'd just jerked up and opened his eyes.

Within seconds, White Streak began snoring again. My heart, currently in my throat, began to make its way back to where it belonged. And I moved out of the bedroom.

Now, back in the dark kitchen, I stood there.

And then as if it were the way I'd planned it all along, I went over and opened the oven. Inside the oven were two pots, one big, one small. White Streak stored them there when the oven was off. I myself had used this system. I grabbed the big pot, opened it, and saw a gun sitting right there. The deadly object fitting in the pot just right. Bingo.

It's not that easy to get rid of a gun. It's not. But beyond that, the human condition often gets in the way. People get an assignment and they sit on it. That's what White Streak had done. He'd gotten an assignment and he'd sat on it.

I put on a leather glove, got a Ziploc bag out of my pocket. I housed the gun, shut the bag, replaced the pot, shut the oven, and walked out the front door.

36

I called the LAPD—Detective Mike Ott. He of the perfect head of hair and the incredibly dry skin. It was late. He might not be on duty tonight. He might be home asleep in bed. Or maybe he'd just answer. Like he did.

"Ott," he said.

That's probably why he became a cop, because he knew it would be cool to answer his phone like that: Ott.

"Ott, it's John Darvelle, remember me?"

"Unfortunately. What do you want?"

"I think I have something that will interest you."

"What is it?"

"You going in tomorrow?"

"Yes, Darvelle, what is it?"

"I'll meet you at the station at eight a.m."

"Darvelle, it's four a.m., what is it?"

"I'll see you in four hours at the station."

I hung up, drove to Mar Vista, and went to bed. Three hours later I woke up, exhausted.

I showered, got dressed, got in the Cobalt, and headed downtown. Depressing, stifling, move-out-of-the city traffic. I would normally never travel at this hour. This was an exception. This was important.

I made one quick stop at a drugstore, then got back on the road, back in the mess. Finally, finally I made it to the LAPD station downtown. I was on time. Right on time. In the elevator, then on the detectives' floor, then in front of Detective Mike Ott's desk.

"All right, Darvelle, what do you got?"

"I have something I think will really help you."

"WHAT IS IT?"

Out of my bag I produced the item I had purchased at the drugstore: a massive bottle of Lubriderm skin lotion.

"This is really good lotion for your skin. It can really help with some of that dryness. Sure, this one massive jug isn't enough for you, but it's a start. If you buy seventeen or eighteen more bottles this size you might have a nice base."

He narrowed his eyes at me. I was sure he was going to come at me. Another cop I knew, a large black man named Anthony Demarus, walked over and began to rub Mike Ott's shoulders. "You want me to punch him for you, Ott? I've always wanted to. I mean *always*. For years. Literally years. As my superior please just tell me to do it."

Ott didn't answer him.

I said, "Hey, Anthony. How're you doing?"

"I'm doing all right, Darvelle. I'm doing all right."

We shook hands and he split.

Ott looked at me. "I know you didn't come all the way down here just to do your little lotion gag. Actually, you might have. But quit fucking around. What do you got, Darvelle?"

I told him the things I'd discovered. The PG symbol, everything about Neese, Jimmy Yates, Danny Baker, Jenny Bickford, the other dead girl Allison Tarber. And, of course, the gun.

I pulled it out of the same bag I'd gotten the lotion out of and put it on his desk.

It sat there still sheathed in a bag of its own. The Ziploc I'd stuck it in.

I said, "That's the gun that Neese's boys held in my face. If that matches with the bullet that killed Suzanne Neal I think we're in business and I think we can put Neese in jail for murder."

I told him how I obtained the gun. Entering White Streak's pad with probable cause, seeing as prior to that point that very same gun had been a couple centimeters away from my face, a couple centimeters away from turning my head into a rather large bowl of linguini marinara. Yes, I might have to switch some of the timing around to make it play in court, but I was comfortable with that.

Ott sat there, not saying anything for probably a full minute. I wasn't sure what he was thinking about; his countenance gave me nothing. Then he looked at me with his cracked, dry skin and said, "Yeah. Let's look into that gun."

I said, dead serious. "I want to be there when you grab Neese. You owe me that."

He nodded. "Yeah."

I left and went back home. I tried to take a nap but couldn't sleep. Three hours later my phone rang. The gun matched the bullet. The gun was the gun that killed Suzanne Neal. Ott told me the plan. Grab Neese the next morning, very early. Provided Ott and his boys determined he was in fact home. The morning was a good time to do this stuff because it was often a surprise, and it was just a less violent time of day. People didn't have time to let the day get on, let their anger rise up. Ott told me he'd call me tonight, at some point, to let me know if it was a go. If so, I'd meet Ott and two other cars at a determined location and then drive to a waiting spot outside Neese's house at 5 a.m. tomorrow. I said fine.

At 9 p.m. that night Ott called me. He said Neese had come home and it didn't appear that he was leaving.

It was on.

"See you very early tomorrow, Darvelle. Don't be late."

I said, "I'm never late."

And I hung up.

Now before I tell you what happened outside Neese's house the next morning, I have to tell you what happened that night. It won't take too long. And you might be surprised. I know I was.

I was antsy, restless, waiting around for the thing that mattered the next morning. So I hopped in the Cobalt and headed out to a bar. I didn't know where I was going, I was just driving semi-frantically, to somewhere, somewhere that I could enjoy an adult beverage instead of pacing around my house, looking at my beautiful Ping-Pong table.

I went to Venice—to Hama Sushi. Not too fancy, not too trendy, just a local spot right on the Venice Circle. Half of the restaurant, the actual sushi bar, was inside, the other half, the bar bar, was outside underneath a vaulted tent. So you were still technically inside, but the outside portion had a patio feel. And was just a little cooler temperature-wise than the inside, the beach breezes sneaking in through the tent.

I hit the outside bar and ordered a Bud Light. See what I'm saying? Yeah, they have Kirin and Sapporo and other Japanese beers, which I actually enjoy when eating sushi, but they also have Bud Light so a guy can properly chill out.

Anyway, I got a Bud Light and I poured it into the small, cold glass they provided me with. That's another thing establishments that get it do. They provide you with a small, cold glass to drink your beer from. Not a large, heavy, warm glass right out of the dishwasher. A small, cold one. Try it. Very, very good.

So, I poured the beer into the glass and took a nice pull. Man, it was good, really, really hitting the spot. Instantly calming me down a bit.

And then, I was just sitting there doing the sit-at-a bar-and-stare-straight-forward thing, when two hands came from behind my head and covered my eyes.

"Guess who?" I heard a voice, an incredible voice, say.

37

I had very little clue who was standing behind me covering my eyes. I knew it was a woman and I knew her hands were cool, but not cold, and that the touch of them was what I needed. She was playing the classic guess-who game but the energy I felt from her touch was affectionate.

"Hmm," I said. "Can I have a hint?"

"Nope."

I grabbed her wrists and pulled them off of my eyes. I then twisted out of my seat, letting go of her hands on the way to standing. I stood now in front of her, no longer physically connected to her, but wishing I was.

It was the nurse who took care of me the night I'd stumbled into the hospital. The woman I'd asked to play Ping-Pong, the Mexican Angel. Nancy. Nancy Alvarez.

"Well, hello," I said.

"Your cuts look a little better."

"Thank you."

"How'd you get them again?"

I honestly couldn't remember. "Can I hold your hands again?"

She smiled and gestured to a woman standing with her, "John, this is my friend Stacy."

Blond, attractive. But nothing like Nancy. Nancy was a vision.

"Hello," I said.

She smiled. Nodded.

Nancy said, "Well, we're out of here."

I said, "Nancy, would you like to stay for a bit and have a drink?"

Nancy said, "You're lucky. Stacy drove."

And then she looked at Stacy and said, "You cool with that?"

Stacy looked at me, then at Nancy. "Sure, Nance, he looks okay."

And then Stacy gave me a friendly wink and disappeared out the door. And Nancy sat down next to me.

We talked. Nancy told me about her job, her life. And I told her about my job, my life. As much as I felt I could share anyway. And then she asked me a question I didn't see coming.

She said, "Why'd you get divorced?"

I looked at her. She was one of those people you trusted after two seconds. She was looking right into my eyes. Jesus. Into my soul. But without judgment. No, it was something else. Compassion? No, it wasn't that either. It was interest. Real interest in another person.

"She cheated on me."

She held me with her eyes and said, "That's happened to me before." And then: "Why?"

"Why?"

"Yeah," she said. "Why?"

"It's a long story."

"How long? I bet it's not that long. What, you work all the time getting obsessed with your cases and banging up your head falling down supposed cliffs so she goes and meets a guy at work or something that's willing to sit and listen to her talk about her marital problems and then one thing leads to another?"

I laughed. "Not exactly. All right, I'll make it quick. Or sort of quick. We met at a party. And we hit it off right away. We spent every day for the next couple weeks together. And then we made a pretty interesting decision. We decided that marriage in many ways is just luck of the draw. We both had some friends in good marriages and some friends in bad marriages, and there was really no rhyme or reason to any of it. We thought: Yeah, you can overthink it and move in together and meet each other's families and go through the completely unproven steps to try and make *sure*, or you can just do it. We just did it. Four weeks after we met we went to Vegas, got married, had a crazy couple days, then came back here and moved in together."

Nancy, still looking at me, scooted her chair closer to mine. "And then what happened?"

I took a breath. "Well, then after a few months, it began to feel a little strange. Like . . ."

"What the hell have we done?"

I laughed. "Yeah. Like what the hell have we done. Which may or may not be what everyone feels like regardless of the circumstances. I have no idea. I just know that's how we felt. Now, let me tell you, there *was* still some magic between us. There was still something *there*. But it was off. It was strange. Like we were two strangers living in a house. And it definitely felt at times like we had made a serious, serious mistake. And then she went to a wedding. Without me. I was on a case. I didn't, *wouldn't*, leave in the middle of it. And, well, she got drunk and slept with an old college boyfriend."

And again, without missing a beat, Nancy said, "Then what happened?"

"She came home from the wedding. And when she walked in the door, I happened to be home. And I looked at her. And she was wearing it all over her face. And I said, 'What happened?' And she told me."

"And what did you say?"

"Nothing. I just listened. Because she had more to say than just that. She said that, ironically, the whole thing had made her sure that *I* was the one for her. She said sleeping with this other dude made our whole life suddenly make total sense. And she said she loved me."

"Did you believe her?"

"Yeah, I did."

"And did you still love her?"

"Yeah, I did."

"So what did you say when you finally said something?"

"I said I'm filing for divorce tomorrow, but you need to get out even quicker than that. You need to get out tonight."

Nancy laughed. "Tell me why you did that. I think you did the right thing, but tell me why, *exactly why*, you did that. You said yourself your situation was weird. And you still loved her. So why not give her a second chance?"

I looked at Nancy. She was beautiful. And I said, "Because I would have never been able to live with myself."

She nodded and thought for a long time. "You know what I think?"

"What?" I said.

"I think when you did that you put the right kind of energy into the universe."

I nodded. I like it when people talk about the universe. I sometimes talk about the universe.

She then said, "You know what else I think?"

"What?"

"I think we should get some sake."

I laughed. "I think you're right."

Nancy ordered a large hot sake and we drank it down fast. We got off the subject of my divorce and we got onto a much better subject—the subject of us having a good time. Nancy ordered a large Sapporo and poured it into two glasses. She then ordered another large sake, poured out two shots of it into small porcelain cups, then dropped one cup in each beer. The little porcelain cups of sake sank to the bottom of the beers, the sake somehow still sitting in the cups even though the cups themselves were in even bigger cups of beer. Ah, the sake bomb, a thing of magic.

"Chug that," Nancy said.

Was I worried about being hungover early the next morning at Neese's? Well, yeah. But, listen, man, you got to pick your spots in life. And this was one of them.

I threw back the bomb, the beer going down first, then the little cup of sake going down last.

It was one of the best things I'd ever tasted and it gave me an instant, slightly hallucinatory buzz.

I said, "Hey, want to go play some Ping-Pong?"

"Do you want to lose?"

"Babe. Babe. Babe," I said. "I rarely, very rarely, lose at Ping-Pong."

And then we were at my house. Hitting some balls. I put on some Pavement, *Terror Twilight*. A beautiful record.

"What is this crap?" she said.

I laughed as hard as I'd laughed in a long time.

"Give it a chance, you'll like it."

We kept hitting Ping-Pong balls. Nancy was pretty okay. She could hit it back. She was more attitude than anything. Which I loved. We played a couple games. I'd keep it close, then take her in the end. After I'd win, she'd narrow her eyes at me and say, "Let's play again."

"We can play all night, you're never going to beat me."

"What if I come over and hit you with this paddle right on both of your cuts and then when the blood is all in your eyes, I'll make you play me. And beat you."

Man, I thought. I really might be in love.

I said, "Unfortunately for you I'd still win."

We went upstairs into my bedroom. The light from the sky came in through the windows and the glass sliding doors. It gave the room a dim glow. Nancy was more beautiful than I'd realized. And then: Our clothes were on the floor, and we were on the bed. I looked at her face, at her intense but soft eyes. At the totality of her beautiful, curvy body.

And we crashed into each other.

Ladies and gentleman, this is what I needed. I hadn't let myself realize the stress and the pressure I was feeling. And now, a release. A release that let it all go. It was a total connection. To her, but also to a feeling, a feeling that came from somewhere else, the heavens, the cosmos.

And then we lay there in each other's arms. And that's when she did something that strengthened even more my belief in the universe. She did something that would help me later in this very story.

She began to trace along my body with the nail of her index finger. She put her finger right in the center of my stomach and said, "If you get shot here the bullet will go all the way through you and out the back of you."

Yes, she was an E.R. nurse. She'd seen it.

And then she traced upward and her fingernail stopped just below my ribs, on my solar plexus. "And if you get shot here the bullet will also rip right through you and explode out your back."

And then she moved her fingernail up to my chest and stopped it right on my heart. "But if you get shot here, right in the heart, the bullet will sometimes stay there. Because the heart is strong. Very, very strong. And it can grab something. Even something as powerful as a bullet. And hold it."

I looked at her. At her beautiful face. At her beautiful skin pressed up against mine. At her fingernail still pressing on my heart.

She said, "I know a P.I. isn't all that you are. You are more than that, I can tell. But you are a P.I.-type. A loner."

I didn't say anything.

"I'm not asking you to fall in love with me. But don't ever forget me."

I thought: That would be impossible.

38

The next morning, at 5 a.m. sharp, there were three cars outside of Richard Neese's house. Down the street a bit but with a line on his heinous Pipe Girl gate. Ott and his partner, Wall, were in an unmarked. Two other cops named Shant and Barker were behind them in another unmarked. And I was in my Mountain Gray Cobalt. Third in line.

The reality was Neese would almost certainly go peacefully. He'd play it cool. He'd let Ott cuff him and take him downtown and he'd have a wry smile plastered on his face the whole time. He wouldn't say a word. He'd just roll along until he got the chance to call his lawyer. That was everybody's best guess anyway. But I wanted to be there when Ott threw out some of the stuff we knew to be true, because that's what would sting Neese, even if he didn't show it. The Pipe Girl story. The gun that killed Suzanne Neal. The fact that the gun was in White Streak's possession and that I'd personally seen the same gun right in my face.

And that right now, right across town, there was another crew picking up White Streak. See, once downtown, Neese would know there'd be another guy in another room getting asked the same questions. And that it was highly doubtful their stories would be the same.

Because once they grabbed White Streak and confronted him with the evidence he'd be in a very tough spot. It would look like *he* pulled the trigger, he killed Suzanne, underneath Neese's command. Which may have been true—that may very well be what happened. But what if Neese had done it himself and just had White Streak get rid of the evidence—which is what I thought.

If that were the case, then White Streak, faced with taking the blame for the whole crime, would have to turn on Neese and tell us what really happened.

And I thought he would. These guys always did. And you had to think a professional criminal like Neese, sitting in the next room over, would make that connection in his head very quickly.

Friends, Richard Neese, as I saw it, was in a serious jam.

And I wanted to see, right up close, the pain doing a dance across his eyes when it all started to come together in his terrible blond-covered head.

It started to rain again. Another light, misty L.A. rain. I moved the focus of my eyes to my windshield. The light little droplets waving around on their way down and landing softly. I watched them float down and hit the glass, hundreds, thousands, millions of them. And then it got a little more serious. It began to break through like it hadn't at Danny Baker's. Drops, not big ones, but real drops colliding with the slanted glass of the Cobalt. Real rain.

I looked at the scene now through the glass. Neese's big gate, the section of the house I could see behind it. And the cars lined up in front of me ready to go in and stick it to Neese. The sky was a purplish blue-gray and the rain gave the scene drama. I looked at everything before me. And, even more so than if it were a bright, sparkling, sunny morning, it was beautiful. The heavy sky. And the rain. The rain coming down. And the anticipation of what was about to happen. I took it in. I took in the scene.

Ott gave me the signal. He'd made contact with Neese and we were headed in. The big gate I'd stared at so much lately opened up. Ott's car drove in. Shant and Barker followed. I cranked up the Cobalt, and just as I too was going to turn into Neese's mountain pad, I instead went straight toward Mulholland.

I called Ott. "Something came up. I've got to go."

"Now?"

"Yeah, now."

I clicked off. Then I swung the Cobalt right on Mulholland and went down the long, winding road, down into the San Fernando Valley, on my way to the Van Nuys airport.

39

Van Nuys airport was a ways away, down into the valley then northwest for a half hour or so. It was early, yeah, but in L.A. it's almost impossible to beat the traffic. But at this hour I *sort of* beat it and made it there in good time. Van Nuys airport was where most of the news helicopters in the city operated out of. Government planes and private planes, for people and businesses, used its two runways as well. I'd never visited it before, but I'd driven by it a million times. I pulled in, found a spot, parked, went inside for twenty-one minutes, then exited and got back in my Cobalt.

Then I went back over the hill, crossing over Mulholland on a different road than I'd taken down, but still not far from where Ott was tersely putting Richard Neese into the back of his unmarked, telling him with that blank cop look that they were just going to go down to the station house for a little questioning.

I headed down the other side of the hill into Beverly Hills.

The house I was headed to had a big gate, like all the houses I'd been to lately seemed to have. But this gate was open, wide open, when I got there. So I drove on in, parked, got out of my car, and headed up to the front door. I was about to knock when the door swung open. It was still pretty early, just 7 a.m. or so. But the woman of the house stood right before me dressed for yoga, ready to head out.

Gina Vonz looked chic and sexy, tights over her legs, a yoga mat under her arm, a Gucci pocketbook over her shoulder, expensive shades hiding her eyes despite the rain.

"The detective—at such an early hour."

"Hi, Gina. Off to do a little morning yoga?"

"You *are* good," she said. "Arthur's in his writing studio. Go on back."

And then she sashayed by me with a smile. She had magic about her. She was sexy, and she knew it. Vonz was right. She could have done more movies. I watched her walk toward her silver Mercedes coupe. She tossed her mat in the back, got in, and disappeared down the driveway, out the open gate.

I walked in the house, shut the door behind me. I walked through all the rooms I'd walked through before. The house felt less welcoming—I felt like a stranger. Maybe the house was just waking up, even though its inhabitants seemed to already be going about their days. No sign of Mountcastle. I wondered where that man-child was.

I went back through the outside patio and reached Vonz's office. I paused for just a second. And then, without knocking, opened the door and went in.

And there was Vonz. Sitting just like he had been the first day I'd met him. Although this time he appeared more at work than usual. He seemed so at ease that first time, posing almost, a few pieces of paper and a pen in front of him, but in an almost unnatural way. This time, he seemed *in it*. Papers askew, pencil in his hand, face twisted into a frown of concentration.

But the concentration was broken quickly after I entered and he gave me that Cheshire smile and said, "John. What a pleasant surprise."

"Mind if I sit down," I said, as I sat down.

He pulled his reading glasses off. "Not at all. What's happening? Evidently something important."

"Why would you say that?"

"You usually call before you come. And you have an urgency about you."

"I always have an urgency about me. You should know that. I'm an impatient bastard. Sometimes to a fault. But I did discover something. And I would say you are right— it's important."

He leaned forward. "Okay. Let's hear it."

"Well, I've kept you up to speed on things as I've discovered them."

Vonz nodded.

"But it's like an hourglass. At the end of the story information starts pouring though at a much faster rate."

I told him everything—with recaps when necessary. Full disclosure on Neese and the Pipe Girls. What happened if you talked. The symbol, as tattoo and as intricate design in a fence. And Allison Tarber. How she connected. How she died. How she might have, scratch that, *did have* a tattoo cut out of her body. That I'd made Danny Baker Talk Show Host as the guy on the balcony the night of the murder. That in that moment I thought Danny might have done it—killed Suzanne. That I was very close to hurting Danny until he confessed everything he knew.

And then I told Vonz that I had discovered Danny had lied and told Neese that Suzanne had talked, without the knowledge that that was a sin she would have to die for. Which then caused me to point the finger back at Neese. And which led me to the gun. The gun that had been in my face at the hand of Neese's henchmen. The smoking gun that matched the bullet that killed Suzanne.

"Jesus," Vonz purred.

"Yeah," I said. "From Jimmy Yates all the way around to Danny Baker being with her right before she was killed, then back to the simplest explanation. The same place I'd been much earlier in the story. The same place I'd been the moment I'd discovered the Pipe Girls and how Neese allegedly controlled them. And then: The gun with a bullet match. Neese and his boys have nowhere to turn."

"So, what happens now?"

"Now? Right now? Richard Neese and White Streak are getting questioned by the LAPD. One of them, or both of them, may have officially been arrested at this point."

"You know what's interesting," Vonz said. "The simplest answer *was* the answer. But you had to go through this complex backstory to get there. You had to go through the other girl, and Danny Baker, and a gun in your face to get there. To get back to your initial suspicion. There's something to that from a storytelling perspective. The person you first suspected based on simple evidence is the one you actually want, but it's not for the simple reason you thought. There's much more to it. Yet, what difference does it make? You're still right. It's like one's gut versus research and methodology. There's some philosophy there worth exploring."

"Yeah, that is interesting, Vonz. Except, it turns out the story's not over. Neese is a bad man and I believe he's responsible for the death of Allison Tarber. But he didn't kill Suzanne Neal. They shouldn't be arresting him for that."

Vonz twisted his face into an almost amused look of confusion. "Now you've got me hooked. Because you just told me that all the evidence you found puts the killing squarely on Neese."

"Yes, but all the evidence I told you isn't all the evidence. There's more—and here it is. Richard Neese didn't kill Suzanne Neal. You did."

Vonz sat perfectly still. He stared at me. It was as if any movement on his part would show feelings or emotions he didn't want me to see.

I said, "It was the cabs that did it. That snapped me off the wrong track and onto the right one. Those cabs honking their horns in New York City. I could hear them through the phone when I talked to you the night I went to deliver your love letter—but wasn't able to do it."

Vonz now spoke, "I'm sorry. The cabs?"

"When I was on the phone with you. The traffic, the cabs. I could hear them clearly and they put me right in New York City. And the image that the sound created kept coming back to me as I pursued the case. When I was driving down the road, or in my office, or even questioning someone, I'd think about those cabs. About a group of cabs at night sitting in New York City traffic honking their horns. I just thought it was one of those images that was so singular, so representative of a place, that my mind was going to it randomly because it was kind of beautiful in a way. Anyone who's ever been to New York City knows that sound. Knows that image. But it wasn't my mind just giving me some pictures for no reason. It was my mind trying to tell me something."

Vonz was about to talk.

"I'm not finished," I said. "See, before I understood what the cabs meant, it was the rain. The rain this morning. I was outside Neese's house with Ott about to go in when it started to rain. At first, it was just L.A. mist. But then, a light rain on my windshield. And I thought: How appropriate. The rain is adding drama to this scene. If this were a movie, a light rain would be just the thing to give the moment some texture, some melancholy, some emotion. And then I thought: If I were directing this scene and it weren't raining I'd insist that we bring in some rain machines to create it. To create the perfect feeling for the moment. And sitting there watching the rain hit my windshield, I realized why my mind had kept going back to those cabs. To those honking cabs in New York City. Those cabs, those sounds, were the perfect effect to make me *sure* you were in New York. To complete the scene. It was a really nice touch. Because without you having to say a word I was one hundred percent sure you were on the street in Manhattan."

Vonz said, "You know, throughout this case, every time I've seen you you've made things clearer for me. But today? You've got me totally confused. What the fuck are you talking about?"

"You never left L.A., Vonz. You tricked me. You made me a player in one of your stories. You took off high in the sky in your gleaming jet for me to see, but you didn't land in New York. You landed in Van Nuys. I went over there this morning and checked. Simple as that. You took off and you landed across town. Who knows how much you spent on that. Who cares? And then, you called me back, not from New York, but from a studio in good old Los Angeles. Put some cab noises in the background and there's no way in hell I'm going suspect you or your house-boy Mountcastle of killing someone *that* night. How could you? You were in New York. I saw you leave. I heard the streets behind you. And you were smart. When I came back to you to tell you what had happened to Suzanne you played to the strongest emotion in all of us. Love. You were in *love* with Suzanne. How could I not look into it? It was someone you loved and I had no reason to suspect you. The noble detective would be sure to feel for you. And look into your story. Then: You kept tabs on me. There was a moment when Neese was actually following me. And I looked in my rearview to see what I thought was a sea of generic cars. Toyotas. VWs. Hondas. But I realize now, not just any Honda. Mountcastle's shitty Honda Civic. The same one he showed up to my office in the first day. So why do that? Why keep tabs on me? It wasn't so Mountcastle could give you the basic details of what I was doing. I was already doing that myself. The reason Mountcastle was following me was because the deeper I got into the story, the more you realized you had to put the murder *officially* on someone else. And in order to do that you had to have every bit of the story. You had to know what, and who, you had to work with. And that was when you made your smartest move.

"The gun. Mountcastle, Mr. Fat But Fleet of Foot, follows me up the mountain that day. Actually, he doesn't follow me up the mountain that day. He follows the two guys that kicked the shit out of me—White Streak and Crowbar. They're not looking for him, they're looking for me. So they don't notice him. And I'm too busy making sure my face doesn't get permanently rearranged to see Mountcastle hiding somewhere. Then they pull a gun on me but it's wrapped in a towel so I can't see it. Mountcastle sees *that* and then you guys get even smarter. It stands to reason that I might assume they didn't shoot me because it was the same gun that shot Suzanne. Turns out that's not the case. Neese hadn't ordered them to kill me. They were just scaring me, with a gun that was even scarier because it was ready to kill, homemade silencer and all. With a gun that has nothing to do with Suzanne. But most importantly with a gun I can't see because it's wrapped in a towel. Which would later help you and Mountcastle out. Of course Neese didn't order the murder of me at that point. When you think about it, why would he? He didn't know what I knew. It would be stupid for them to pop me at that point—my initial conclusion, by the way. But as long as I came back to suspecting they didn't shoot me because the gun would match the gun that killed Suzanne, you were in business. And as long as I went back eventually and looked for the gun—which I did—you were going to be able to put the murder right on Neese. So I show up at Jumbo's that night. You hire a second detective to make sure I'm there tracking White Streak. I see that detective's ridiculous Hummer, but I don't connect it. Not until later. So while the second detective is watching me watch White Streak at Jumbo's, Mountcastle goes and puts the actual gun that shot Suzanne in White Streak's apartment. The second detective doesn't know what's going on—it's just a simple tail. So he could never talk and get you guys in any real trouble. He doesn't know anything. Meanwhile White Streak has no fucking clue the gun that shot Suzanne is even in his apartment, but what difference does it make as long I go over and find it? And when I do find it, I can't tell that it's not the gun that was in my face that day because the gun that was in my face that day was covered up with a towel. So it all fits. The bullet matches. I confirm that these same guys had the same gun in my face. And Neese goes down for the murder. And you get away with everything.

"Problem is, you made a mistake. The cabs. I realized, when it all hit me, that they were just too *loud*. That's why I'd kept going back to them in my mind. Through the phone, they were just too loud. Too hot. Over the top. Too *present*. A rookie mistake for such an esteemed talent. It was the most important thing on your list—to make sure I thought you were in New York. But you overcooked your sound mix, Doc. I know the area you said you were standing in. Outside of Pete's Tavern. There isn't that much traffic there. And yet it sounded like you were in the middle of Times Square on New Year's Eve. You didn't respect your audience, Vonz. You made it too obvious. And as a result, that one little hole in your story was big enough for the truth to fit through. Neese isn't the one who's going to prison for Suzanne's murder. You are."

Vonz looked at me for a long time. He didn't say a word. He was trying to determine if the information I had was provable. He was thinking, sure, I could prove he didn't leave. But could I prove he killed a woman?

I said, "How can I prove it? That's what you're thinking, aren't you, Vonz? Listen. You're a brilliant guy. But you're not a criminal. If they take down Neese for it, sure, you'll get off. But once I tell Ott my story, they're going to recomb Suzanne's apartment, recomb White Streak's place, and they're going to find evidence of you and Mountcastle being there. And no matter how careful you were when you bought that gun, now that we know what to look for, we will put that purchase on you. We will find where you got it. There's no getting out."

He shifted in his seat. I didn't like it. I pulled my gun and put it on him. His eyes lit up. And he sat very still.

"Before we continue this story," I said. "I want you to answer some questions."

I pulled my gun off him and let it rest by my side. "Why did you do this? Why did you go to all this trouble? It can't simply be because you wanted Suzanne dead. There's so many other ways to murder someone. So why do it this way? Why make all these people your toys? Did you need some fresh material for a screenplay? Or are you just crazy?"

Total silence in the room.

I continued. "Answer me this. Were you a client of Suzanne's? Did you know she was a Pipe Girl? Or did you have an actual relationship with her?"

Vonz spoke. "I had no idea she was a pro. I met her on a movie set, just like I said. And I had a brief relationship with her. But everything you told me about her, her secret life, you discovered, John. I knew nothing about the Pipe Girls, Richard Neese, the punishment for talking. I learned about it from you. From you telling me. And from Mountcastle following you and telling me about your moves."

"You realize you just all but confessed to me."

He knew what he was doing. He *wanted* to make that mistake. He had a plan. I looked forward to seeing what it was.

I said, "Did your wife know?"

After a long pause Vonz said, "Nope. Just me and Paul. As for turning around the plane that day, I just got a fake emergency business call as soon as we took off from Santa Monica, then told Gina the only runway we could get was in Van Nuys. It's pretty easy to fool people when they aren't looking."

Okay, so now he had confessed. I didn't feel the need to tell him that.

Vonz looked at me dead in the eye and said, "I want to tell you a story, John."

"Sure. But it better be about why you did this. That's the only story I want to hear."

He nodded and leaned back in his chair.

"I grew up in Brooklyn. And when I was a teenager I discovered the movies. I'd go to the theater in Brooklyn, or I'd go into Manhattan, to Times Square, and watch two, three, sometimes five movies in a row. It was literally a transformative experience for me. The stories, the magic, it was so powerful for me. I couldn't believe that an art form could take me away like that. I would leave the theater so moved, even by movies that, looking back, weren't particularly special. But they were all special to me. I went back every single weekend for years. The sets, the stories, the lights, and the performances would take me to a place of near nirvana. And then, of course, I had to make movies myself. So I set about learning the art of moviemaking. And writing scripts. And understanding character, and story, and story arcs. And then, of course, I moved into shooting, making and editing films of my own. And I loved it—I loved being a part of this world. It was just thrilling to me. To read a great script, to write a great script, to conjure up ideas and twist and turns. And then to create shots and sequences that evoked images, memories, emotions. Once I got pretty good at it, I came to realize that I was doing it all in the name of two things. One, to give myself that feeling I had as a kid in Times Square. And two, to give someone else that feeling. That rush of story. Of an unpredictable yarn told with light and sound and pictures. Like magic."

Vonz paused. And I said, "Answer my question, Vonz. Why did you do this? Why did you kill a young girl?"

He held up a finger and nodded. "How long have I been doing what I set out to do? Thirty years, give or take? Thirty-five? Three and a half decades. Something like that. Well, over the last few years, something happened. The magic died. The scripts I read, the scripts I wrote, even the movies I made . . . I wasn't the kid in Times Square anymore. Everything was dead. If I read a script someone else wrote, I knew what was going to happen before I turned the page. If I wrote a script, the next scene would appear to me without even having to think about it. Not because it was the right scene to put next. Fresh, unexpected, inevitable. But because I had done it so many times that according to the system I and the whole industry had built, the predictable, obvious scene *had to* come next. Because that's the pattern we have established. All movies are the same. One obvious story beat after the next. That's how I felt. Nothing was fresh. Nothing engendered that feeling. That feeling that was so special to me. All the stories I was involved with were now just patterns in a predictable matrix. If a guy gets dumped, the next scene he's at a bar drowning his sorrows. If a guy goes to war, a few scenes later he has a poignant moment with a civilian living in the country he's shooting up. If a man starts living by night instead of by day, at some point he sees something about himself amid the darkness that's as bright as the sun. On and on and on and on. I couldn't find a story that broke me free. And I couldn't invent one either. And as result, I began to die. I began to die inside. And I knew the only thing that could save me would be art. Would be *my* art. Would be finding a way to have that feeling again. Would be creating something new, something unpredictable. Something magical and thrilling.

"And so I thought: What if I could set a story in motion that was *real*. And not just any story. Not a story about a teacher who takes a job at a school and changes some lives. No, a story with drama and mystery. A story with the greatest stakes there can be—life and death. And best of all, a story that wasn't cooked up by a tired filmmaking professional. Me or somebody else. But rather, one that I set in motion, but that would play out from there for real.

It would run on its own inertia. And it would take twists that I couldn't predict because I would no longer be the author. Life would be. I thought: It would be a new form of art that I could watch, not on a stage or a screen, but in the actual world around me. I thought: I'd be blindsided by the developments. I'd have no idea what the characters would do next. Imagine that! Imagine the excitement I had, John! See, when you would report to me, or when Paul would tell me what you were doing, it was the only time I've felt alive in years. My ability as a storyteller had died, but now because I had come up with a new way of experiencing a story, I was able to see and feel the magic I had as a young boy. Sure, I had to set it in motion, and as things progressed and I learned about Neese and his operation, and the other people in Suzanne's life, I had to plant a few things to put the murder on someone else. But that didn't ruin the experience. It made it better. I was involved. I was helping. But in a totally new way. I had the feeling again. I was experiencing, I had indeed created, a new art form. I was a kid again. And it saved my life."

"But it took someone else's, Vonz. You killed a girl for your own amusement. I should have known you were a wee bit bent when you told me you went down to the Amazon to research that movie. Another way to look at that trip is that you got your jollies by watching a bunch of tribesman kill themselves. Let me ask you this. Did you pull the trigger or did Mountcastle?"

"Paul helped me, as you know. And I trust him—totally. But I wouldn't ask him to do that."

Vonz sat there. He had admitted to me fully now that he was a cold-blooded killer. I could see both his hands but I got the sudden signal from within to stand up and get ready. I got up out of the chair, and moved behind it, still facing Vonz.

I put my gun on him again. "Let's go down to the police station, Vonz."

He held up both his hands. "Please, let me finish."

I took the gun off of him.

Vonz continued, "I didn't want one part of this story to happen. When I hired you, I didn't want to like you. But I did."

"Shut up, Vonz. Don't patronize me."

He continued. "It's trite, I know. But just hear me out. See, my feelings became bifurcated. I didn't want you to figure out what was really happening. Of course I didn't—I was behind it. But at the same time, I liked you, you were my story's hero, so I was pulling for you. To my own detriment. And that was yet another level of excitement for me. I was almost pulling for my own demise because the *art* took over. That is the power of story, of art."

"Who cares about art, Vonz? You killed a girl. That's what you don't see."

"Who cares about art? If I may, I think this is where you are the one who isn't seeing. Art is what gets us all through life. Art has helped the human race survive since we began. Pictures, sparks to the imagination, stories. Neanderthals were drawing and writing on cave walls. To move, inform, or entertain others, but also to understand their own condition. Art is the reason that we don't all kill ourselves. It's the outlet that allows us to be human. John, you're not going to like what I'm about to say."

"I haven't liked almost everything you've said so far."

"John, artists, like me, are among the most important figures, maybe *the* most important figures, in all of human existence. On the level of the greatest scientists, the most profound thinkers, the most spiritual holy men."

"I've told you this already, Vonz. You're a killer and a sociopath. But you're also a megalomaniac. You don't even realize what you're saying. You don't realize how ridiculous you sound."

"John, the human existence is a struggle. Art is what gets us through. From the first time a person is affected by circumstance. Any conflict. Any tension. Big or small. Art is what gets us through. The first time you fall in love. The first time you get your heart broken. The first time you suffer a real loss. It's art that helps you understand, heal, get inspired to keep going. Isn't there a song out there or a book or a movie where every time you hear it or read it or see it you are transported? I bet there's a song out there that for twenty, thirty years, *every time* you hear it, you're taken to a better place. A place of power and emotion. A place that helps you understand the world. A higher place. Think about that. Is there anything else that's created out of thin air that can even come close to that magic? John. Yes, I killed someone, but look at what I gave life to. A new art form. How often does that happen?"

"Are you finished? Or are you ready to go to jail?"

"I want you to understand where I'm coming from. Do you? I know you have it in you to understand."

"Vonz, you killed a young woman. You took her life. It doesn't matter if I understand."

He took a contemplative breath and said, "John, how many people are killed every year, every day, every second on this planet? And why are they killed? Why? Well, murders happen over money, over betrayal, over ego. But let's go bigger than that for a moment. How about religion? How many people die over religion? And the killers? When it comes to religion? They just say, 'I believe one thing, you believe another, so I have a right to take your life.' Or they say, 'My god is this, your god is that, so all the people in your village, town, city, all have to die.' Since the beginning of time, millions of people have been killed this way. And here's the thing: Millions of people *accept* it. People just say, 'Yep, I think the same thing as those killers, so it's okay what they did.' And how about war? How many people have been killed in wars? Sure, lots of wars are *about* religion, but plenty aren't. Plenty are about money, or oil, or land, or freedom. Some of those things are noble, some of them aren't. But, either way, people are killing other people in the name of something they believe in. They are making the judgment that it's okay based on *nothing*. Based on: Our group of people thinks one thing, your group of people thinks another. And entire countries, entire sections of the planet, *modern cultures*, get behind these wars. They support the killing. They legalize it though political documents that set the rules of civilized culture. But the other way to look at it is, millions of people all over the world have no problem with murder. They just go about their lives while people are dying all around them. Right? And you know why? Because everyone has done one simple thing. They have shifted their minds to a belief that in certain situations it's okay to kill. It's as simple as that. A subjective opinion.

"Now, I decided to take one life. Not in the name of religion. Or money. Or power. But in the name of art. Something I think that most people with a soul would agree is *bigger*, is more important, than all those other things combined. So you may not think that what I did was right. But why are *you* right? All these other people all over the world since the dawn of time are killing people constantly, in all of the ways I just mentioned. All the time! Right now! And you, John Darvelle, don't do anything about it. But me? I made something beautiful. Something new. And, while you don't do anything about all those other murders, you want to condemn me for this one."

Vonz looked at me. He wanted me to respond. So I did.

"Vonz, that's a long way to go to try and get away from the one thing you'll never escape. The thing *you* don't get. You think you are better than other people. You think you are better than Suzanne Neal. And you know what? You aren't. You're a smart guy. And a great artist. But right above that is the truth. You're a low-rent killer. And an entitled piece of Hollywood shit. And you are going down."

Vonz gave me a judgmental look. Then he stood up, took a deep, defeated breath, turned around, and looked out the window.

I held my gun at my side. Waiting. Waiting for something to happen.

And then: The door to his office opened. It was Mountcastle. Dressed in his schoolboy attire, now with a man-purse satchel over his right shoulder. He'd returned to enter into the story once again.

I said, "Enjoy the view, Vonz. I don't think the one you'll have in prison will be quite so lovely."

Mountcastle frowned at me, suggesting he was ignorant

as to why I'd make a remark like this. Mountcastle, still playing the game.

Then he said, "Mr. Darvelle. Mr. Vonz has a meeting. Are you wrapping up?"

I didn't answer. I was still looking at Vonz's back.

"Mr. Darvelle?" Mountcastle said.

Mountcastle was in my periphery, but I was keeping my eyes on Vonz.

I saw Vonz's left eye in the reflection of the window. He wasn't looking out onto his beautiful patio, he was watching me. Watching me in the reflection. Watching me like he had from the beginning.

I looked at Mountcastle. He was pulling something out of his bag with his left hand. Yes, a gun. Then back at Vonz, who was pulling something out of his right blazer pocket. Another gun.

Vonz whipped around, pistol in his right hand, trained on my chest. I grabbed Mountcastle's left wrist, twisted it, and yanked him toward me. His hand dropped the gun, and as I pulled him, his body responded instinctively. He moved toward me quickly, his feet dancing, responding deftly, like always.

I positioned Mountcastle in front of me.

Vonz didn't have time to call off his shot.

He pulled the trigger and a bullet went right into Mountcastle's chest.

Right in his heart—where it stayed.

Before Vonz could pull the trigger again, I raised my gun and put a hollow-point bullet through his forehead. And now, the window that he'd just been pretending to look out was no more. The bullet had come out the back of his head and exploded through it, sending slivers flying out, catching the sun now shining through the rain clouds and stabbing the bright grass beneath. Only the window's edges remained and they were no longer transparent, no longer any kind of portal to the colorful flowers and foliage outside. No, the edges were bright red and opaque with the liquid insides of Arthur Vonz's skull.

The blood began to move down the sharp shards still hanging on to the frame.

And then:

Mountcastle dropped.

Vonz dropped.

I stood, and watched them die.

40

Nine days later I was back at my office. Here's what had transpired since I stood over those two dead bodies on the floor of Academy Award–winning director Arthur Vonz's office.

I called Ott and told him to come to Arthur Vonz's house—right away. I told him that two people were dead, and he didn't need to hear much more. He put Neese and White Streak in a holding cell, then came to Vonz's house with an entire investigation team.

Ott looked at the scene, taped it off, and told everybody not to fucking move. He then pulled me aside and said, "Talk."

I told him my version of the story. Slowly. Clearly. Calmly. He listened. He didn't rush me, he didn't interrupt. When I finished he nodded, then ordered his people to sweep the scene.

And then I went down to the LAPD, to give Ott and his superiors the full story again. I told them exactly what had happened step by step. I got some crazy looks. But as my story progressed, and after a couple days of investigation, the LAPD began to realize that I wasn't the crazy one—Vonz was.

Because the plane story checked out. Mountcastle hiring the second detective checked out. And the gun that killed Suzanne Neal checked out. Turns out it was bought in a pawnshop in Indio, California. The proprietor of the pawnshop, a man named Glen with a tattoo of a target in the center of his forehead, described the person who had purchased the gun as "A pale big blobby guy. Kind of looked like a little kid in the face."

Arrogance. That's what Vonz and Mountcastle had had. They never assumed anyone could track the killing back to them. They never thought anyone would ever be talking to Target on His Forehead Guy. So when it came to the purchase of the smoking gun, they were sloppy. Two sloppy moves. The cabs and the gun. And as a result, they were both dead.

The problem then became Neese. Because while he didn't kill Suzanne, I believed, and Ott eventually believed, that he did kill Allison Tarber.

Or at the very least ordered her to be killed.

So, based on my information, Ott reopened the Allison Tarber case. And guess what? Her mom knew where she got a certain tattoo. And the tattoo artist confirmed that it was the PG pyramid. And then Ott took another look at the evidence gathered at Allison's accident scene. Sure enough, in the residue found under her fingernails there was more than just the dirt and the dust of the Santa Monica mountains. There was some of White Streak's DNA. Turns out, at some point during White Streak's despicable act Allison had clawed at his skin just enough to get a tiny bit of it under her nail. When confronted with this, White Streak ratted out Richard Neese for a shorter sentence.

They always do.

White Streak was arrested for murder. Neese was arrested for murder, for organized crime, and for running a prostitution ring called the Pipe Girls.

Eventually, White Streak would get twenty years. Neese would get life.

For the record: Prostitution was never the issue. I never hated Neese for that. What I hated him for was enforcing his system through threats and murder. For that he needed to go down. And he did.

Now. I want to tell you a few other things before we end the story. Specifically, two quick stories about women.

First, about a week after Neese and White Streak got arrested I was at home one night chilling out back by my pool drinking a Budweiser and listening to some relaxing, melancholy Leonard Cohen. "So Long, Marianne." My doorbell rang. I opened the door to see Linda Robbie, real estate badass, cougar to the core.

I said, "Linda, please, come in."

She was wearing a beautiful khaki-colored trench coat and high heels.

She said, "Do you have any white wine?"

I said, "You know, I think I do."

I uncorked a bottle and poured her a nice cold, crisp glass.

She took a sip and looked me in the eye and said, "I helped you a lot on this case."

"Yeah, you did," I said.

She undid the belt on her trench coat and it dropped to the floor. She was wearing a bra that barely contained her enhanced chest and a tiny, and I mean tiny, thong. She looked amazing.

"I think I helped you so much that I'm entitled to a demand or two," she said.

I nodded and replied, "What did you have in mind?"

She said, "Do me."

I walked over to her and kissed her on the lips. It felt good, better than expected. Then I did a deep knee bend so that my face was right in line with the front of her minuscule thong. I wrapped my arms around her ankles, grabbed her trench coat that was on the floor behind her, and stood up.

I was now essentially hugging her, her coat in my hands behind her. I wrapped it back around her and tied it in the front.

"It seems like we're going backward."

"Linda, I can't do this. Not now anyway. I'd like to. I'd really like to. And maybe someday we'll get our chance. But I met somebody special during this case. And I'm going to see her soon. And if you were her, you wouldn't want me to sleep with another beautiful woman right before I saw you. Right as I was just getting something started with you. Right?"

"Dammit, Darvelle. I wanted you to squeeze my tits and slap my ass. Not appeal to my heart."

I laughed.

"But you're right. I wouldn't want you to sleep with someone as beautiful as me, right before you saw me."

I thought: That line actually makes sense. Sort of.

Linda said, "Call me if it doesn't work out. The second it doesn't work out."

She threw back her wine and left.

And the second story happened just today. I was sitting at my desk. The big slider was open. The sun was coming in, the breeze, with a just a hint of chill. Just a hint of colder weather on the way. It was perfect—a beautiful golden Los Angeles afternoon. I picked up my phone and called Nancy Alvarez.

"Yes?" she answered.

"Remember me?" I said. "You made me promise to never forget you. But can you say the same? Have you forgotten me?"

"Hmm. I see your name here on my phone but it's not ringing a bell."

"Can I take you to dinner tonight, gorgeous?"

"You got lucky when you beat me in Ping-Pong."

"I'll take that as a yes. I'll pick you up at seven."

And then her voice softened and she said, "I'll be ready."

Now. The story's almost over, but not just yet. There's a few more things I want to tell you. There's one last chapter before I let you go.

41

I sat at my desk after hanging up with Nancy. I was feeling good, excited to see her, excited for my date. And then I just sat there thinking. My feet up on the desk. My eyes looking out the slider. The golden light fading. The golden light going to gray. I was thinking about the case I'd just closed. About the journey I'd been on. About how so often you don't know something for sure until you really, really look. But the thing was, now that my investigation had come to a close, I did know some things for sure. And that was a good feeling. And, sitting there, I realized I knew *other* things for sure too. Yes, I do know that there are some other things in life that I believe to be absolutely true. I want to tell you about a few of them. So here goes.

If you ever almost die you will realize how much you want to live.

You have no control over what physical or intellectual gifts you are given. But you have total control over how hard you fight.

When you're one hundred percent sure of something, there is a possibility, a great possibility, that you are wrong.

When you take off in an airplane at dusk and you can just start to see the twinkle of the lights in the city below you, and the plane is rocketing skyward, and the horizon line is going from a blue-purple to a dark blue, no matter where you are headed, there is a sense of promise.

I'll take John, John Paul, Robert, and Jimmy over John, Paul, George, and Ringo any day.

If you ever find yourself standing outside a crowded restaurant in the hot sun on the weekend waiting to be seated for *brunch*, it may be time to rethink things.

When professional Ping-Pong players stopped using thin, dimpled hard paddles and started using thick, slick soft paddles, the sport gained some rubber, but lost some soul.

If you can learn to keep a secret you will be among a very small select group of people.

When you go see your favorite band live and they do the *acoustic version sung a cappella* of your favorite song to try and make it special, it isn't special. It's a bummer.

And lastly, the hunt. The Hunt. The Hunt to solve The Problem. When you are on the hunt, when your mind is locked into a search for *the answer*, it can be anything, a math problem, where your lost wallet is, where your destination is, trying to determine the first thing you need to do, trying to get the final touches just right, trying to figure out who, just exactly who, killed a beautiful young girl in Santa Monica, when you are on the hunt, you are in a different and special place. When you are on the hunt, your mind and your body and your consciousness are *engaged*. And that is good. When you are on the hunt to solve the problem, that special place is in fact a higher place. My friend, you are connected to a powerful and empowering force. And the things that trouble you, or fill you with anxiety, or stress you out, go away. They disappear because you have killed them with your absorption. When you are *not* on the hunt, you are the one who is dying. You are not unleashing your focus on the world. So false and phony and pedestrian troubles enter your mind and try to confuse and weaken you. But when you are on the hunt, that never happens. Because you are dialed in. Locked in. Living. Yes. You are alive. The hunt is connection and commitment. It is energy and power. It is passion and love. Yes, the hunt. The Hunt. When you are on the hunt, you are happy.

THE END

ACKNOWLEDGMENTS

On the professional front:

A big thank-you to Michael Signorelli, a top-shelf editor and a believer from the beginning. And another big thank-you to Erica Spellman-Silverman, an agent who knows what she's doing and calls it like she sees it.

Also, thank you to Tara Carberry, Hannah Wood, and Amanda Ainsworth.

On the personal front:

Thanks to my mom, my sister, Priscilla, and my brother, Rich. I'm lucky to have you as my family.

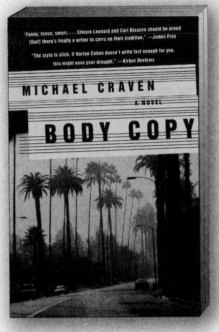